ARIANA

A Gift Most Precious

ARIANA

A Gift Most Precious

a novel

Rachel Ann Nunes

BONNEVILLE BOOKS™
Springville, Utah

ISBN: 1-55517-646-1
e. 1

Published by Bonneville Books
Imprint of Cedar Fort Inc.
www.cedarfort.com

Distributed by:

Typeset by Kristin Nelson
Cover design by Barry Hansen
Cover design © 2002 by Lyle Mortimer

Printed in the United States of America
10 9 8 7 6 5 4 3 2 1

Printed on acid-free paper

Library of Congress Cataloging-in-Publication Data

Nunes, Rachel Ann, 1966-
  Ariana : a gift most precious : a novel / Rachel Ann Nunes.
      p. cm.
  ISBN 1-55517-646-1 (pbk. : acid-free paper)
  1. Mormon women--Fiction. 2. HIV-positive persons--Fiction. 3.
Friendship--Fiction. 4. Mormons--Fiction. I. Title.
  PS3564.U468 A88 2003
  813'.54--dc21
                            2002154246

DEDICATION

To TJ, my best friend and biggest fan. Thank you for giving me Jewels (my computer) and for never giving up faith in my abilities.

SPECIAL THANKS

To Jean Hanvey, for sharing touching experiences
with her premature son, Wyatt.

Books by Rachel Ann Nunes

Ariana: The Making of a Queen

Ariana: A Gift Most Precious

Ariana: A New Beginning

Ariana: A Glimpse of Eternity

Love to the Highest Bidder

Framed for Love

Love on the Run

A Greater Love

To Love and to Promise

Tomorrow and Always

This Time Forever

Bridge to Forever

This Very Moment

Daughter of a King (picture book)

Ties That Bind

Twice in a Lifetime

PROLOGUE

My name is Ariana Merson Perrault, and I am twenty-eight years old. As a child in Paris, my twin brother, Antoine, was my world. He was fearless, adventuresome, and engaging, and everyone fell in love with him the minute they saw him. But my beloved brother died nearly eleven years ago, when we were six months short of our eighteenth birthday. Early one rainy morning, he was hit by a car on his way to school and died instantly. I should have been with him that day; perhaps I would have been able to protect him. Though I no longer feel guilty for his passing, I still miss him.

His death broke our family apart, and I turned to drinking and drugs to dull the pain. Then I met the dashing Jacques and fell in love. A week after we met I became pregnant; three months later we married. I vowed to do what was right for my baby.

We argued about drugs, and Jacques left me when our daughter, Antoinette—or Nette, as we called her—was three months old, the day before my nineteenth birthday. After our separation, I struggled to make a life for myself and went back to school. When our daughter was eight months old, Jacques came back into my life, swearing that he had changed, only to take away the most precious thing I had. In a drugged state, he gave Nette heroin, trying to alleviate her teething pain. She went to sleep and never awoke. I had been at school that dreadful, stormy night and blamed myself for leaving her. It was only then, when my life seemed at its end, that I finally agreed to listen to the Mormon missionaries, as I hadn't when Antoine died two years earlier. It took a long time, but I forgave my first husband for what he had done . . . and finally, I forgave myself.

A year and a half after my baptism, I met Jean-Marc, who was serving a mission in Paris. He encouraged me to serve one myself, and after our missions we married. When we were sealed in the Swiss Temple, it was the happiest day of my life. Our twin babies, Marc and Josette, were born after a year, and their brother, André, was born three years later.

I am not the only one who has come a long way. My best friend,

Paulette, was there the night my baby died. She had been heavily into drugs before, but Nette's death caused her to plunge even deeper into the abyss. Years later I found her during my missionary service, lying half dead on a cobblestone sidewalk that lined a street in Bordeaux. With the help of the ward there, she left the drugs behind and embraced the gospel. She married Pierre, Jean-Marc's brother, and less than a year later they had a daughter, Marie-Thérèse. Since then, she has been a model member of the Church and my best friend.

I feel the devastating past Paulette and I share has made our love for each other and for the gospel flourish. It may seem strange to those who did not live my life, but I am grateful for those experiences. This doesn't mean I wouldn't change the fact of my daughter's death; if I could somehow take it back, I would, in an instant. But so much good has come of her death that I recognize the reasons for it, which in turn dulls the pain. With the help of the Spirit, I have reached many people because of my experience, sharing the gospel of Christ with them and seeing their lives change for the better.

I know I'll see my brother again, and my daughter. Until then, I have a husband I adore and three lovable children to replace all I have lost. The Lord has been good to me these past four years, and I've been happy, if not perfectly content. I may have even begun to take my happiness—and my faith—for granted.

Perhaps that's why the time has come for me to be tested once more.

CHAPTER ONE

The fluorescent lights hurt my eyes, already burning from the tears I had shed the night before and again today. Around me, people moved with purpose; only I sat slumped motionless against the wall, waiting to hear if she would be all right. I hadn't been to the hospital except for the times I'd had a baby . . . and when Nette died. The memory made me suddenly afraid that Paulette, too, had come here to die. *Please tell me she's all right!* The thought was a silent prayer.

It was what Jean-Marc would term a perfect ending to a really rotten day. Of course he wasn't here to say it, and even if he were, I'd be too angry to listen. *It's all his fault,* I wanted to mutter, but I knew I had no one to blame except myself.

The carpet in the waiting room was brown instead of the unsightly orange that had lined the floor in the hospital where I had lost my daughter; the observation offered meager comfort. A nurse at the nearby desk glanced up at me from the paperwork in front of her. She smiled kindly, but I felt it was more from habit than from any feeling of compassion. Her smile didn't reach her tired eyes, and I knew she would much rather be home with her family than working the night shift.

Even at this hour, the lights on the hospital phone winked furiously. I wondered who could be calling so late and what emergencies had driven them from their beds. The wild blinking echoed the raging emotions in my heart and contrasted sharply with the quiet intensity around me. Crossing my arms over my chest, I rubbed the flesh under my long-sleeved shirt for warmth, ignoring the chestnut-colored jacket thrown carelessly across my lap. I wondered if Paulette was dying—or perhaps the baby she carried inside. Even as the thought came, I prayed more fervently for it not to be so. Paulette had been through too much already. Besides—it was impossible to stop the selfish thought—I needed her, especially since Jean-Marc had walked out on me last night, suitcase in hand. I still didn't understand how I had let that happen.

Though my current troubles had begun months ago, they had come to a climax the morning before. I had been in the kitchen frying eggs, wishing I had earplugs to block out the clamor the twins and André made as they banged their spoons against their dishes in raucous discord. André's rice cereal sloshed out of his bowl, making the high chair tray look like a war zone. I think he put more cereal *on* his body than *in* it.

"Good morning, Ari," Jean-Marc had said from the kitchen doorway. My husband's trim figure was smartly dressed in a dark-gray suit, a wool and polyester blend. On his face was the familiar grin I adored. He crossed the room and gave me a kiss.

Peering into the shiny metal surface of the toaster oven, I ran a quick hand through my dark-brown hair that was cut short to fall in wisps about my neck. I noted with satisfaction that I hadn't really changed all that much since Jean-Marc and I had met while he was serving his mission here in Paris. My laugh lines were deeper and I was more experienced, but that was all.

I turned to see Jean-Marc trying to get the baby cereal out of André's ears. Our son cried and tried to push the cloth away.

I walked over. "There, there, André. Poor child." I took the baby out of the high chair and away from Jean-Marc. "There's no hope, honey. He needs a bath."

He threw the cloth at me, but I ducked and it landed on the stove. We both laughed and hugged each other tightly. André objected loudly to the squeeze.

"See you tonight," Jean-Marc said, releasing me.

"But I've got breakfast nearly ready," I protested. I usually didn't bother with more than a few croissants and hot chocolate, but I had wanted to make this day different. Jean-Marc adored eggs in the morning—a habit gained from one of his American missionary companions.

He sniffed the air appreciatively. "It smells good, but I really have to go. Your father and I are visiting the new branch today and we want to get an early start. He's probably waiting outside. We'll grab something at the corner bakery on the way."

I sighed. Sometimes I hated the fact that my father, Géralde Merson, was president and partial owner of the bank, and that Jean-Marc was rising ever higher in the bank hierarchy. "But you'll be home early, won't you? Remember our date?" There was an adult dance at the church building, and we were going. We hadn't been out alone together for months, and I had finally taken a stand and made plans to attend. My mother would baby-sit our four-year-old twins and one-year-old André.

"Yeah, I remember." He bent to kiss the children. "You guys are getting so big," he cooed. Briefcase in hand, he was nearly at the door before our son stopped him.

"Wait!" little Marc yelled accusingly. "Prayer. You forgot!"

Jean-Marc returned and stood against the wall, bowing his head as Marc prayed. He kissed us again and jogged down the hall. "Goodbye!" He tossed the word over his shoulder like a bag of laundry. I felt a little upset at his hasty departure, but was determined to enjoy myself that night, and I wouldn't be able to do so if I held a grudge.

The time for our date came and went with no word from my husband. While I was hurt, I wasn't really surprised. I tried to call the bank, though I knew it was almost a hopeless endeavor. Jean-Marc spent most of his workdays out of the office with clients or on the phone, staying long after closing. At least the receptionist was still there.

"This is Ariana," I said when she answered. "I need to speak with Jean-Marc."

"He's not here. Shall I transfer you to the other branch?"

"Yes, thank you." But he wasn't at the second branch either, and they didn't know where he was. I left a message and hung up. Next, I called my mother to tell her I didn't need her to watch the children after all.

My anger simmered inside me more hotly than the soup I made the children for dinner. "Bedtime," I said when they were finished eating.

"I'll get the Book of Mormon!" Josette shouted.

"No, me!" Marc was out of his chair in a flash.

I read them the story of how the brother of Jared made sixteen small, transparent stones to put in the eight boats, and how they shone when the Lord touched them with His finger.

"And then Jesus showed Himself to the brother of Jared," I explained, "because he had so much faith."

"I wish I could make stuff light up," Marc said.

"Where are those rocks now?" asked Josette. I didn't know and told her so.

"I bet Daddy knows," Marc said.

I rolled my eyes. "We'll ask him tomorrow. It's Saturday."

"Saturday! Maybe we can play tiger!" the twins shouted. Saturday morning was the one time Jean-Marc usually spent with the children—or had, up until a few months ago. The children would come into our room and wrestle on our bed until finally hunger took control, and Daddy got up to make breakfast. Then I would enjoy a leisurely bath alone, without any peering eyes. I wondered that the twins still remembered.

"And aren't we going to the Saint-Martin tomorrow?" Marc asked.

"Daddy promised," Josette added quickly.

The Canal Saint-Martin in Paris was the world's only underground urban canal. We had promised to take the children there months ago after they had seen a special about it on television. We had already changed the date twice because of Jean-Marc's work.

"Then we'll go," I assured them.

It took another half-hour to put the children to bed. It wasn't an easy task alone, but one I had grown used to in the past year. And all the while my resentment built inside me until I wondered if I might explode.

Jean-Marc came home around ten. "Are you still in your pajamas?" he joked when he found me in bed reading a book. With his green-brown eyes twinkling, he looked vital and alive.

I glared at him.

"What is it?" he asked. Suddenly realization dawned, and he smacked his forehead with his open palm. "The church activity! I forgot. I'm really sorry, Ari."

"It's okay," I murmured untruthfully, as I had so many other times.

"Well, I practically closed the deal I've been working on," he said, looking relieved. "Tomorrow I'll wrap it up."

"Tomorrow?" I felt my eyes narrow. "But it's Saturday, and we're taking the children to the Saint-Martin canal. We've been planning this for months. They're so excited about it; we can't let them down again."

Once more he smacked his forehead. "I forgot about that. I can't do it, Ari. We'll go next time. They'll understand."

I pictured the disappointment on the twins' faces when they learned their father had once again canceled on them, on us. The anger I'd held in check for months boiled to the surface as I got out of bed and began to pace around the room. "They'll understand that your work is much more important than they are," I said acidly. "Or me."

"I'm working for us," he retorted. "As soon as we're set, I'll slow down. I'm only doing it for—"

"We don't need your money! We need *you*! The children, especially." Now that I had begun, I couldn't stop the hot torrent of words. "I'm sick of waiting in line for time with you. Home is not just where you come to sleep! I see the man at the corner bread store more than I see you!"

"That's not fair," he said. "Stop stalking around like an angry bull, and let's talk about this reasonably." He tried to draw me close, but I was sick of listening to "reason" tinged with his bias. Besides, his touch always affected my judgment. I pulled away.

He released me and ran a hand through his hair. His face had grown stiff, and I felt a wall forming between us. "We've been through this before, Ari. It's only for a short time."

"Is it? I'm not so sure. Not even my father, who *owns* the bank, works as much as you do. He at least came home at night before Antoine and I were in bed. Tell me, how often do you see your children? Saturday mornings and Sundays? Yes, that's about it. And half the time on Sunday you're at church meetings. You're not around or available at the important intersections of life. You sleep here, but that's all." I put my hands on his shoulders and stared into his eyes. "Jean-Marc, we need you *now*, not ten years from now. In ten years, if the children haven't learned to trust you and go to you with their problems, they won't *ever* do it. It'll be too late!"

He took my hands from his shoulders and held them. "It was for this new branch, Ari. That's all."

"And what was your excuse last year?" I took my hands from his, threw open the closet, and pulled his suitcase down from the top shelf, driven by my anger. "Maybe if you don't want to be with us, you should leave," I said, thrusting it into his arms. "Maybe our children would see you more if you didn't live here."

I was trying to make a point, trying to show him how serious the situation had become. He wasn't just a man who worked overtime during deadlines, but a man so obsessed with his job that he neglected his children, his family. Me. I was through simmering about it; the time had come for a change.

I met his eyes and saw hurt there, but it seemed deeply buried beneath his own anger. "Fine," he said through gritted teeth. "I'll leave."

His words pierced me. My insides seemed to tear apart as I watched him hastily throw a few things into his worn case. I loved him. What was I doing? What were *we* doing? Weren't we married for eternity? I wanted to throw myself into his arms and tell him I didn't mean what I had said and beg him to stay.

But I *did* mean what I'd said. We had been sealed in God's temple for eternity, but I didn't want to live my life alone, waiting for eternity to come.

He clicked the suitcase shut and left the room, pausing momentarily at the door, but not looking back at me. His jaw worked and he seemed about to speak, then he shook his head once and stalked down the hall, leaving whatever it was unsaid.

I couldn't believe he was actually leaving. He wouldn't do that. He couldn't! I waited in our room for him to come back. He didn't. Tears came, searing and painful. *What have I done?* But even as the question came, I resolved to see it through. I had to protect my children.

By losing their father? The accusing words seemed to come from the oppressive silence.

I was almost relieved when a cry came from the twins' bedroom. Unlike little André, they still had difficulty sleeping through the night. I wiped my tears on the long sleeve of my nightgown and went down the hall, wondering how I would tell them tomorrow that not only was their daddy not taking them to the canal, but that he wouldn't be coming home at all. Perhaps I would take them by myself. The sad thing was that they might not notice the difference.

CHAPTER TWO

"You can see her now."

I started at the voice, and looked up to see a nurse standing over me. At once the sights, sounds, and smells of the hospital came rushing back, firmly pushing aside the raw memories of the night before. I stood and followed the nurse down the hall to a room where Paulette lay on a tall bed, seeming very small and weak despite the mound of her stomach. She had an oxygen tube in her nose and a machine monitored her vital signs. An IV dripped steadily into her arm. She seemed to be unconscious, or perhaps sleeping.

I glanced up at the doctor, who stood near my friend. He was an older man with white hair, sagging cheeks, and sad brown eyes that made him look like a basset hound. He was tall for a Frenchman and very thin. He studied a chart with an engrossed expression, then said something quietly to a nurse who replied with an equally soft voice. It was all I could do not to yell at them to speak louder. I bit the soft inner side of my cheek and moved restlessly in the doorway, finally drawing the doctor's attention.

"Hello," he said, his eyes coming to rest on my face. "I'm Dr. Flaubert."

"I'm Ariana Perrault, Paulette's sister-in-law."

"You were with her when she collapsed?"

I nodded and swallowed hard, forcing my feet to take a few steps into the room.

"Tell me exactly how it happened." I had told the nurses before, but it seemed Paulette's doctor wanted to hear for himself. I was happy, at least, that they had found him. With her difficult pregnancy, Paulette was better off in the hands of her own doctor than a stranger.

As I spoke, guilt once more assailed me; it was my fault Paulette was here. This morning I had decided to take the children on our outing without Jean-Marc, rather than to see their disappointment. Knowing that her husband was out of town on business, I called Paulette to ask if she and her daughter, Marie-Thérèse, would like to go with us.

Paulette was my sister-in-law and best friend, and had been for years. She and Pierre used to live in Bordeaux, but had moved to Paris after Pierre sold the family grocery store to a larger competitor who had a chain of stores throughout France. Now he worked for that same company, overseeing the stores in Paris and surrounding areas. His mother had retired and still lived in Bordeaux with her youngest, Lu-Lu, who was twenty-two.

"Want to come?" I asked, after explaining where we were going. "Please?"

Paulette was expecting her second child after three disheartening years of trying to conceive. She had been sick this time, almost to the point of being bedridden, but since she was five months along now, she had begun to feel better. "Canal Saint-Martin?" she said. "I'd love to. Marie-Thérèse has been wanting to go ever since she heard you were taking the twins."

"Are you sure you're feeling up to it?"

She laughed. "Not really. I've gotten a cold from somewhere and a cough as well, but I can't spend the next four months doing nothing. I'm coming, Ari."

I hung up the phone and looked down into the eager faces of the twins. "They're coming with us," I said.

"What about Daddy?" Josette asked, her large brown eyes luminous.

"Yeah, I thought he was taking us," Marc added.

I frowned. "He's working." Both little faces drooped. "But we'll have fun anyway." I ruffled their dark-brown locks and tickled their stomachs until the sadness vanished. It didn't take long; they were accustomed to their father's absence.

"It's underground!" Marc said importantly when he had stopped laughing. "We get to ride on a boat! And underground for two kilometers!" He stumbled slightly over the last word.

Josette glared at him, unimpressed. "I know, I know." She turned to me. "Mom, don't you think we should go get André? He's awake. I heard him a little while ago."

I started guiltily. Oh, yes, André. My youngest was so well-behaved that I sometimes forgot he existed at all—quite a treat after the rambunctious twins. He had just turned one, and had only recently weaned himself from nursing.

"Go get dressed," I said to the twins, backtracking down the hall to the baby's room. "Make sure it matches!" I added. "And bring a jacket." It was mid-May, and though the day would most likely be pleasant, the underground canal would probably be chilly—if I remembered anything from my days of exploring Paris with my twin brother, Antoine.

André was awake, standing up inside his crib, waiting patiently. When he saw me, he smiled and jumped up and down, holding out his arms in anticipation.

"Good morning," I sang, picking him up and kissing him.

"Ma-ma," he said, grinning. Then he continued babbling, as if explaining something unquestionably important. I didn't understand his baby-talk, but pretended I did. Otherwise, he would become so frustrated that I would never get him calmed down. It was his only true short-coming, and I loved him for it. Besides, I couldn't really consider it a shortcoming; after all, each of us craves understanding.

After taking care of André, I showered and exchanged my nightgown for chestnut-colored pants and a matching jacket; the dark colors served the dual purpose of setting off my brown eyes and announcing my disheartened mood to the world. Part of me kept listening for Jean-Marc's step, but it never came.

When we arrived in front of Paulette's apartment, only five minutes away, she and Marie-Thérèse were waiting outside. Marie-Thérèse held her favorite doll in her arms—one Paulette had made for her at last year's Christmas Homemaking meeting. She was four and a half, four months older than the twins, with light-brown hair, brown eyes, and a slightly upturned nose. Taller than the twins, Marie-Thérèse took after her mother's side of the family rather than her father's. The cousins greeted each other eagerly, but as Paulette and Marie-Thérèse slid into the car, my friend's face darkened. "What's wrong?" she asked. "You're wearing brown. That's your best color, but you only wear it when you're upset. What's going on?"

I shook my head slightly, moving my eyes toward the children.

"Okay," she agreed. "For now. But you won't get away with it for long."

I smiled. She was really a good friend, and I loved her. I was closer to her than anyone, even Jean-Marc, though that hadn't always been the case. Once Jean-Marc and I had been best friends—and once I had wished Paulette dead. I shook away the unwanted memories.

Paulette sneezed and drew out a tissue to blow her nose. I studied her anxiously. She looked thinner than I remembered her being even a few days earlier. Her brown hair hung limply on either side of her face; it also seemed thinner somehow, though surely a few days could make no real difference. Her stomach poked out hugely from her thin frame, dominating the scene. Though she was only five months pregnant, she looked almost like a caricature in an artist's chalk drawing. There were several who worked along the Seine, mostly taking money from the many tourists, and only last week Paulette and I had had our portrait done. When the artist finished, her stomach had taken up nearly the whole page, though in reality was small compared to most pregnant women. It was just because she was so thin that her stomach jutted out so tellingly.

I drove to the yacht harbor near the Place de la Bastille where the canal tour began. The children were competing to speak louder than each other, and the din grew until I wanted to shout at them to be quiet.

"Children," Paulette said in a composed but firm voice, "you all need to calm down a bit or we won't be able to find a parking place, and we won't go on the tour. It takes concentration to find a place to park." The children grew silent and I was amazed, as I always was with Paulette these days.

We finally parked and made our way down the sidewalk to the canal, where several boats floated in the water. We didn't have a long wait, as the tourist traffic hadn't reached its peak, and were soon comfortably settled in a medium-sized craft. A group of other people had joined us—mostly tourists—and Josette was already talking enthusiastically to a woman seated on the bench next to her. Marc peered over the edge of the boat, making me nervous, and Marie-Thérèse sat quietly between me and her mother, playing with André, who was cuddled on my lap.

Before entering the corridor leading to the nineteenth-century tunnel, we sailed under the roundabout and the lofty, 180-ton Colonne de Juillet—Column of July—where the names of the five hundred who had died during the 1830 revolution were inscribed. Once we entered, the light faded and we had to blink several times before our eyes adjusted. There were skylights positioned every fifty meters that cast a misty blue light into the passageway. It was a romantic setting, and I found myself missing Jean-Marc.

Above us we could see the stone base of the Colonne de Juillet, which served as a crypt and contained the bodies of those whose names were etched in the towering column above ground. The canal was more than impressive, and I settled down eagerly for the three-hour ride. Nostalgic memories of my twin brother softened the longing I had for my husband.

"Did Jesus make this?" Josette asked, coming to stand beside me.

"Actually, this used to be an open canal," I explained. "But then a long time ago, the people lowered the canal bed and covered it over."

"Why?" asked Marie-Thérèse.

I shrugged. "I think they wanted to use the space above for cars and buildings."

"But Jesus told them how, didn't He?" Marc said. He still stood near the side, but at least now his feet didn't leave the boat's floor in his eagerness.

Paulette and I glanced at each other, trying to hide our smiles. This was one of those great teaching moments, one of the times I was so grateful to be a member of The Church of Jesus Christ of Latter-day Saints. At least I knew what to tell my children.

"Yes," I said. "Jesus is the source of all knowledge. Every great idea man has comes from the light of Christ. Every invention ever made."

"Even boats?" Marc asked.

"Even boats," I affirmed.

When the canal ride came to an end at the Bassin de la Villette, we made our way to a bread shop to buy something for lunch. The small boulangerie was filled with different breads and I ordered two baguettes. As the lady handed me the long bread, the children clamored for *pain au chocolat*—bread with chocolate baked inside.

"Okay, okay," I said. The lady at the counter smiled and rang up my order. I paid and waited outside while Paulette ducked into the shop next door for cheese and fruit. Purchases in hand, we walked down the street until we found a bench overlooking the canal and settled on it. The children scampered on the cobblestones nearby, eating and trying to attract the pigeons flying overhead.

Paulette dabbed at her nose with the tissue she carried in her hand. "So what's up?" she asked. "You've been going around all day glowering and looking like you lost your best friend."

I scowled. "Maybe I have."

"Jean-Marc?"

I nodded.

"He loves you, Ariana."

I wasn't so sure. After all, he had left. And not knowing where he was and who he was with drove me crazy.

She put her arm around me. "I'm here for you, you know."

I leaned my head on her shoulder. "Thank you, I do need you."

"I'm glad."

Something in her voice made me look up. Her eyes had the faraway glaze that signaled a return to the past. "Don't," I said softly. "Leave the past alone. We're happy now."

She smiled, her hands moving to her stomach. "Do you remember how I longed for this baby?"

I remembered well. After having Marie-Thérèse, Paulette had been unable to conceive until five months ago.

"I worried I wouldn't ever have another child," she continued. "I think I must have felt like Queen Marie-Antoinette. Do you remember what she did?"

"What? You mean how when she couldn't conceive, she took the child of a peasant woman to raise as her own?"

"Something like that." Paulette's laugh was low and husky.

"You'd never steal a child," I said, smiling at the idea.

"No," she agreed. "But I wanted to. I understand Marie-Antoinette's need."

"I remember reading that she was criticized for doing it," I mused. "And later, that child—a son—became one of her worst opponents during the Revolution."

"But that's because she neglected him after finally having her own children," Paulette said. "I would never neglect any child. Not now, anyway."

And I knew she wouldn't. Once she had been able to discard the heavy weight of the drugs, Paulette had uncovered the inner part of herself that was good almost to the extreme. At times I envied her.

"So what happened with Jean-Marc?" she asked, returning doggedly to the subject of my husband.

I shrugged and looked away. "I'm not sure. Let's walk, okay?" I knew I was hiding from the issue, but Paulette would let me, at least until I felt I could talk about it. That was one of the reasons she was such a good friend.

We walked for a short time, until Paulette began wheezing. "We'd better head back now," I said. She nodded and coughed into a handful of tissue. Her coughs and sneezes had become more frequent during our outing, causing her frail body to shudder with each exertion. It didn't take me long to realize that she had come today because of something she had heard in my voice more than any desire to leave her warm bed. Suddenly I was anxious to get her home.

We took the metro back to near where we had parked the car. On the train, André sat on my lap, yawning. The girls were also tired and sat languidly across from me next to Paulette.

Marc stood on the seat and tried to climb the bars next to it. A man standing and holding onto the bar in the crowded train eyed him indifferently, but I grabbed my son and pulled him down, shaking my head. He frowned, huffing emphatically. I hid a smile in André's hair. Marc was impulsive and wild, just like my brother had been. Antoine had always hung on the bars, especially to amuse me. The memory made me warm.

After leaving the metro, we walked the short distance to our car. Near where we had parked there was a short stone wall encircling several trees, the only greenery in sight. Marc immediately jumped up on the wall and stuck his hands in the dirt. Then he stood up, extended his arms for balance, and began walking the length of the wall.

"Get down, Marc!" Josette cried.

"No!" Marc said, sticking out his tongue. He started to lose his balance.

I dropped André into the car and rushed to grab Marc. I was too late. He fell to the cobblestone sidewalk, his head making an ugly cracking noise as he hit, face first. There was a brief second of stunned silence before he started to wail. I turned him over to see a small river of bright red coming from his chin.

"Here." Paulette shoved a wad of tissue in my hand, and I held it tightly against the wound. Marc was still crying, and I pulled him onto my lap and cuddled him.

"Try to lie still," I said. "Let me see what's happened." He tried bravely to obey, letting me remove the tissue and take a peek. My insides churned at the sight of the deep gash.

"That's definitely going to need stitches," Paulette said.

Marc started to cry again, louder this time. I soothed him as best I could. "It's all right. I'll be there with you."

I held him on my lap as Paulette drove to the hospital. Once there, she sat with the children in the waiting room while I talked to the nurse. I wished I could call Jean-Marc, but even if my pride would let me, I had no idea where he was.

At last the doctor arrived, an older man with graying hair and a kind face. He looked like someone's grandpa, and Marc gazed at him trustingly.

"Let's put this over your face so the light won't hurt your eyes," the doctor said gently. In his hand he held something that looked like a sheet of white wrapping paper with a hole cut in it to expose the chin area. I knew its real purpose was to hide the sight of the shot needle they would have to use. Despite the doctor's gentleness, Marc screamed as he received the injection of painkiller in his chin. He clutched my hand, and tears squeezed out of the corners of my eyes. I wished I could spare my little boy this suffering.

After the stitches were in place, I went into the waiting room. Paulette was sneezing again and her face glistened. I felt her forehead. "You have a fever," I said.

She groaned and clutched her chest. "I thought I was feeling strange, but I figured it was being here at the hospital."

"Come on, I'll get you home."

Marc fell asleep in the car on the way, sporting a row of tiny stitches on his chin. Josette watched over him, occasionally smoothing his forehead. Maybe she would be able to protect her brother as I hadn't my own.

We were nearing our area of town when Paulette started coughing violently. In the tissue she clutched in her hand, I saw blood. She was in no condition to be alone. "You're coming home with me," I said.

"I don't want to get in the way," she murmured. "I'm sure Jean-Marc is waiting for you."

I gave a short, bitter laugh. "No, he won't be." She gazed at me, a question in her light-brown eyes. "He left last night with his suitcase," I explained quietly.

Her eyes grew sorrowful, but she said nothing as another bout of coughing shook her.

The apartment was ominously quiet when I finally succeeded in opening the door with my key, burdened by Marc's sleeping form. I felt my hopes dwindle; Jean-Marc hadn't come home. I laid Marc in his bed, disturbing him only enough to remove his shoes. I was sure he would wake up before I finished dinner; a small accident like this wouldn't cause him to lose his appetite.

"Mommy, come quick!" Josette's worried voice called from the bathroom. I hurried from the twins' room and found her and Marie-Thérèse watching Paulette, who sat on the edge of the tub, hunched over the toilet. The water inside was red.

I pushed past the anxious girls and little André, who stood in the doorway. "Are you all right?" I said, reaching out to Paulette.

"I feel so tired," she said, "and my chest is hurting."

She looked exhausted. Her face was pale against the red of her lips, stained with bright blood. A streak of crimson marked her cheek.

I pulled some tissue from the roll and wiped her face tenderly. "Can you walk?"

"I think so."

"Let's get you to bed, and then I'll call your doctor."

Paulette gasped in pain as I put my arm around her and helped her to the door. She pasted a smile on her face as we passed the children, but Marie-Thérèse wasn't fooled. She watched her mother without speaking, her eyes plainly showing fear.

We were nearly to the bedroom when Paulette collapsed in the hall, unconscious. I nearly dropped her as her weight sagged against me. The children started to cry.

"Wake up, Paulette!" I cried, gently slapping her face. There was no response. She lay on the floor, pale and still.

"It's going to be all right," I said to the children as I ran to the kitchen and called the ambulance.

I had been terrified—more terrified than I had ever been since the night my firstborn had died. Nette had been so young, only eight months. And now, as I stood next to Paulette's bed, the vivid memories of my daughter's death vied with the more recent ones of Paulette's collapse.

"Then we waited until they came and got her," I found myself saying to the doctor, closing my eyes for a moment to gain composure. It made no difference; open or closed, I could still see Paulette's inert body on the white sheets, and Nette's as well.

"I took the children to my mother's and came here," I added, though the doctor couldn't possibly care about such details. "Is she going to be all right?"

Dr. Flaubert shook his head. "I don't know yet. She's stabilized for now, but there's something wrong. She seems to have pneumonia, but it shouldn't affect her the way it has. She's normally a healthy person. We're going to know more in a few hours when the test results come in."

Guilt ate at my insides. I shouldn't have hauled Paulette on my family outing. The cold in the tunnel couldn't have helped.

"Could she die?" I asked.

"She's in very serious condition," the doctor replied, his jowls shaking as he spoke.

I wished he would give me a straight answer. "But could she die?" I repeated.

He nodded slowly. "Yes, she could. The next twenty-four hours are crucial."

I didn't dare ask about the baby, but thoughts of that innocent spirit tortured me. I didn't know what Paulette would do if something happened to her baby.

CHAPTER THREE

I called my apartment just in case Jean-Marc had come home, telling myself it was for Paulette. I needed to find someone to give her a blessing. There was no answer, and I hadn't really expected one. Next, I telephoned the hotel where I knew Pierre would be arriving later and left a message at the desk. After calling the bishop for the second time that evening and again receiving no answer, I left a message on his machine. I didn't know Paulette's home teachers' numbers, or my own, nor could I find them in the book. The point was moot anyway, as I had run out of change and had left my checkbook at home. For all their smiles, the nurses weren't allowed to let me use the hospital phone.

Giving up, I settled into a chair, refusing to leave Paulette's bedside the rest of the night. Occasionally she awoke, and each time she clutched at her chest as pain racked her body.

"Why does it hurt so much?" I asked the nurse who went mechanically about, filling the doctor's request for additional tests. Her gray-speckled hair was swept on top of her head in a tight bun, and her thin lips were pursed in disapproval. I wondered if, like the woman at the desk, there wasn't somewhere else she would rather be.

She withdrew a needle from Paulette's arm, full of dark-red blood, before replying. "Pleurisy," she said. "A complication of pneumonia. It's very painful, but should get better in a week or so."

"Stay with me until Pierre comes?" Paulette asked during one of her short lucid periods.

"Of course I will."

"You're such a good friend," she murmured. "Much better than I ever was to you."

I knew she was thinking of Nette, and how she hadn't been able to prevent her death. Though she knew I didn't blame her and that God had forgiven her for being drugged up that night, she still remembered it with a certain degree of pain. As did I. But our Savior, who had endured so much more, helped us survive even the most severe bouts of memory. I opened my mouth to comfort her, but she was already asleep.

Pierre came in about seven o'clock Sunday morning, his short black hair tousled and a worried expression on his face. He closely resembled Jean-Marc except that he was taller, and his large eyes were a simple brown instead of my husband's unusual green-brown color. He also had an ample waist, whereas Jean-Marc had always been slender.

"Is she all right?" he asked, as he came into the room. Paulette was sleeping.

"But you were supposed to be out of town!" I exclaimed.

"When I called to tell the hotel I'd be delayed a day at my first stop, they gave me your message. I drove all night to get here." His eyes never left Paulette's face as he spoke. "How is she?"

"It's pneumonia," I said. "The doctor says she's stable for now, but—"

"Oh, thank you, Father," Pierre whispered, falling to his knees at the foot of the bed. He stayed there for a full minute in silent prayer before adding aloud, "I don't know what I'd do if something ever happened to Paulette."

Tears gathered in my eyes as I remembered how they had first met. Paulette, a drug addict, and Pierre helping her to overcome the insufferable craving that ate at her body. His love for her and forgiveness of her past was what had saved her in the end, when her testimony of the gospel hadn't been strong enough to sustain her.

I remembered, as if it were yesterday, how he had proposed to Paulette. She had been off drugs for a month and was living with his next-door neighbor, Elisabeth. We thought we were over the worst of her drug problem when a large sum of money came up missing at the Perraults' grocery store, where Paulette worked. Pierre called me as soon as he discovered the missing money, and my missionary companion and I went to his house immediately. I remember wishing that Jean-Marc was not still serving his own mission in Paris so that he could be there to help us.

Together we went to Elisabeth's, where we found the outside door ajar. Paulette was alone in her room, staring at an empty suitcase on her bed.

"Going somewhere?" Pierre asked. His voice clearly showed his suffering.

She nodded, not speaking, and slumped to the bed in complete abjection.

"You took the money from the store," Pierre said. It was not an accusation, only a fact.

Again she nodded. She reached for her brown handbag, lying on the bed next to the suitcase.

"No, I don't want it," Pierre said hoarsely. Both Paulette and I stared in surprise.

"Everything I have is yours, Paulette," he continued. "Everything. Including my heart." In two strides he crossed the space separating them. "Marry me! Please. I love you!" He sank to the brown carpet, clasping her hands and burying his face in her lap. "Just don't leave me. Or—" his voice broke. "Or if you do leave, please don't go back to the drugs. At least I'll have the comfort of knowing you're alive somewhere."

She gaped at him. "You still want me after what I was going to do?"

"I love you." His words were simple, yet the emotion behind them struck me like a blow to the stomach, filling me with longing for Jean-Marc. Suddenly, I was embarrassed to be in the room with them.

Pierre left then, as if knowing he could say nothing more to convince her. He paused at the door. "I'll be at the store, waiting," he said softly.

After his departure, she sobbed in my arms as if her heart would break. "Were you really going to leave?" I asked her.

"I—I don't know. I hadn't decided. I do know that I wasn't going back to the drugs, but I was uncertain about the future and what I would do."

"And now?"

She sniffed. "I love him. It will break his heart if I leave."

"Then don't leave."

She stood quickly. "I've got to go to the store."

I smiled as she ran out the door. I had never doubted she would stay. I suspected she had unconsciously been testing Pierre to see if he really did love her, despite her faults. And both had passed the test. I didn't blame her for wanting to be sure; an eternity was a long time to pledge undying love. Pierre was very special to have seen beyond Paulette's rough exterior to the real woman beneath.

"Ariana!" Pierre said, jolting me back to the present.

I looked up, the memories fading. "Yes?"

"I'd like to stay with her, but where's Marie-Thérèse?"

"At my parents'," I said. "I guess I'd better go and get her. And my own children. They'll be wondering about Paulette."

Pierre stood up. "I appreciate your being here, and for taking care of Marie-Thérèse. I'll call you the minute I know anything."

I nodded, remembering that it was my fault Paulette was here in the first place. I wished Jean-Marc was there to hold me, to stave off the chill that cloaked my heart.

"She hasn't had a blessing yet," I said as I left. "But the bishop should be by when he gets my message." I wondered if Pierre would ask where his brother was, and what I would say.

"Thanks. I'll take care of it." He sat in my vacated chair and turned his attention back to his wife. I was relieved that in his preoccupation he hadn't asked about Jean-Marc.

I called my parents from the lobby to let them know I was coming, but to my surprise, my mother wasn't there. "She took the children back to your house to get them dressed for that church of yours," my father told me. His voice sounded a bit mocking. "She decided to take them herself when we called and couldn't get hold of Jean-Marc." His words took on a joking tone when he said, "Where is that boy, anyway? I haven't seen him since he left work yesterday afternoon with our newest clients. He was supposed to call me and let me know how it went."

"Well, you know more than I do," I said. "I haven't seen him since Friday night. We had a fight."

There was a pause before my father asked, "What are you saying? You mean he's not at the hospital with you?"

I shook my head, though my father couldn't see. "No," I said in a small voice. "I don't know where he is. He doesn't even know Paulette is sick."

"I'll look for him, Ari. If that's what you want." My father's voice sounded angry.

"Would you? I—" I broke off, not knowing how to explain what had happened without sounding like I was whining. Then I began to wonder if my father's interference would only make things worse between Jean-Marc and myself.

"Don't worry. I'll find him." A loud click sounded in my ear.

It was nearly eight o'clock in the morning when I arrived at my apartment building. I pushed my card in the small box that would automatically open the huge metal door of the underground parking garage. It was very dark inside, lit only by the overhead lights, which were quite weak compared to the brightness of the morning sun. I came to a quick stop in our numbered spot, sprang from the car, and strode across the rough cement floor, anxious to get home.

Since we lived on the eighth floor, I was glad we had an elevator. Once it had broken and I had lugged André up the steps, listening to the twins complain about how their legs hurt. They would never know what real pain was, at least not for many years. I put my key in the lock and opened the door. The smell of cooking food wafted around me, pulling me into the apartment.

"Mommy!" Josette, named for my mother, Josephine, came running into the small entryway. She was dressed in her church clothes, but her feet were bare. "I missed you!"

"I missed you, too," I said, hugging her.

"Grandma made a cake," Josette informed me with an air of importance. She turned and yelled at the top of her voice, "Marc, come and see! Mommy's here. She's going to eat some cake with us!"

Marc came running from the bedroom, with little André toddling behind. Both smothered me in hugs and kisses. They didn't look any worse for not having had me around for the night.

"There's no cake until after church," my mother said, coming from the kitchen. She was fifty-three, but looked younger. Her body was slender, with just a slight thickening at the waist. Only the thin streaks of gray in her dark locks and the deepening wrinkles around her eyes and mouth gave any indication of her true age.

"Oh, Mother, I'm sorry it took so long."

"That's all right, Ari. I'll admit, though, it's been a long night." She let out a weary, lingering breath and walked to the arched opening off the entryway leading to the sitting room. She sank to the sofa while I opened the blinds to let in the morning sun. Instinctively, I checked my answering machine. There were no messages from Jean-Marc, only one from the bishop saying that he and the home teachers were on their way to the hospital.

"How is Paulette?" my mother asked when I settled on the love seat across from her.

"Where is Marie-Thérèse?" I asked before replying. As if in answer, the little girl appeared in the doorway, clutching the doll Paulette had made. She wore one of Josette's dresses, and it was short for her taller frame. Her face was pinched and red-looking.

"Is my mommy going to die?" she asked, her bottom lip quivering slightly.

"Goodness, no!" I exclaimed, jumping up to wrap my arms around her. Until she asked the question, I didn't realize that my faith in the matter was so strong. "Of course not. Your father's giving her a blessing, you know. She's got pneumonia, but now that she's in the hospital, everything is going to be all right." I thought I was telling her the truth.

Marie-Thérèse seemed relieved, and I felt bad that I hadn't been there to comfort her earlier. I hugged her again, more tightly. Marie-Thérèse was actually lucky; in a few weeks her mother's problems would most likely be over, but mine with Jean-Marc wouldn't be solved quite so easily.

"But she will be in the hospital for a few days," I added.

"Then does Marie-Thérèse get to stay with us more days than one?" Josette asked, her eyes bulging with excitement.

"Yes," I said.

She squealed enthusiastically. "Oh Marie-Thérèse, can you believe it? You're going to stay a few nights with us. Finally, I won't be the only girl here. Mommy doesn't count, 'cause she's a mom."

"Yeah, yeah, we already heard," Marc said. "We're right here. You don't have to tell us what she said."

Josette ignored him. "Come on, Marie-Thérèse. Let's go play dress-up. I'll be Princess Jasmine, and you be the prince."

"The prince has to be a boy!" Marc protested.

Marie-Thérèse frowned. "I don't want to be a boy."

"You can be a princess too, and Marc can be the prince."

Her brother hit his forehead in dismay, reminiscent of his father. "Then I'll have to marry both of you!"

"No, André can be the other prince," Josette said.

"He's too little," Marc protested.

"I can tell him what to say."

I watched them with a smile on my lips. My mother stood. "Right now, you'll all go into the kitchen and sit at the table. We're going to eat that breakfast I made. Then we'll go to church. Afterwards, we'll have cake."

My mother was a small woman, as was I, but rarely did her words go unheard by my children, even when she didn't have cake to bribe them. The authority in her voice was unmistakable.

"Thanks, Mother," I murmured as the children raced to the kitchen. We followed at a more sedate pace.

She smiled. "I've enjoyed being with them." Her eyes took on a faraway look.

"Are you thinking of Antoine?" I asked.

She nodded. "Marc is a lot like him."

"I've noticed," I said dryly, pointing at Marc. We had arrived in the kitchen in time to see him teetering on the counter, reaching a hand toward the cake cooling on top of the refrigerator, supposedly out of the sight and minds of certain little four-year-olds. He stepped on the butter on the counter and lost his balance as it squished between his toes. He shrieked as he fell, but I was fast enough to catch him as I hadn't been during our outing the day before.

"I told him not to." Josette sighed and shook her head, hands on her little hips. I saw my mother swiftly covering her smile. "And I told him not to go up on the wall yesterday. But he did anyway. Boys never listen, do they, Mommy?" Thinking of Jean-Marc, I couldn't have agreed more.

"Marc, how many times have I told you not to climb on the counter?" I asked, setting him down. "You'll cut your chin open again if you're not careful. Didn't you learn your lesson yesterday?" I didn't suppose he had, but I had to say it anyway; as a mother, it was my duty. Just as it was Marc's to ignore me.

"But I was seeing if the cake was cold yet, so we could put on the icing." He grinned at me engagingly, and despite my resolve, I melted. He was so like the brother I had adored.

"Go sit down," I said firmly. He ducked his head and obeyed.

While the children ate, I went into my bedroom for a change of clothes. Mother followed me with André, though she knew I needed to shower. "I already fed him earlier," she explained.

My blinds were pulled shut, and the yellow light coming from the overhead lamp cast strange reflections on my mother's face. Surely these shadows were what made her look so despondent.

"What's wrong, Mother?"

"Nothing." But she sighed.

"Tell me."

Her smile was wistful. "I never could hide anything from you, Ariana." I didn't speak, but simply waited for the rest.

She heaved another sigh and sat on my bed, sinking her head onto André's tousled hair. "I want to be baptized."

I nearly slammed my finger in my dresser drawer. "You do? But that's wonderful!" I sat beside her, throwing my arm around her shoulders. "I've waited so long to hear that!" It had been four years since my parents had agreed to listen to the missionary discussions. My mother had attended church with me often, especially in the last year. I hadn't pushed her, but had prayed constantly that she would accept the truth. Now it seemed as though she had.

"Why aren't you happy about it?" I asked.

"Oh, Ariana, I'm not like you. From the moment you first knew the Church was true, you forged ahead, not letting anyone persuade you otherwise."

"The Church explained Nette's death," I said softly.

"And Antoine's."

We were silent, and only the cars in the street below broke the quiet.

"When did you first know you wanted to be baptized?" I asked.

"I don't know. It's been a long time now—years. I keep waiting for your father. I thought he would accept the gospel and we'd be baptized together. But he's no closer to accepting it than he ever was."

"Does he know you want to be baptized?"

"No. I haven't had the courage to tell him."

I understood why. My father was a forceful man, and assured of his own place in the world. He considered religion a weakness.

"I'm tired of waiting. I want to be baptized, and I want to go to the temple."

"Then you will, Mother. But you'll have to tell him."

She sighed. "Why are men so blind to the truth?"

I snorted. "Tell me about it. Jean-Marc's so busy with work that he doesn't seem to have time for me. Sometimes I feel home is where he goes only to shower and change his clothes."

"It should ease up after the new branch is settled. You'll get used to being married to an important man. I had to."

He left me," I said abruptly.

"Oh, no! He can't have!"

"That's what I thought," I agreed.

She set André down and hugged me. "It'll be okay," she murmured.

Would it? I knew if it were up to me, it would be over now. As it was, I couldn't help the gnawing questions. Where was my husband? Could there be someone else? I didn't really believe this last thought. Jean-Marc might be obsessed with success, but he was a good man.

"And we thought marriage ended the struggles." My mother cast me a wry smile.

"The honeymoon is over, huh?" I added. "And the work begins?"

"I guess so."

I glanced at my watch. "I'd better get going or we'll be late," I said. I couldn't help hoping that Jean-Marc would be at church.

The phone rang, and I flew to the kitchen to answer it.

"Hello, Ariana?"

My hopes plummeted. "Hi, Louise." It was Jean-Marc's mother, not him.

"How are you?"

"Great. And you?"

"Well, I'm worried about Paulette. Pierre called and told me what happened."

"She'll be fine," I said. "She has to be."

"Where's Marie-Thérèse?"

"Here, with us."

"Oh. That's good." She was quiet, but I sensed there was something she wasn't saying.

"So was there another reason you called?" I asked mildly.

She heaved a sigh. "It's Lu-Lu. She's fed up with dating only members. She says there's not enough around. It's gotten worse since she started working as a secretary for that construction company. And now she's going out with this guy she met at a nightclub—Philippe, or something. She brought him home, and I don't like him."

"She's twenty-two now. You can hardly tell her who to date."

Even over the phone, I could hear Louise bristle. "Well, she still lives under my roof!" It was the same argument my parents had used on me all those years ago when I had started drinking after Antoine died. I had simply moved out, thinking to free myself of their constraints. It was the worst thing I could have done, and I didn't want Lu-Lu to rebel as I had. She was old enough to be on her own, but not if she parted from her mother in anger.

"She'll get through this, she just needs some time. Don't be too hard on her."

"I thought perhaps you could talk to her. You know, share your experiences with her. She's young for her age, and I'm afraid she'll make a mistake."

I wanted to tell her that mistakes were how we all learned, but I knew only too well how those errors could slice deep into your soul. Look what had happened to me only two days ago—and I was a mature twenty-eight. Still, I wanted to help, if I could, spare my sister-in-law the pain I had endured in my youth. Lu-Lu was immature and had always been shy, and it seemed she was finally breaking out of her shell—but not in the way her mother expected.

"So I thought we'd come down to help Paulette. Or you with the children. If Lu-Lu thought she was needed . . ."

At long last I understood why Louise had called. "You want to get her away from this guy?"

"I guess that's it." Louise's voice was subdued.

"I can always use another hand. Taking care of four children under four is not an easy task. Tell her you're coming to visit for a few weeks, and see if she'll come.

"Will you talk with her when we get there?"

"I'll try." But I wouldn't have listened to anyone when I was younger; I hoped Lu-Lu was smarter.

"We'll leave tonight and be there tomorrow," Louise said.

"Why don't you take a plane?"

I could almost hear Louise shudder. She hated airplanes. "No, I like to drive. Besides, it will give Lu-Lu and me a chance to talk."

Or you a chance to preach, I couldn't help thinking.

"We'll see you tomorrow," Louise said. Already, she sounded happier. Strangely, I too, felt more content. Maybe things would work out.

I hummed as I drove through the streets, crowded even on Sunday. Ahead of me, I could see my mother's car. Since I planned to stop at the hospital after church, she drove herself. We were nearly at the chapel when an idea occurred to me. Paulette's mother, Simone, should know about her daughter. I veered to the left, turning away from the church, and drove to a poorer section of Paris where Simone lived. I had once lived there, too.

We stopped outside a run-down apartment building that had to be at least a hundred years old from the appearance of its worn cement exterior. Clothes hung out of windows and on thin lines dangling over the cobblestone road. Some of the windows had small balconies with rusted metal railings that couldn't be trusted to hold anyone's weight. I was glad my children didn't have to live here.

The streets were safe at this hour, but I still searched to be sure there was no apparent danger. "Come on, children." They filed out and gazed around in curiosity. Marc kicked at a pile of loose cobblestones, scattering them. Similar mounds were strewn the length of the street, mixed in with refuse.

"Someone needs to fix this road," Marc said.

"Leave the cobblestones alone," I warned, worried more about his church shoes than the rocks.

"It stinks, Mom." Josette pinched her nose.

I hefted André onto my hip. "Follow me, and stay close."

The outside door to the building was ajar, and I could see the lock was broken. The mailboxes just inside the door were rusted and peeling. A foul odor assaulted our senses, and more trash lay strewn about.

"It's dark in here," Marie-Thérèse complained.

"It's not far."

Like the hallway lights, the elevator was broken and had been since I had stayed with Paulette for three months before my first marriage ten years ago. But I hadn't noticed how bad it actually was until I had found a better life. Everything looks pleasant when you are using drugs. I hurried up the stairs, ignoring the way my high heels seemed to stick to the stained marble that had deep grooves worn into its surface.

Simone lived on the second floor, so we hadn't far to climb. As I knocked on the door, the children clung to me in the murky darkness of the hallway. They weren't really scared, more thrilled to be in such a curious place. I knew the building and this adventure would be echoed in their play for many weeks to come.

The door opened, a slice of light cutting through the dark in the hallway, and a woman with greasy dark-blonde hair peered out at us. Her colorless eyes seemed unfocused, giving a rather vague feeling. She was taller than I but slightly stooped, so we appeared near the same height. I knew her to be in her mid-forties because she had given birth to Paulette when she was sixteen, yet she looked much older.

"Wha'd ya want?" she asked. The smell of alcohol was on her breath, and in her hand she held a thin homemade cigarette. I wasn't surprised.

"It's Ariana, Simone. I've come to tell you something about Paulette."

"Oh, Ariana," she said, squinting into the dark. "Come in." She backed up and opened the door wide. I took a few steps forward and the children came with me. The hallway inside the apartment was brightly lit, but in a terrible chaos. Papers, empty containers, bits of food, and various articles of worn clothing lay haphazardly strewn around, and a thick coat of dust covered everything. "Ya could have called, ya know. I got me a phone now." I couldn't miss the trace of pride in her voice. She picked up a heavy black phone that stood on a tiny table positioned under a mirror in the hall and put it to her ear. She muttered an expletive. "Stupid phone company disconnected me again!"

I shifted André's weight to the other side. "Paulette's in the hospital." That got her attention. Her face turned to me. "Why?"

"She has a severe case of pneumonia. I'm taking her daughter to see her later, after church. I thought perhaps you'd like to come with us."

Simone stared at the children, her gaze settling on Marie-Thérèse. "Yer Paulette's daughter?" she asked. Marie-Thérèse nodded.

"Why, I ain't seen ya since ya was about two years old, still a baby practically. Not really my fault, ya know. Yer mother don't want to bring ya here. I ain't good enough fer her no more." Her way of speaking clearly showed the accent of the small French village where she had been raised, as well as a lack of formal education, but this latter was mostly an act. She was smart, perhaps one of the most clever people I had ever met.

"That's not really true, Simone. You and I both know she's tried to see you. It's you that has refused."

Simone ignored me. "Come 'ere, child. Let me see ya better." She reached out a bony hand, but Marie-Thérèse took a step back. Simone didn't seem to mind. "Ya look 'xactly like Paulette when she was yer age. A spittin' image." She repeated the last sentence, this time adding a word I would have preferred she not use, especially around the children.

"We really have to be going," I said, retreating into the dark hallway. "Church will begin soon. Would you like us to come back for you?"

The older woman shook her head. "No. She don't want to see me, or she would've called."

"Your phone's disconnected," I reminded her.

Simone glared at me in annoyance. "I ain't up fer preachin' today. That's all she ever does." She reached for the door. "It was good seein' ya, Ariana." I thought she might have added a thank you, but if she did, it was muffled by the slamming door.

"That was my grandmother?" Marie-Thérèse asked once we were back in the safety of the car.

"Yes."

"Mother told me all about her, but I didn't think she'd look like that."

"How?"

"Sad. I don't know. Like she doesn't have anyone."

I pondered Marie-Thérèse's words on the way to church. Children could be so perceptive. I wanted to explain how Simone's lifestyle had distanced her from her family, but I didn't know how much Paulette wanted Marie-Thérèse to know about the past. And there was also the matter of Simone's refusal to come with us. Paulette would be hurt if she knew.

"I think we'd better not talk about our visit with Simone until your mommy comes home from the hospital," I said to Marie-Thérèse.

"Why?" the older three children chimed.

"Because Simone didn't want to come and see Paulette at the hospital. I think that might hurt her feelings, don't you?"

They thought about it, then three little faces bobbed up and down. "After Mommy comes home from the hospital, I'll tell her," Marie-Thérèse said.

"We'll both tell her. And perhaps your grandmother will let you visit her again, now that she knows who you are."

"I want to. She smells funny, but I like her."

"She swears, though," Marc said. "We have to tell her not to."

We arrived at the church and piled out of the car. I scanned the parking lot, but didn't see my husband or any of the company cars he sometimes used. For the first time, I wondered if our argument would lead to a more permanent separation. Perhaps he had been waiting for an opportunity to leave. The thought sent cold shivers to my heart.

"Where's Daddy?" Josette asked. It was the first time any of them had mentioned their father that day.

"Hurry kids," I said brightly, trying to distract Josette. "We'll be late." To my relief, she didn't pursue the thought.

My mother's wave attracted my attention. She stood on the cement sidewalk in front of the main entrance to the church. Near her was Marguerite, my longtime friend who had befriended me during the years I had been estranged from my parents. Marguerite and her husband owned several cafes and an apartment building here in Paris.

"Ariana!" my mother cried as they rushed up to me.

I set André down, and he toddled on alone. There were no other members in sight, confirming my idea that we were late. "What is it?" I asked, fearing the worst.

She glanced at the children, who were already scampering to the chapel doors. They were out of hearing range, but even so she lowered her voice. "It's Pierre. He called from the hospital. Paulette's awake, and they want to see you. He says to come immediately— with Jean-Marc. He says not to bring Marie-Thérèse."

"Is Paulette all right?" I asked quickly.

"He wouldn't say."

"Maybe she's having her baby," Marguerite suggested.

"So early?" my mother said. "She's not due yet."

"No. She's got another four months," I said, frowning. "But maybe the pneumonia is causing early labor."

"Pneumonia? Is it bad?" Marguerite asked. I had assumed my mother had already told her about Paulette's condition.

"Bad enough. She's stable but in serious condition. The doctor said the next twenty-four hours will tell."

Marguerite was quiet. "Michelle died of pneumonia." She was talking about her only child, who had died long before I knew the family.

I felt my eyes widen in surprise. "But I thought she died of drugs."

"It was the drugs, but the actual cause was pneumonia. If it hadn't been for the drugs . . ." Her voice faded and she looked away, concealing her regrets.

"Have you seen Jean-Marc?" I asked. My mother's gaze was sharp, but she said nothing. Both shook their heads.

"You'll have to go without him," my mother said.

I hesitated. "But the children . . . and I was going to teach Paulette's Primary class." I taught Relief Society once a month, but my lesson had been the week before.

"I'll take care of the class," Marguerite said.

"And I'll watch the children." My mother gently pushed me back the way I had come. "They'll be all right. Take as long as you want."

I knew my mother was serious. She always carried one of the twins' old car seats in her car for André, just in case it might be needed. With kisses for the children I made my way hastily back to my car, casting my eyes about once again for Jean-Marc. My heart called out to him; I missed him more than I had imagined possible.

I drove through the streets of Paris, fearing what I might find awaiting me at the hospital. Still, whatever it was, I felt confident I could handle it alone; after all, I had already faced more tragedy than most people did in a lifetime. It didn't matter that Jean-Marc wasn't with me.

I didn't understand then that refining fires sometimes had to be repeated many times, and that we couldn't change the consequences of our earlier choices. I especially didn't fathom that even I could not face this next challenge alone.

CHAPTER FOUR

The hospital halls were oddly quiet, menacingly so, and I seemed to see everything sharply and acutely as if in slow motion. The wheelchairs against a wall were bigger than life, the feather designs on the wallpaper more alive, and the occasional spot on the brown carpet seemed to rivet my attention. The nurses at the desk near Paulette's room looked up as I passed, staring at me with fixed eyes until I glanced in their direction. Immediately their gazes dropped, as if unwilling to meet mine. I walked on and felt eyes on me again, curious and scrutinizing, but when I turned abruptly, they jerked their heads away and focused on their paperwork.

I was sure I imagined their stares and silent refusals to meet my eyes, but nonetheless an overpowering apprehension hung over me. Quickening my pace, I was relieved to see Paulette's room. I rapped on the partially closed door, even as I pushed it open.

The scene made me stop short. Paulette was lying back on the bed. This time she wasn't using the oxygen, but the IV still dripped into her arm. Her eyes were open and she breathed steadily, if somewhat roughly. In all, she appeared much better than that morning, but there was something disturbing about the way she stared into space, seeming not to see anything.

I coughed and Pierre, sitting on the edge of the bed with Paulette's hand in his, glanced up. He said something inaudible to Paulette, who started and looked over at me. Her gaunt face crumpled, and she began to cry with heartrending sobs.

I rushed across the room. "What is it, Paulette?"

Her eyes were red-rimmed. "I have AIDS," she said unsteadily.

I felt my eyes grow impossibly wide, and my heart hammered in my ears. Surely this was some kind of hideous joke. AIDS? Acquired Immune Deficiency Syndrome? "No!" My voice came as a gruesome whisper.

She nodded. "Probably from a dirty needle years ago, or . . ."

Or prostitution. My mind completed the sentence she couldn't—or wouldn't—finish. Paulette had done many things in the past to get drugs after Nette's death. But that was over now; she had repented and been forgiven. I couldn't believe the past could come back to haunt her future. It wasn't right.

I glanced at Pierre; his red-streaked, swollen eyes and ghastly pale visage confirmed his wife's words. His overwhelming grief made him appear close to death himself. "Oh, Paulette!" Tears cascaded down my cheeks in silent torrents, and my shoulders convulsed.

She held out her arms and I went to her. We hugged. It felt strange because she turned her head, as if not wanting me to see her tears.

After a long while, she pulled away. "Marie-Thérèse and Pierre have to be tested. The doctor has agreed to do it today so we'll have the results by morning." The words were matter-of-fact, but I struggled for breath; somehow oxygen seemed to elude me. Marie-Thérèse? Pierre? But of course. AIDS was a highly contagious disease. How could they *not* have it?

"The baby?" I asked carefully.

Pierre sighed. "She has about a thirty percent chance of contracting the HIV virus. If we had known earlier, they could have given Paulette a drug that might prevent the baby from getting it. It could be too late, but the specialist has started Paulette on the drug in the hopes that the baby doesn't already have it."

A thirty percent chance of contracting AIDS! Nearly one in three! The same odds must also apply to Marie-Thérèse. Even now she could have the latent HIV virus in her blood.

"We'll know tomorrow," Pierre said bleakly. "There's a chance that—" He couldn't finish the sentence. The slim possibility that one of them might not have the disease made it too painful for hope.

I wanted to scream out the unfairness of it all. Innocent children! And Pierre, who had never done anything wrong, except perhaps to love a woman back to life. Was that so evil?

The silence in the room was far from tranquil. I could almost feel Paulette's and Pierre's hearts pounding out their hopeless despair. My own feelings threatened to drown me with sorrow. I thought it could get no worse until Paulette spoke again, and it seemed as if my world had been torn from beneath my feet, causing me to fall into an endless void.

"You need to be tested, too. And your family."

"What!" The word felt ripped from my throat.

Paulette closed her eyes and raised a hand to wipe the stream of tears. Pierre reached out to her, but she gently pushed him away.

He faced me. "Dr. Flaubert told us about the AIDS this morning. He called in a specialist who explained that AIDS is the end result of having the HIV virus. AIDS can set in anywhere between six months and eleven years after being infected with HIV. They begin to call it AIDS when a patient has signs of two or more sicknesses they call opportunistic diseases. The virus is usually contracted through sexual intercourse, from exposure to contaminated blood or blood products, or from a mother to her child before or during birth. But HIV has also been detected in tears, saliva, urine, and breast milk. It isn't probable, but remotely possible that it could be spread through those things as well."

I said nothing, feeling inundated with information that couldn't possibly have anything to do with me. Then I understood why Paulette had turned her face from me during our embrace. It wasn't because she hadn't wanted me to see her tears, it was because she worried she might give me HIV—if I didn't have it already. After all, she had done drugs with my first husband, had perhaps shared needles with him. Who knew when she had become contaminated? Perhaps I, too, had the virus in my blood, a last bitter present from Jacques. I felt myself backing away from the bed.

HIV in blood? Yesterday, hadn't I taken Paulette to the hospital while she was spitting blood? I had put my arms around her, never thinking I might be exposed to a disease that inevitably kills.

HIV in saliva? Hadn't my children and Marie-Thérèse shared suckers countless times during their young lives?

HIV in urine? Years ago, hadn't I changed Marie-Thérèse's diaper or cleaned up her mistakes when she was potty-training?

The thoughts raced through my mind with a velocity that made me stagger. Had HIV been passed to my own children and Jean-Marc? Were all those I love destined to die?

It was all I could do not to run from the room.

"I'm sorry," Paulette whispered.

I seemed to remember vividly when she had said those same words the night Nette died.

"I've got to go find Jean-Marc," I managed to say. "He has to know."

Pierre nodded. "The doctor wants to test us all. Could you bring Marie-Thérèse later? We're lucky to be in a hospital that does the tests in its own lab. In some clinics it takes a week for the results. Here they even have a wing for AIDS patients."

I nodded numbly. "I'll bring Marie-Thérèse."

"And don't tell her anything yet," Pierre added. "We want to be the ones."

"Of course."

Once out of their sight, I ran down the hall. Spotting a bathroom, I ducked inside and began washing my hands and arms with the strong-smelling soap, over and over again, as if to wash Paulette's touch from my skin.

AIDS! She had AIDS! Paulette was going to die!

And perhaps take all of us with her.

The hot water seared my skin, but I didn't stop scrubbing, not even when my arms turned red from the heat and tiny beads of blood oozed from the broken flesh. Steam rolled up, covering the mirror and dampening my skin. I sobbed hysterically, and mascara-laden tears blocked my vision and streaked my face. It wasn't fair. It just wasn't fair! How could the Lord let this happen?

I was in the bathroom for a long time, and when I finally emerged, I felt frail and shaky. I passed the nurses' station, once again feeling their eyes on me. Now I understood; they remembered my being with Paulette that morning. They had known about her having AIDS, and they felt pity for us all.

My mind was in too much turmoil to go home. I drove to the Quai of Montebello that ran along the Seine River, opposite Notre Dame. In my growing-up years, this had been one of my favorite places to come with my brother. I walked along the parapets where the booksellers' stalls were located. The stalls were really only large boxes bolted to the stone wall of the quay itself. At night, the boxes would be locked.

My attention drifted from the stalls to the river. I stopped to stare down into the water that lapped softly at the base of the wall below. It held many memories for me, mostly happy ones. Life was good, every minute so precious. Was it now running out?

I wasn't afraid of dying; part of me even longed to be near my brother and Nette. But I was terrified of leaving my children without a mother, or of watching them suffer.

Why had this happened?

I watched the boats pass by, staring at the rippling wakes they left in the water. Paulette and I had both come so far. She, especially, had changed her whole life to accept the gospel. She had repented of her sins and been forgiven. What kind of justice was this? I wanted to scream and cry out my pain to my Father, but something inside was also angry. He could have prevented this! Logically, I knew there had to be an explanation, but perhaps I wasn't ready yet to hear it.

Leaving the river, I made my way to my car. I drove slowly, ignoring the impatient honking of the cars behind me. Like in the hospital, I seemed to see everything under a strange, intense light, as if through a magnifying glass. What was it about death that made life suddenly so precious?

Before I realized where I was going, I found myself near the cemetery where Nette and Antoine were buried. I parked and made my way languidly up the cobblestone path. My foot occasionally hit a loose stone and sent it flying, echoing loudly over the quiet graveyard. I sat on the bench opposite my daughter's grave, my eyes soaking up the quiet green of the grass and trees. Her tombstone was a twin to my brother's; both were made of gray stone with carved scrollwork decorating the top and stood nearly as high as my waist. Afternoon sunlight reflected through the leaves and onto the stones and the names carved there, inlaid with gold.

Usually I visited my daughter's grave on the second and fourth Wednesday of every month, right after lunch. I always brought the children—much to the caretaker's dismay—and told them stories of little Antoinette and my life before they were born. I didn't want them ever to forget their older sibling and the pain drugs could cause. Knowing about their sister could only keep them on the right path.

It wasn't the original cemetery where Nette had been buried during my estrangement with my parents, but after my marriage, my father and I had her moved next to Antoine, after whom she had been named. There I could talk to them both and remember the happy times. Oh, I knew their spirits weren't in the ground beneath the headstones, but coming here gave me a focus, a time out of the real world to concentrate on spiritual things.

As today was Sunday, there were more visitors than I was accustomed to seeing on my bi-monthly trips. Most carried flowers for their loved ones. I paid them no heed, but let my head slump into my hands. Tears came again, and I rubbed my eyes as to stop the torrent. I had no idea how much time had passed since I left the church, nor did I have the energy to check my wristwatch.

Someone sat down on the bench beside me, and I stiffened. Who would dare to intrude on my sorrow? I darted a glance in the newcomer's direction.

"Hello, Ari." My father slid closer and put his arms around me. "Today's not Wednesday, you know," he murmured against my hair. The cemetery was the one place my father and I met alone. The first time it had happened by accident, but when he discovered four years ago that I visited Nette's and Antoine's graves twice each month, he began to visit on the same days. Sometimes his work wouldn't allow his regular visits, and I would be there alone with only the children and my thoughts for company. Occasionally I was unable to make it at the right time, and he would be alone. It didn't matter; there was always the next time we would visit.

I had never told anyone except Jean-Marc of the time my father and I spent together at the cemetery—not even my mother, though she probably knew, if not from my children then from my father. It was special, a time for us to be together and talk, or just to sit in comfortable silence as the children played nearby.

"Paulette has AIDS," I said, my voice hoarse. I wasn't expecting much sympathy from him. He had warned me all my life about drugs and the consequences of using them. To him, it might even seem a kind of justice.

In thinking this, I misjudged my father. "I'm sorry, Ari," he said. "It doesn't seem fair."

"You already knew?"

He nodded gravely. "Pierre called after you left. He was worried about you. Your mother took Marie-Thérèse to the hospital, and I came to look for you. I hoped to find you here." He held me tightly, smoothing my hair with his strong hands.

"Thanks for coming," I said after a while. "I just couldn't go home. How can I tell my children their favorite aunt is going to die? I haven't even gathered the courage to tell them Jean-Marc has left me."

My father chuckled. "That's not how I heard it."

"What do you mean?" I asked hotly, drawing away from him.

"Jean-Marc told me you threw him out."

"But I didn't—" I stopped. Well, maybe I had. "I was just trying to make a p—" But that didn't matter now. The point was that my father knew where Jean-Marc was. "Where is he?" I demanded.

He shook his head, his voice dripping irony. "For a couple that claim to be married for all eternity, you two aren't communicating very well."

"I never said I was perfect," I retorted. "Just tell me."

"All right, all right." My father raised his hands as if fending me off. "But I'll tell it my way." I sighed and settled back on the bench, knowing I would have to hear the whole story, instead of the part I was most interested in.

"I was very angry after we talked this morning. As I dressed, I planned all the things I would say and do to Jean-Marc once I found him." He paused. The sunlight seemed to reflect off his chiseled features and his graying temples. His trimmed moustache was still a shiny black, and seemed to soften his strong face. Not for the first time, I noticed that my father was a handsome man. "Luckily, I calmed down a bit," he continued. "By the time I arrived at the bank, I had begun to think there might be another explanation for his behavior."

"Then he's at the bank?" I said.

He frowned disapprovingly, but I thought I saw a twinkle in his brown eyes. "I remember how before your marriage, Jean-Marc disappeared and didn't call you for two months," he said as if I hadn't spoken. "He ran away then for a reason, and I thought maybe he might have one in this situation. So when I found him asleep on the couch in his office, I didn't kill him at once."

I smiled despite myself. "And?"

"And he told me you two had a fight, and that you practically threw his suitcase at him. What else was he supposed to do but leave?"

"That's not the way it was at all," I said. "I felt I had to do something. He's never home. He works more than you do. He neglects the children. And me. It's been going on for years, though I've been so busy with the children, I didn't recognize it until now."

"I'm not the one you should be telling this to."

"But I tried to tell him, and that's why he left."

My father said nothing, but gazed out over the tombstones. He put his arm around my shoulders. "You know, your mother and I married very young. She was only nineteen, and I twenty."

I held my breath in frustration; I had heard this story many times, and I didn't see what it had to do with my situation. However, I had learned that there was no stopping my father once he started. But as he continued, the love in his voice made my resentment fade.

"We were both only children, born late in life to our parents, and they objected to our getting married so early. But your mother was so beautiful, and I knew that having her as my wife would only give me more purpose, make our lives fulfilled. I was right. I worked hard—and you can see where I am today.

"That's not to say we didn't go through troubles. During those first seven years, we tried to have a baby, but it didn't happen. Your mother grew sad, and I didn't know how to help her. I worked harder to earn money, and it was that money we used to pay for fertility treatments."

"And the treatments got you Antoine and me," I said. My mother had been twenty-seven when she had us, a year younger than I was now.

He smiled. "Yes, but even without the drugs we could have had you both. Your mother's line has a history of fraternal twins—her own mother was one, as you know. We'd wanted a son, but when we got an extra surprise, it was the happiest day of our lives. By that time our parents had died, and I thought that we had already faced the biggest trials we would ever face. Until Antoine was killed."

I saw tears on my father's thick lashes and looked away, embarrassed in spite of our closeness.

"What I'm trying to say, Ari, is that I've learned a lot in my fifty-four years of life. Each day has its hills or mountains, and how each person deals with those problems is different, especially if those people happen to be of the opposite sex."

"What do you mean?"

"Well, for instance, a woman will say, 'André needs a diaper change,' and another woman will understand that the first woman wants her to change the diaper. However, a husband will think, 'Oh,' and go about his business, while the wife becomes angry because he's not doing what she asked. But he thinks that if she had wanted him to change the diaper, she would have said, 'Will you change his diaper?' I see this miscommunication at the bank all the time. In fact, we have a class on it now. Employee relations, you know."

"Jean-Marc has to know how I feel," I said.

My father nodded. "I think he does now. And maybe he did before, but he didn't realize how large the problem has grown."

"Then I did right," I said, "by . . . uh . . . kicking him out." Even as I said the words, I felt ashamed.

"Maybe. But it still doesn't explain why he feels he has to work as hard as he does. There must be some reason. And simply knowing your feelings might not make him change."

I found I didn't really care if the problem between us was solved at all. I only wanted Jean-Marc to come home. Paulette was dying of AIDS, and I felt my reaction to his working late was trivial now. At least he was alive, and I was, too. We could go from there. I refused to consider that one or both of us might have contracted HIV.

"So now what?" I asked.

He sighed. "First, you have to realize that not everyone faces trials the way you do. You tend to go at them head on; Jean-Marc backs away and thinks about it first. One way isn't necessarily better than the other. I've done both in my life, and both have consequences. But one thing I do know is that you can only change yourself, not your spouse. Change has to come from within a person because he wants it. And I learned this the hard way." His voice held memories of the past. A sudden, deep sorrow emanated from him, and I knew it was because Antoine was lost to him forever. While my father had some belief in God, no manner of begging, pleading, or talking on my part could make him realize that he could be sealed to Antoine, that we could be an eternal family.

"What can I change?" I asked, wanting to wipe the sadness from his face. "I haven't been nagging."

He cocked his head back and stared into the blue sky. A white cloud floated across the sun and cast a shadow over us. "That I don't know." He grimaced slightly. "Just when I think I have it figured out, your mother changes the rules."

I bit my lip, knowing that though my mother had not told him of her desire to be baptized, he obviously sensed something in her demeanor.

I kissed his cheek. "Thanks for your advice," I said. "When will I ever know as much as you?" I added lightly.

The sadness vanished, and again I caught a gleam in his eyes. "When you're as old as I am, perhaps," he said. "But don't forget that I'll be older then, and I'll still know more than you."

I laughed. One part of me questioned how I could do so in light of Paulette's illness and my own marital problems, but reality seemed far away right then. I stood, crossed the soft grass to Nette's tombstone, and ran my finger over the gold-colored indentations of her name. The edges of the carved stone felt rough against my skin.

I nodded at Antoine's stone, then joined my father. Together we walked back down the path to the black cast-iron gates that separated the graveyard from the world.

"Are the children at your house?" I asked when we reached our cars.

"No. At yours. With Jean-Marc."

My heart seemed to skip a beat. "He's home?"

"I dropped him and the children off before I came here. He wanted to come with me, but," my father's face broke into a wide grin, "I thought he should get a taste of being alone with the children for a while."

I hugged him. "Thanks, Father."

"That's what I'm here for," he said, opening my door.

Smoothing my brown linen skirt around my knees, I slid into the soft bench seat in my car. My father hesitated. "When I talked to Pierre, he said you all needed to be tested tomorrow. And that his and Marie-Thérèse's results will be ready. We'd like to be there, your mother and I."

"I'd like you there," I said softly.

He nodded and closed the door. With a short wave of his hand, he turned and strode to his own car.

On the way home, my mind drifted to Paulette. *Jesus Christ had died for our sins*, I thought, *including hers.* I believed that with my whole being; the past was over and gone. Yet why, after Paulette had embraced the gospel and become new, did the past still have the power to destroy her? It simply didn't make sense, and I needed to understand why.

CHAPTER FIVE

In my eagerness to see my husband, I fumbled for the keys in my purse. Finally, I opened the door.

"Mommy!" My children ran to me, and I hugged them.

"Why are you crying?" asked Josette, reaching up to wipe away a tear. I caught her hand before it touched me. Until I knew more about HIV, my family would have to take precautions.

"Because I love you so much." They didn't seem to think my answer strange.

"I love you too, Mommy," the twins answered together.

I felt eyes on me and looked up to see Jean-Marc watching us from the kitchen doorway, a wooden stirring spoon in one hand. He wore rumpled suit pants and a white and gray pinstriped shirt. His hair wasn't combed as neatly as usual and he looked tired, but the green-brown eyes were the same, except today they held no mirth. I stood up and took a few tentative steps toward him. He met me halfway, and we clung together in a tight embrace.

"I missed you," he said, burying his face in my hair.

"I missed you, too." My words sounded like a sob.

He held me back enough to see my face. "After I talked to your dad this morning, I went to church. When I didn't see you there, I got really scared. I couldn't believe it was over between us. Please forgive me!"

I put my finger on his lips, stilling the words, then kissed him. It was enough just to have him back. He responded fervently, until my head swam from lack of oxygen. For a moment time suspended, and I was happy and right where I belonged.

"Were you two fighting?" Josette asked.

We broke away to see three curious faces staring up at us. Jean-Marc coughed delicately and moved into the kitchen, drawing me with him. Dipping the spoon he still held into the enormous pot of soup I had made Friday night, he stirred slowly.

"We're just happy to see each other," he said. His eyes searched my face. "I wish I could have been there for you last night," he said quietly. "How is Paulette?"

"We need to talk," I said.

He looked startled. The spoon dropped from his hand and sank out of sight into the soup.

"Stay here, children," I said firmly. I grabbed Jean-Marc's hand, leaving the spoon submerged in the soup.

"Why?" Marc asked.

"Stay here!" I repeated. They stared with wide eyes as I led Jean-Marc into the hallway and toward our bedroom. The tears were coming, despite my attempt to stop them.

"I know about the AIDS," Jean-Marc said. "I was at your parents' when Pierre called. We went there after church."

"It's not that."

"What's wrong, Ari?" Jean-Marc came close and reached out to touch my face.

"Don't!" I said, remembering the HIV.

"What's wrong? You're scaring me!" He cocked his head back and studied me, his expression unreadable. "I'll be with you through this, Ari. I love you."

I shifted my eyes to the floor. "I hope so," I said softly, "because Paulette's not the only one who may have the HIV virus."

"Pierre!" Jean-Marc looked as if someone had punched him in the stomach and he couldn't find his breath. He slumped to the bed. "Of course! My brother is going to die, isn't he?"

"They don't know, but he probably has it as well. He's probably had it for years."

Jean-Marc put his head in his hand and cried, the tears seeming to dissolve all the problems separating us. My heart went out to him, but I had to tell him the rest. "Marie-Thérèse and Pierre are being tested today, and we need to go in for a test, too."

His eyes grew wide as he reeled from the shock. I tried to comfort him, but he stood up and paced the floor. "No," he said. "It's not possible. We're fine."

"We have to believe that, but we still have to be tested. Tomorrow morning, when the lab opens."

"No." His voice sounded oddly detached. "We don't need to. God wouldn't do this to us."

"Nor to Paulette. Yet she has it."

"But we've lost too much already!"

At first I thought he was referring to Antoine and Nette, but from his distant expression, I realized he was thinking of his father. I didn't know much about the man's death, except that it had been from a heart attack. Jean-Marc had never talked about it, saying only that he didn't remember the event very well. I believed he blocked it out; sometimes it was easier to hide pain than to deal with it.

"We need to be tested," I repeated. "And to learn more about AIDS—if only to help Paulette and Pierre."

I thought he might hug me then, and reassure me that everything would be all right, but he didn't. He shook his head. "No. I'm not going."

"But we have to know."

"I do know, and I'm not going!" He pushed past me and into the hallway. He didn't stop when he reached the kitchen.

Leaving! Not again. I followed him, stunned. He picked up his briefcase and opened the apartment door.

"Jean-Marc!"

"I've got work to do. I'll be home later."

"On Sunday?" I said. He never went to the office on Sundays. "It can wait. We have to talk about this."

"No, we don't."

"You're running away, darn you!" I called after him. "Come back!"

He paused in the hallway, eyes pleading. "Let me go."

I softened, remembering what my father had said about the different ways people handled problems, and how I couldn't change him. The only thing I could change about this situation was my attitude. "When will you be back?" With these words he would know that I wanted him back.

"Later."

"Okay." I kissed my hand, then blew on it.

He caught the imaginary kiss with his hand, touched his mouth, and smiled unsteadily. "I love you, Ari." He pushed the elevator button and stared expectantly at the closed double doors.

"Jean-Marc?" An idea had come to me, a flash of memory. One that perhaps could help both of us.

He turned to look at me, eyes guarded. "Yes?"

"Once, you promised me never to try to solve the important things yourself. You said we'd do it together. Do you remember?"

His shoulders slumped. The elevator chimed as it opened, but he made no move toward it. His briefcase slid to the floor as the doors slammed shut again. When he spoke, his voice was teary and full of memories. "Yes. It was when I proposed. I said you were a queen, and I'd do my best to become your king." His eyes met mine and his voice sounded ragged. "I haven't done too well, have I?"

I gave him a watery smile. "Maybe not tonight or in the past few days, but there's still time."

He walked over to me and hugged me tightly. "What would I ever do without you?"

"Is that why you're afraid of our getting tested? Are you afraid of losing me?"

"Well, it's like this." He held up his hands in a cupping motion, his voicing breaking as he spoke. "Friday morning I felt as if everything was right here in my hands, and now it's suddenly slipping away, and I can't stop it." He opened his fingers and stared down at them.

"What can we do?" I asked him. He probably didn't know, but to ask him might get us both on the right track. He was a priesthood holder, and I had faith that he would rise to the challenge. I wasn't to be disappointed.

"Pray," he said after a long pause. "We need to pray together. And let's start a fast tomorrow."

Jean-Marc retrieved his briefcase and grabbed my hand, holding tightly, as if afraid to let go. We went inside our apartment and turned to face the three pairs of eyes, wide and scared-looking, watching us from the kitchen doorway.

"Come here," Jean-Marc beckoned to them. He led us into the family room where we knelt in a circle, holding hands. The twins were strangely reverent, as if somehow sensing the importance of the moment.

"Dear Heavenly Father," Jean-Marc began. He prayed for Paulette, Pierre, and their children, then he prayed for us. Instead of imploring the Lord to make us free of the HIV virus, he asked that God's will be done, and pleaded for the courage to accept his will.

I was proud of Jean-Marc and the example he set for me and the children. He wasn't perfect, but then, neither was I. We were both merely doing our best.

After the prayer, Josette asked, "What's wrong with Aunt Paulette?"

I looked to Jean-Marc and he nodded once, sharply.

"She's got a disease called AIDS," I said. "There isn't a cure. And she's going to get very sick."

"You mean die?"

What could I say to my little girl, kneeling on the ground and watching me so intently? She knew little of life and nothing of death—not yet. Eventually she would have to face it—when Paulette died—but surely I could protect her a while longer. I pulled her onto my lap.

"Not right now, honey. Now that the doctors know what she has, they can give her medicine to help her. But like I said, after a few years, she'll be very sick."

Josette's eyes filled with tears. "But does Marie-Thérèse know?"

"Her parents are telling her now."

"I'm going to keep praying for Aunt Paulette," Josette said.

They had more questions and we answered them to the best of our ability, trying not to scare them but to be truthful. Then Jean-Marc told them about our having to be tested.

"It's just to make sure we don't get sick," he said. He looked at me as he added, "We need to know."

"Could we die?" Marc asked. He didn't seem frightened, only curious, as if dying might be an adventure.

I didn't know what to say. Once I would have reassured him, but now I couldn't. While it was unlikely that Marie-Thérèse or Paulette could have given him HIV, my own life before being baptized might very well have given him this terrible legacy.

Jean-Marc came to my rescue. "I don't think we should worry too much," he said. "We're all going to be around for a long time. Except, of course, if the tiger gets you. Rrrr!" He flopped onto all fours and pretended to bite Marc's neck.

The twins screamed in delight, their young minds already discounting any danger, but André came to sit in my lap as if sensing I needed something to hold on to. He was a blessing, one I had often taken for granted. I cuddled him, vowing not to make the mistake again. I would cherish each day with all my children. We watched Jean-Marc and the twins playing on the floor until they tired of the game. At last they stretched out on the mauve carpet, panting.

"Now can we get the spoon out of the soup?" Josette asked suddenly, bringing a smile to our faces. "Marc was going to do it, but I wouldn't let him."

"Good for you, Josette. Yes, we can get it out. Does anybody want soup?"

While they were eating, I called the hospital to speak with Pierre.

"Should I come and get Marie-Thérèse?" I asked.

"No; Paulette's asleep, and I'm going to take Marie-Thérèse home tonight. We'll see you tomorrow morning. I'll bring some clothes for Marie-Thérèse, and perhaps you can watch her for a few days."

"Of course," I said. "We'd love to have her." My voice wavered. If it turned out Marie-Thérèse had HIV, maybe I wouldn't be so willing.

"Thanks, Ariana."

"Would you like to talk with Jean-Marc?"

"What would I say?" he asked. "It's better to wait until tomorrow. Until I know."

I hung up and went to put the children to bed. The twins went peacefully, but we had waited too long to put André in his crib. The little boy cried irritably as Jean-Marc tried to change his diaper and dress him. Jean-Marc looked upset, but I knew what to do when André acted this way.

I took André from Jean-Marc and whirled him around the room, singing the theme from the latest Disney movie. His tears disappeared, replaced by a smile. I laid him down and tickled his toes softly. In between the tickling, I got him ready for bed. It really wasn't difficult to deal with André; you just had to keep him occupied. The twins had been more exacting.

"I didn't know he ever got like that," Jean-Marc said as I kissed the baby and tucked him under the covers in his crib.

"How many nights have you been here to see how he acted?" I said without thinking. Jean-Marc frowned. "It's because he's tired," I said, relenting. "He doesn't normally do this. There's been too much excitement here tonight."

"Too much for all of us," he said. He peered into the twins' room. Already they were snoring gently.

"Thank you for staying," I said, moving to stand beside him.

"Thank you for reminding me of what I should be doing." He held my hand tightly and glanced back into the darkened room, not looking at me as he spoke the next words. "Ari, are you afraid?"

I nodded. "I am."

His smile flashed so briefly that I wondered if I had imagined it. "Good. Then it's okay for me to be afraid." He laughed, but without mirth. "It's funny how it takes a crisis like this before you realize how much you have to lose." He spoke the words in my own heart.

For a long time we said nothing, simply stood in the doorway, watching the sleeping children. Then Jean-Marc reached out to me and drew me close. Our lips met, and for a short time everything was right with the world. We made our way to our bedroom, lit only by the thin moonlight streaming through the blinds. We embraced tightly, neither of us wanting to let go, silently sharing our hopes and fears as only eternal companions could. Whatever the outcome, we were in this together, and nothing—not even death—would defeat us.

I knew my thoughts were brave; in the reality that Paulette and Pierre were living, there would be much more hardship and sorrow. But tonight, I would not borrow others' troubles. Tonight I would be with my husband as if eternity were already ours.

CHAPTER SIX

We awoke early Monday morning to go to the hospital. Jean-Marc made breakfast while I readied the children. The tension in the air was palpable, and André, normally so cheerful, was cranky and crying. Jean-Marc tried to comfort him but was unable. I took the baby from his arms, and after a few minutes he was quiet. Jean-Marc seemed angry, but I didn't understand why. I assumed he was worried about the tests.

We were ready to leave when the doorbell rang. "Who could that be?" I muttered. Jean-Marc opened the door to reveal Louise, a suitcase in either hand.

"I'm here," she announced. She dropped her cases and hugged her son, kissing him several times on each cheek in the French custom. "A young man let me in the door downstairs so I didn't have to buzz you. He was coming out as I arrived."

Jean-Marc darted a questioning glance over his shoulder, and I shrugged apologetically. In the upheaval caused by Paulette's AIDS, I had completely forgotten about Louise's visit.

"Grandma!" shouted the twins, rushing forward with outstretched arms. Jean-Marc stood back to allow them room.

Louise was a plump woman in her late fifties. She had lustrous dark-brown hair that showed no signs of graying, though I knew she had help from her hairstylist to make it so. But the youthful hair matched her indomitable spirit. She had been widowed when Jean-Marc was seven, and for many years had been the backbone of their family, not only managing their grocery store, but supporting both sons on their missions.

"Ariana, as beautiful as ever," she said, coming forward to kiss me.

Jean-Marc and I stood silently, neither of us knowing how to tell her the news about Paulette.

"Where's Lu-Lu?" I asked.

"She went in to work today to finish some things and to tell them she'll be gone for a week. I told her it was a family crisis and that they'd understand if she called from here, but she insisted." Louise sniffed.

"She's taking the plane later today. She said for me not to worry about picking her up either," she added tersely. "Lu-Lu said she knows how to use a taxi."

It seemed that Lu-Lu really was growing up, and her mother wasn't enjoying the process.

Louise heaved a frustrated sigh. "I need to rest. How about showing Grandma to a chair?" she asked the children. Unlike my own mother, she had a few health problems, including an ulcer, varicose veins, and painful arthritis. It had been a relief for her when Pierre had sold their store and she could retire.

"But we're going to the hospital for a test," Josette said.

"Yeah, they take your blood out and everything," Marc added with relish.

Louise glanced up at us, instantly understanding that something terrible had happened. "What's going on?" she demanded.

"It's Paulette," I said.

"The baby?"

I shook my head, glancing at Jean-Marc for help.

"Paulette has AIDS," he explained gently. He repeated everything Pierre had told me at the hospital, leaving nothing out. "Now we all need to be tested."

"Oh, Jean-Marc!" Louise lost her composure and began weeping. He hugged her for long moments as she sobbed.

"I'm going with you," Louise finally said through her tears. She wiped her large hands over her red face, as if to cover the fact that she had been crying.

It was a very subdued group that filed into the hospital. My parents were there waiting, and each picked up one of the twins. With a flash, I remembered how they had picked Antoine and me up at that same age. How young they had been then! And how certain of the future. But Antoine died, and now they were afraid of losing someone they loved again.

The antiseptic smell of the hospital drifted into my nose and seemed to settle in my stomach, making me feel nauseous. I was grateful to feel Jean-Marc's arm around my shoulders; there were no walls between us now.

The nurses at the lab drew blood quickly and efficiently. Little Marc watched in fascination, but Josette squeezed her eyes shut tight. Neither cried, nor did André, but all of the adults had tears in their eyes, stemming from fear of the virus and not from the needle.

"If you call after nine in the morning, we'll give you the results," the nurse said, removing her gloves. Her voice was clipped and remote, making me want to shake her. Our whole lives hung in the balance, but for her it was just another test.

"Thank you," said Jean-Marc.

"Will you stay home to call with me?" I asked quietly as we moved down the hall. He seemed surprised at the question, but I had to know.

"I'll take the whole morning off," he said.

We went to see Paulette. They had moved her to another wing where all the patients were terminally ill, including many with AIDS. To me, even the corridor smelled like death. However, the nurses we saw didn't stare at us with pity, and their smiles were genuine. I guessed Paulette was lucky that at this hospital they were equipped to deal with her sickness.

"Your mother and I will be in the waiting room," my father said. Once more he held Josette in his arms.

Jean-Marc looked at the twins. "You stay with Grandma and Grandpa."

"But I want to see Marie-Thérèse," Josette protested.

"She's coming home with us," I said. "You and Marc can play with her then."

"And remember, I'll not have any horsing around here," Jean-Marc warned, staring pointedly at Marc.

"Okay," the boy said, the picture of innocence.

"Would you like to leave André with us, too?" my mother asked.

"No, he won't understand anyway." I held my baby tightly.

Jean-Marc's arm went around my shoulders again, and I was comforted.

As we approached the room, our steps slowed in trepidation. Louise knocked and, at a faint sound from inside, pushed open the door. Paulette lay curled on her side with one arm covering her face. She breathed heavily, and once again we could hear the hiss of the oxygen in the quiet of the room. Pierre, by her side, was strangely calm. His face was still pallid, but the red eyes had disappeared. Marie-Thérèse sat on his lap watching her mother sadly, eyes red and puffy as if she had been crying.

Pierre stood up as we entered, and Marie-Thérèse slipped to the floor. She didn't run to play with André or to greet her grandmother as she normally did, but simply regarded us gravely. Jean-Marc stepped forward and silently hugged his brother. No one spoke for a long moment, and the tension in the room built.

"Well?" It was Louise who broke the silence.

Pierre's face was visible over Jean-Marc's shoulder. His lower lip quivered, the only sign of his inner turmoil. He broke away and hugged his mother briefly before speaking. When he did, his voice was low, almost a whisper, and very hoarse. "Marie-Thérèse doesn't have the virus," he said.

"But you do," Louise stated.

He nodded. "I do. Of course, it may be years yet until . . ." His voice dropped away as if he was too tired to finish the explanation, or as to say, "What difference could my words make? It won't change the fact that I'm going to die." The unfinished sentence and the tragic calm on his face revealed more about what he was feeling than anything he could have said.

I didn't know what to do for him. My mind grasped at the only consolation it could find. Marie-Thérèse at least would live! I handed André to Louise and knelt to hug the little girl, unable to stop the tears. "Oh, thank you, Lord," I whispered over and over, hugging her. She clung to me with one arm; in the other she held her rag doll.

"I'm okay, Aunt Ariana," she whispered. "It's Mommy who's sick. But she's going to get better." Her words showed me that like my own children, she had no real understanding of death or the illness that had her mother in its fatal grip.

"Why don't you go out in the waiting room and see your cousins?" Jean-Marc suggested. "They're with Ari's parents," he said in further explanation to Paulette and Pierre.

A smile lit Marie-Thérèse's face. Jean-Marc moved to the door and opened it for her, then walked with her down the hail, making sure she was delivered safely into the care of my parents. When he returned, Louise spoke.

"What about the baby?" She had tears on her worn cheeks, but she maintained her composure. She gave André back to me and walked to the head of the bed. One rough hand touched Paulette's hair gingerly.

"They won't know until she's born, unless we want to take a test that may cause her to abort early," Paulette said sadly. "We don't want to risk it."

A knock at the door came and Louise opened it. A nurse entered, carrying a tray of food. She was short, with skin the color of dark chocolate and full lips painted a rich red. "How are you today, Paulette?" she asked kindly.

Paulette groaned, but she let the nurse help her to a sitting position. "I'm not hungry," she said petulantly.

"I know, but you have to eat to keep up your strength. If not for yourself, then for your baby."

It had been the right thing to say. Paulette began to eat, without appetite, but steadily.

The nurse chattered happily as she went about her work straightening the pillow, checking the charts, and watching the monitors. "It looks like you're holding steady," she said cheerfully. "That's a good sign."

"This is Giselle," Pierre said to us. "She's been assigned to Paulette."

"Glad to meet you," I said sincerely. She was certainly a lot better than the silent, mean-looking nurse who had taken care of Paulette before.

"And you are?" Giselle's face seemed to shine with a happiness that should be out of place in this room. Instead, I found her manner refreshing.

Pierre made introductions. Giselle looked at each of us intently, as if putting our faces in her memory. "It's nice to meet you all," she said. "It's good to see Paulette has so much support." She turned and faced the bed. "I'll be back in a little while for your tray, and to take your temperature and blood pressure before I go off shift. The doctor also wants another blood sample. We need to get you up and home, don't we?"

Paulette nodded, but I could see the fear in her face. Giselle did too. "It's all right," she said. "AIDS is a terrible disease, but you can have a good life for as long as you have left. It's what any of us try to do, really. It's all in the attitude."

I was beginning to like this nurse. She was exactly what we needed.

"We're all here for you," Jean-Marc said after Giselle had left. "Tell us, please, what can we do?"

Pierre looked at him gratefully. "There's nothing now. Just taking care of Marie-Thérèse has been a big help."

"Has she had a blessing?" He motioned to Paulette.

Pierre nodded. "I gave her one yesterday morning."

"Will you watch Marie-Thérèse again, Ariana?" Paulette asked, her spoon pausing in mid-air.

"You know I will."

"Could everybody leave so I can talk with Ariana for a minute?" Paulette asked. The group nodded and filed out the door. Only André stayed with us. He put his hand in my short hair, tugging gently. I pushed his hand away and kissed his forehead.

I waited, but Paulette didn't speak. "So what now?" I asked.

"I'm afraid, Ari," Paulette said. "I mean, I'm going home when I'm over the pneumonia, but I'm afraid of getting Marie-Thérèse sick. For Pierre it's too late, but for her . . ."

"I won't do it," I said, knowing what she was going to ask. "Marie-Thérèse needs you now. She needs to build memories that will last a lifetime, after you're gone. I won't take that away from her."

"Memories of me being sick? Of me wasting away until I die?" Paulette bit her lip to stifle tears. "What good could that possibly do my baby?"

"During the bad days, I'll gladly take her home. But don't leave her yet. You have to give her time to adjust. You could have years left. You can't push her aside."

"Not even to protect her?"

"She wouldn't understand. Besides, you've had this for years, and she hasn't gotten it. And now that you know, you can take precautions."

"I'm so afraid," Paulette repeated.

"Just love her like you've been doing. We'll get through somehow."

Tears gathered in the corners of her eyes. A big drop fell and splashed on her white cheek. "Why, Ariana? Why? I can't figure it out. I thought I was forgiven for my sins, but now I have to pay for them. And so does my family. I don't understand why!"

Those were the same thoughts that had tortured me the day before after leaving the cemetery. I still didn't have an answer, so I said nothing. I stared at the floor, unable to help my best friend. Then an idea came. I knew it was the Spirit whispering to me, though I hadn't asked for aid.

"Give it time," I said. "I don't know why, but I have faith. The Lord loves you, Paulette. He does."

"Will you help me?"

I wasn't sure what she was asking. If I would help her understand? Accept? Help her with Marie-Thérèse? Or was she asking if I would help her to die? I thought I might be able to help her with the first three, but never the last. I couldn't help her die, surely she wouldn't ask that.

"Whatever you need, Paulette," I heard myself saying. "I love you." I wanted to hug her, but didn't dare.

She laid her head back on the pillow. "I love you too, Ariana."

There was nothing more to say, so I turned and walked to the door. I paused. "Get better, huh? You and I have more memories to make, too."

She gave a short laugh, and to my surprise, it sounded genuine.

When I joined the others, Jean-Marc and my father had already left for work. I felt strangely deserted, though I had known all along that Jean-Marc was planning to leave after our tests. I envied him for being able to bury himself in work, and thus not having to think about the possible test results.

"Is there anything we can get for you?" I asked Pierre.

He shook his head. "No. Thank you."

"I'll come back later," Louise said, "to see how she's doing."

"Thanks, Mom." Pierre kissed Marie-Thérèse, then took a few steps backwards. He pointed over his shoulder with his thumb. "I gotta get back to her now. I don't like to leave her alone."

We started slowly down the hall. The twins had overcome their temporary shyness and begun to investigate their surroundings. Accompanied by Marie-Thérèse, they darted in and out of cubby-holes, hallways, and everywhere else they could imagine. I felt like a puppet on a string, with my head jerking from side to side as I tried to keep track of the youngsters. I gave André to my mother and barely managed to stop Marc from going into another patient's room. I grabbed firm hold of my children's hands, and Louise took Marie-Thérèse's. In Louise's other hand she carried a small suitcase for my niece. Linked together, we walked to the elevator.

"Wait!"

I turned to see Nurse Giselle waving at us. We stopped and waited for her to catch up. She was breathless when she arrived, and her wiry black hair puffed about her face. With one hand she patted it down, and with the other she held up a thick booklet.

"It's nearly everything you need to know about AIDS," she said. "I find it helps when everyone in the family knows what to expect. Dispelling any misconceptions can get rid of unnecessary fears, while telling you what to look out for. For example, because the HIV virus has been found in tears and saliva, people suppose they can be infected by getting a little bit on them. But the truth is, you'd probably have to drink a quart or more of either liquid before you were at risk of infection. At least that's what they taught me in nursing school." She pushed the booklet into my hands. "This tells it all."

"Thank you." I meant it. Her comments about the tears were especially useful. I felt foolish now, though my fear had been real.

"Have you had many patients die?" Louise asked.

Giselle nodded, her expression sober. "Yes. I have."

"How can you stand it?"

"I make their last moments comfortable," she said. "That's all I can do. The rest is between them and God."

"Do you believe in God?" I asked. The question was instinctive for members like me, who lived in places where there wasn't a large population of Latter-day Saints.

"I do. If anything, working here has helped me to believe that."

"Why?"

"Because I see the peace most of my patients achieve before death. And on their faces after they die. Only God can give them that."

"What religion are you?" asked Louise.

Giselle smiled. Her face was sweet and innocent-looking. "Just of God. That's all."

I wanted to ask her if she had heard of our church, but she glanced at her watch. "I have to go. I need to check on Paulette and give her some medicine." She smiled again and left.

I drove home, feeling lighter than I had expected. Giselle's moving testimony of God's existence had strengthened my own, even if she wasn't a member of the Church.

Thank you, Father, for reminding me, I prayed silently.

The twins argued in the back. André in his car seat and Marie-Thérèse in front both sat silently.

"Mommy," Josette said, "Marie-Thérèse is going to live with us forever now, isn't that right? Marc doesn't believe me."

"Stop arguing now," I said firmly, glaring at them in the rearview mirror. "Marie-Thérèse will live with her parents for a long time to come. Meanwhile, she is always welcome to come to our house to play. She's part of our family."

I stopped the car at a red light as I finished speaking. Louise glanced over and our eyes met. We both knew Paulette didn't have very long to live compared to a regular life span, even if it might seem a long time to a child. What did the future hold? What of Pierre? And what of the unborn child who may or may not have the HIV virus? I was willing to take care of Marie-Thérèse; I loved her already as my own. But to take the responsibility of a sick infant? To place my own children at risk? I didn't know if I could do it. I couldn't even admit to myself that I didn't want to. It was too much to ask of anyone.

I sighed, pushing the thoughts away. For now, I would take one day at a time. Until the uncertainty of our own tests was over, there would be no point in planning for the future.

CHAPTER SEVEN

I was unable to function normally the rest of the morning. I found myself staring at nothing for long periods of time. When my children spoke to me, I would come out of my trance, only to realize that an hour had passed, and I couldn't remember what had kept me so absorbed.

Finally, I shook myself and concentrated on playing with the children. There were a million things I should be cleaning around the house—a pile of dirty dishes, a tower-high mound of laundry, dust and bits of paper everywhere—but they seemed unimportant now. Instead, I played the brave hero in my children's make-believe game of prince and princess, cutting down pretend foes and protecting them as I might not be able to do in reality.

Josette and Marie-Thérèse draped sheets over their heads and the lower part of their faces; Marc and André wrapped towels around their waists. André tripped repeatedly on his towel during the sword fights, but he didn't cry. He rarely did.

At noon we had a picnic lunch in the bedroom, and afterward, they fell asleep on the blanket as I read them a story. I had a twin on each arm, with André squeezed in next to Josette, his head on my stomach and his short legs thrown casually over his sister. Marie-Thérèse slept next to Josette.

I set the book down and lay back on the pillows. My arms felt stiff, but I didn't move. I wished this moment could last forever, that we would never have to face the reality of tomorrow and the dreaded test results.

I kept telling myself that I didn't feel sick. But then, neither did Pierre.

"Ariana?" Louise called softly from the hail.

"Yes?" I extracted myself carefully from the sleeping children. For all my care, André, who had been the first to sleep, awoke and held out his chubby arms. I picked him up and went into the hall.

"I'm making vegetable soup, if that's okay," Louise said. "Then I'll go back to the hospital. I'd like to take some for Paulette. That hospital food didn't look too appetizing."

"I'll help you," I said. "We'll make extra to serve with the turkey breasts I'm making for the children's dinner." Jean-Marc and I wouldn't be eating, since we had begun a fast after lunch.

While we worked, Louise chattered about how Lu-Lu had changed, how she had suddenly become outspoken and had taken to staying out late.

"Maybe she's trying to find herself," I said.

Louise stopped peeling the potatoes. "I think she might be involved in drugs."

My heart must have skipped a beat because I suddenly felt dizzy. I sank abruptly to a chair, staring at André, who sat on the floor playing with a truck and a few miniature people. He wasn't much older than Nette had been when drugs had killed her.

"Will you talk to her?" Louise asked.

"Of course." But I feared it might be too late.

Jean-Marc came home before dinner that evening, carrying a huge bouquet of my favorite white roses. I was content to have him home, whatever the reason. Together we fed the children, and afterwards we washed the dishes, read the Book of Mormon, and had family prayer. Then we set up the cot we kept under Josette's bed for Marie-Thérèse, and kissed each child good night. In his room, André curled up in his crib and slept immediately, but the twins seemed to take their father's presence as sign of a holiday, and it was difficult to get them and Marie-Thérèse settled. Because of the test we were more indulgent than usual, and they pushed for full advantage, even while not understanding the cause. After a bathroom trip and two drinks of water each, the suddenly dehydrated children finally fell asleep.

The excitement of the evening wasn't over. Louise came home, her face more drawn and weary than I'd ever seen it. "Paulette is dying," she confirmed as we went into the sitting room. "I can see it in her eyes. I'll never forget the look; I remember it so well."

As he hugged his mother, Jean-Marc's eyes were haunted. "We'll get through this together," he murmured. "We're a family."

"Your father was in the hospital for three weeks before he died. He had the same look. Do you remember?"

"No." His whispered voice was slightly self-accusatory.

"How long does she have?" I asked. "Do they know?"

Louise sighed and sank to the couch. "The specialist can only tell me the statistics. That's one of the problems with this disease: it affects everyone differently. He did say that once AIDS sets in, most people die within three years—some a lot sooner. He worries that Paulette has had it for quite some time. Evidently, Dr. Flaubert has been treating Paulette for a variety of what he calls opportunistic infections, without recognizing what was causing the problems in the first place. She's had anemia, bacterial infections, and now pneumonia, which is the leading cause of death among AIDS patients and quite often the first symptom to develop. It wasn't the doctor's fault, really. He didn't have any reason to assume she was at risk for AIDS. She never told him about being involved with drugs."

"So what does that mean? Is Paulette coming out of the hospital or not?" I asked. "What does the specialist say?"

"Dr. Medard, his name is Dr. Medard. But he doesn't know. Evidently, people with AIDS get a special kind of pneumonia. At least now that he knows what she has, he can treat it more effectively. But it depends on how far gone her body is. He believes she'll live a couple of months. Longer if she gets over this infection."

"If?" I could hardly believe what I was hearing. I had thought we would have years to come to terms with Paulette's illness.

"What about the girls?"

"Paulette's had HIV for at least six years," Louise said. "Apparently, people can have it up to eleven years before it develops into AIDS. It's transmitted through sexual intercourse, so Pierre," her face seemed to collapse, "had almost no chance to test negative. But according to the doctor, like with Marie-Thérèse, the baby has around a thirty percent chance of having the virus. Had they known sooner, they could have given Paulette a drug that helps prevent it from spreading to the fetus. They are giving it to Paulette now, but we'll have to wait and see how the tests come out."

I hadn't been asking that question exactly; Pierre had already told me about the drug to help the baby and about it possibly taking the HIV virus eleven years to become AIDS. What I wanted to know was who would take care of the girls when Paulette was gone. I knew Pierre wouldn't be able to do it; he would be fighting for his own life.

"Paulette's being pregnant is another difficulty," Louise continued. "They have to be careful of what they give her because some drugs can hurt the baby."

"Paulette doesn't deserve this," I said.

"No," Jean-Marc agreed. "No one does."

We sat in forlorn silence, broken only by the occasional chiming of the grandfather clock my parents had given us for our wedding.

"I guess it's time for bed," Jean-Marc finally said.

"I made up a bed for you in André's room, Louise," I said. "If Lu-Lu gets here, she can sleep on the couch bed."

"I'm going to wait up for Lu-Lu. She should be here by now. Besides, she'll need to be told." Louise's face showed her worry, one I understood well. It wasn't every day a person learned their brother was going to die. My own world had been shattered when Antoine had been killed.

We started nervously when a loud buzzing broke the silence in the corridor—someone ringing at the outside door downstairs.

"It must be Lu-Lu," Louise said.

Jean-Marc got up from the couch and shuffled to the intercom box in the hallway near the door. Static sounded as he pushed the button. "Who is it?" he asked.

I couldn't make out the answer, but another buzz signaled that Jean-Marc had pushed the button that would open the downstairs door.

"It's Lu-Lu," he confirmed as he came back into the room.

A short time later a quiet knock sounded at the door, and Jean-Marc went to open it. He returned shortly, followed by Lu-Lu. They were not alone.

"Hi everyone," she said, giving us a wave with her hand as she stood under the arched entryway. She was a feminine version of Jean-Marc, with the same green-brown eyes as her brother. Her short figure was lean and fit, and her dark hair was cut short, similar to my own, but it was newly highlighted with red. She had a thin nose and a wide, laughing mouth. She didn't usually talk much, but I had never seen her without a smile—until tonight.

"This is Philippe Massoni." She motioned to the stranger beside her, a tall youth with shaggy brown hair and a scruffy beard. I could almost swear her words were slurred.

Louise stood. "What are you doing here?" She addressed the man directly, her words almost an accusation.

"When he heard I was flying to Paris, he decided to visit friends himself." Lu-Lu's expression was triumphant.

"We have a family crisis," Jean-Marc said stiffly, standing next to his mother. "No offense meant to you, Philippe, but we need to talk with Lu-Lu."

"But that's what I've come to tell you." Lu-Lu nearly propelled Philippe into the room. The blue eyes that marked his family as likely originating in the northern part of France were dulled, his faded jeans and T-shirt reeked of smoke, and there was a faint aroma of alcohol on his breath. I joined my husband and mother-in-law in opposing this man. I would never forget those smells; they reminded me of Jacques, and of Paulette the way she had been before joining the Church. None of us was ready for Lu-Lu's next statement.

"Philippe has asked me to marry him."

We gaped in shocked silence.

"And you said?" Louise finally found her voice.

"I said yes."

"That's great," Jean-Marc said softly. "And what temple will you be getting married in?"

Lu-Lu blinked, and her defiance faded. "Uh, we don't know where or when yet. We've only decided tonight."

I saw the uncertainty in her, even if the others could not. She didn't want to marry outside of the temple, but she felt she didn't have a choice. Maybe she thought her love might change Philippe; indeed, love might change him if anything could. The only obstacle would be if Philippe didn't want to change. My father was right when he said that change had to come from within.

"Well, there's no hurry to decide anything," I said lightly. "We have a problem you need to know about."

"Is it Paulette?" Lu-Lu realized we were serious about the family crisis, that we weren't just trying to get rid of Philippe.

"Yes." I looked at Louise and Jean-Marc, but they said nothing. "She has AIDS," I said gently.

Philippe jerked, and Lu-Lu began to cry. She rushed into her mother's arms.

"Maybe I'd better go," Philippe said after her tears had subsided. He looked uncomfortable. Louise sniffed, and I knew what she thought of Philippe for running out on Lu-Lu at a time like this.

Lu-Lu didn't object. "I'll see you tomorrow." She kissed his cheek.

Philippe nodded toward me and Louise. Jean-Marc held out his hand, but Philippe hesitated.

"It's okay," Jean-Marc said. I could see his eyes glinting in the soft light of the sitting room. He had a half-smile on his face, the one he wore when he teased the twins. "We don't have the virus." He waited until Philippe took his hand. "At least we don't think we have it; we'll find out in the morning."

Philippe pulled his hand away as if he had touched hot coals, then tried to hide it by pulling on his beard.

"Silly," Lu-Lu said, smiling through her tears. "You can't get it from shaking hands."

Philippe didn't seemed convinced. He turned, and Lu-Lu walked with him to the door. "Nice to meet you," he mumbled over his shoulder.

Louise looked about ready to explode, but I cautioned her. "Let it ride for tonight," I said. "We'll decide what to do later." It wasn't really our choice, I knew. But our actions could force Lu-Lu into a quick decision—one she might regret. Lu-Lu was coming back into the room, so there was no time for further discussion. I was glad to see Louise purse her lips and say nothing.

While Jean-Marc explained the details of how we had found out about Paulette, I went to the kitchen to make hot chocolate, forgetting for a moment about our fast. It was really an excuse to escape the tense conversation in the sitting room. As the milk heated, the phone rang.

"Hello?"

"Ariana, it's me," my mother said. Her voice was rough as though from crying.

"Is something wrong?"

"I just wanted to talk with you."

"You told Father, didn't you?" I waited for a response, then prompted, "And?"

Usually my mother was full of words, but tonight I had to drag them from her.

"He got angry. Said he wouldn't allow it."

"And you said?"

"I said I was going to do it anyway, and he said that if I loved the Church more than him, then I should be baptized. Then he went into his study."

I wasn't surprised; Father always retreated to his study when things didn't go as he planned. He liked to control the world around him, and he became upset when someone altered or disagreed with what he believed was right. "Give him time," I said, gently fingering one of the white roses arranged in a large vase in the middle of the table. Their sweet smell contrasted sharply with the horror that had come into our lives, and I was grateful to be reminded of beauty in the midst of our ugly reality.

"I don't have any choice, do I?" my mother said bitterly.

But she did have choices; we all did. Except Paulette.

"The Church is true!" my mother continued. "I can't deny it any longer. But I love him. We've been through everything together, and our love is stronger now than it has ever been. I can't lose him, yet I feel torn. I want to follow the Lord! Doesn't God come first?"

I was unsure what to tell her until I remembered my father's face in the cemetery. "Father loves you," I said. "As much as you love him. He has to come around."

"I don't know, Ari. He's so stubborn."

"Well, so was I." We talked more, until the despair faded from her voice.

"Are you still coming over tomorrow?" I asked finally. "To be here when we find out the test results?"

"Of course. Our fighting has nothing to do with you. You're calling the hospital at nine, aren't you?"

"Yes."

"We'll be there for you."

"Thanks."

The milk had long since boiled over onto the stove, and had actually put out the fire underneath the gas burner. "I have to go now, Mother. I love you. Will you remind Father about tomorrow?"

"As if he'd forget. But I'll tell him."

I hoped my request would at least force them to talk. Perhaps it might even draw them together and help my father rethink his objection to my mother's baptism. Regrettably, the thought held little hope.

I cleaned up the milk and had started to relight the burner when I remembered the fast. Guiltily, I switch off the gas and went instead to check on the children. The twins' bedroom door was ajar, and I pushed it open wider with my hand. The light from the hallway cut into the room, illuminating it enough to see my children and Marie-Thérèse sleeping peacefully in their beds.

I kissed each soft cheek, marveling at how peaceful they were, how like small angels. *How could Jean-Marc stand to be separated from them so much?* Josette opened her eyes, and her hands went up and around my neck. "I love you, Mommy."

"I love you too, honey." I kissed her again.

Next, I checked on André. He was curled under his blankets, his small head using a stuffed bear for a pillow. The twins would never have fallen asleep alone at that age; I'd had to rock them or pat their backs. But André seemed to prefer to sleep alone.

I went into the sitting room and bid good night to Louise and Lu-Lu. After helping them settle in, Jean-Marc and I retired. A short time later, Jean-Marc's soft snores came quickly and before I knew it, I drifted off to sleep. I had scarcely reached the point of oblivion when a whiny sob reached my subconscious mind and compelled me to wake. It sounded like Josette.

I groaned and rolled from the bed, nearly falling despite the night light in the hall. Jean-Marc's eyes fluttered, but he didn't wake. He never did when the children called, or if he did, he never acknowledged it, as if he felt it was somehow strictly a mother's duty to stay up at night with the children. It hadn't bothered me until André was born, and I had spent most of the nights nursing him and still getting up with the other two. I began to resent his indifference to my dilemma. It seemed one more part of his drawing away from his family.

In the twins' bedroom, I found not Josette but Marie-Thérèse crying and clutching her doll. I sat on her bed and drew her close, rocking her until she slept. She had stayed many times before at our house, but I understood that tonight was different. It wasn't just for fun.

"Life isn't always what we expect," I murmured, stroking her cheek. "Sometimes we need to take one day at a time."

CHAPTER EIGHT

Thin light filtered in through the curtains early Tuesday morning and woke me. I had been dreaming that someone was shining a light into my eyes, but it was only the bright May sun. Birds called loudly to one another in the few trees outside our apartment building. I started and glanced at the clock radio by my bedside. It was only seven—not yet time to call the hospital.

Jean-Marc's soft laugh came from the pillow beside me. He had his elbow bent, propping up his head as he gazed at me with his laughing green-brown eyes. "You are so beautiful," he said. The love in his stare was unmistakable. "I'm so lucky to have you."

I hoped he wasn't feeling emotional because he had some tragic insight about our forthcoming test results. I rolled over next to him. "How long have you been watching me?"

He kissed my nose. "Long enough to know how much I love you."

"I love you, too." I pushed him back on the pillow and laid my head on his chest. I could hear his heart, a calm and steady thumping.

"They're up! They're up!" Marc hurled himself on the bed, yelling with abandon as only small children can do. The others followed Marc, jumping onto the bed and throwing themselves on Jean-Marc excitedly. Even Marie-Thérèse, who didn't appear to remember crying the night before, joined in the wrestling. Someone had helped André out of his crib, and he covered both Jean-Marc and me with slobbery kisses. Far from shattering our peace, the children only added to our special moment.

I loved mornings like this. They were what reminded me of why I had wanted a family in the first place, why Jean-Marc and I had fallen in love.

"I'm going to get you!" Jean-Marc snarled. The twins screamed and jumped to the other side of the bed, but André catapulted himself into his father's arms, growling like a lion cub.

"I know, I'll get Mommy!" Jean-Marc crawled over to me with André still hanging on his neck. He started to bite my arm, working his way up. "Yum, yum." He licked his lips.

"Help!" I squeaked. The twins and Marie-Thérèse were on him in an instant, pulling him off me and laughing almost hysterically when he turned and nibbled on them instead. We played for half an hour before forcing ourselves out of bed. Then I fed the children while Jean-Marc showered and dressed. Louise and Lu-Lu sat in the kitchen with us but refused to eat, and I knew that like Jean-Marc and me, they were fasting.

I was in the bathroom getting ready when the doorbell rang. "It's your parents," Jean-Marc came to tell me. I had him zip up the white dress I had chosen to wear, not only because I could bleach out any stain, but because it made me feel pure, not at all like someone who might have a fatal disease.

Together we walked to the sitting room, where Lu-Lu had already made up the sofa bed and now sat silently opposite Louise. My parents still stood, both wearing serious expressions. I smiled and hugged them. There had been a time when they weren't there for me—when Antoine died—but that was all in the past.

"Let's sit and talk," I said.

But it was suddenly hard to find conversation. The minutes ticked slowly by in the oppressive silence. The grandfather clock near the window didn't miss a beat; its pendulum swung back and forth with a steady, unchanging rhythm. I seemed to have to remind myself to breathe. Only the children didn't seem affected. They ran in and out of the room, playing a game that made sense in their minds, if not in ours. Though she played with the others, Marie-Thérèse was not her normal, smiling self, but withdrawn and subdued.

"It's nine, Ari. Do you want me to call?" Jean-Marc picked up the phone on the table beside the lamp near the window. It was the phone he had bought last Christmas when I complained about having only one extension in the kitchen.

"Yes," I said in a hollow voice. André toddled to the couch and climbed into my lap. I wrapped my arms around him, and for once he didn't struggle at being held too tightly.

My gaze flitted from my parents, to Louise, and to Lu-Lu before settling on Jean-Marc. In the silence of the room, my breath seemed loud.

"Yes, I'm calling for the results of my family's blood tests yesterday." He gave the nurse the information and waited. I closed my eyes and said a quiet prayer.

I saw the relief on his face before he spoke the words. "Negative. All

negative!" He glanced around the room at the faces of our family before
his eyes came to rest on me. "It's negative, Ari."

I smiled, feeling my lips quiver with emotion. "The phone, Jean-
Marc," I reminded him.

He stared at the receiver in his hand before understanding. He put it
to his ear. "Hello? Are you still there? Thank you. Thank you so much!"
He set the phone in its cradle and came to hug me. I met him halfway
across the room.

Louise was sobbing with relief, as was my own mother. Lu-Lu said
nothing, but tears rolled onto her cheeks.

"What do you say we go and celebrate?" my father asked, putting his
arm around me and squeezing. "An early lunch for all of us. Or a late
breakfast—whatever. I'm starved."

"That's because you've been fasting since yesterday," my mother
said.

"What!" I didn't trust what I was hearing. "I thought you didn't
believe in all that stuff."

My father's face changed color slightly, but I couldn't tell if it was
from embarrassment or anger. "I don't believe in 'all that stuff,'" he said
stiffly. "But I do believe in God. I have since before you were born."

"But he doesn't believe in baptism." My mother's voice sounded
resentful.

"I don't need a little water to get me to heaven," my father retorted.

"But you do." Mother wasn't giving up easily.

"And I don't need to go to church every week to show I believe in
God," he continued as if she hadn't spoken. She glared at him and he
glared right back. She opened her mouth to speak.

"Whatever made you do it, thank you," I said quickly. My mother's
mouth clamped shut.

"So are we going to eat or not?" Jean-Marc said. "I take it you're
treating, eh Gèralde?"

My father slapped him on the back and chuckled. "I am, my boy. I
am."

"Are we going too?" Marc asked me.

"Of course, but not in that." For the first time I noticed his clothes—
a green T-shirt, purple shorts, and dark-blue socks without shoes. Josette
was worse, dressed in a yellow and white striped dress layered over her
pink fairy princess costume, with dark-blue flowered pants poking out

beneath. In her hand she held two pairs of socks, one a deep red and one a light pink, and her white Sunday shoes.

"Which go better?" she asked me. "I think the red is the prettiest."

Brightest was what she should have said.

I glanced at Marie-Thérèse, who wore a pink jumpsuit. It seemed she was the only child in our family with any fashion sense. Either that or Pierre hadn't packed much variety in her little suitcase.

The men were already heading out the door. "Uh, Jean-Marc," I said, "look at *your* children."

He stopped and stared, a smile playing on his lips. "Colorful," he said finally. "But not quite right for a nice restaurant. Back into the bedroom."

It took a short time to get the children presentable and matching. Jean-Marc tried putting on Josette's tights, but she cried because the toes weren't right. I ran from the bedroom where I was gathering diapers for André. "I'll do it," I told Jean-Marc. He seemed relieved.

Minutes later, we were ready to leave. But the joy of our good news was partially diminished as I worried about my parents. Once before, at Antoine's death, our family had been torn apart. Could my mother's love for the Church and my father's rejection of it do the same thing now?

Once our early lunch—or breakfast, rather—was over, my father and Marc went to work. I was amazed at how much better I felt, knowing that my babies and husband were healthy, that I hadn't unknowingly given them HIV.

In the spirit of celebration, I changed from my white dress and packed a snack to take to the playground nearby. The children were exuberant, and I wished I could share their innocence.

"Will you come with us?" I asked Louise as I helped the children into their play clothes. Lu-Lu had already disappeared somewhere with the infamous Philippe.

"No, I want to wait for Lu-Lu," she said wearily.

Once outside, I breathed in the late May air appreciatively. Though the stark heat of summer was not yet upon us, the air was warm with the scent of flowers coming from the landscaped beds in front of the apartment building. I pushed André in his stroller while the twins and Marie-Thérèse skipped on ahead.

The playground wasn't very big. It featured a small sandbox filled with very fine sand surrounded by a cement barrier. To one side of this stood a swing set with two swings and a slide. Below it, the dirt was covered with more sand, coarser ground than what was in the sandbox. That was all. Cement sidewalks with scattered benches made up the rest of the play area. There was no green anywhere; in France, grass was for decoration, not for play.

"I'm going to dig to the bottom this time." Marc's voice was determined as he started for the sandbox. "I have to know what's there."

I smiled. My brother Antoine and I had done the same thing at our own playground. The sand had been deep enough to reach our shoulders, the bottom paved with cement. But I wouldn't spoil the surprise. One day my son wouldn't tire of digging, and then he would discover the secret for himself.

My thoughts floated back to Paulette and AIDS. She and Pierre were both going to die! I still couldn't come to terms with it. Hadn't Paulette been forgiven for her terrible past? I had always believed that the Atonement was expansive enough to cover any sin, no matter how grave, aside from murder and denying the Holy Ghost. Any sin. The Savior suffered the pain Paulette bore now, and also that which was to come. Then why did she have to go through the agony as well?

For the first time since my marriage, I had a serious question that I was unable to answer with any Church doctrine I was familiar with.

"Mom, it's raining!" Josette tugged on my sleeve.

So it was! I looked up and saw André in the sandbox, sitting contentedly in the large hole Marc had made. With chubby fingers, he patted a large handful of sand into his hair. My oldest son was now building a mountain or a volcano, his goal to reach the bottom of the sandbox discarded for another day. Marie-Thérèse sat on a swing, staring at the sand, her rag doll in her lap.

The rain fell faster, and soon the warm cement was dotted with dark spots where the drops hit and splashed. I breathed in the pungent smell of the wet pavement. I loved the smell now, though once I had despised it for the memories of death it had brought. Those days were over, replaced now by new experiences. A fleeting memory came to mind of a romantic evening when Jean-Marc and I had slept in the rain on a roofless balcony in a hotel near the ocean where we had gone on business several months after our wedding. That was the night I was sure the twins had been conceived. The recollection filled me with tenderness.

Marc began to dance in the rain. Marie-Thérèse left the swing and ran over to him, laughing. André stood up in his hole and fell down again, a smile on his face. Yes, the rain could be a marvelous thing.

I took Josette's hand and whirled her around. She laughed. The others came to join us—even André, who didn't trust his legs on the sand and came crawling.

The smell of wet cement was stronger now as we danced and laughed. The other mothers in the playground were hustling their children away, but we stayed. It was warm, and I saw no danger in letting them play. At least Marie-Thérèse was smiling.

We were soaked by the time we reached the outer door to our building, and covered in wet sand. We stomped off as much as we could outside, but still the children's faces sported adorable splotches of sand, especially André, who wore it in his hair as well.

On the eighth floor, Louise opened the apartment door for us. "Goodness, I didn't realize it was raining! Come on, let's get you four in the bath." She led the children down the hall. I began to follow her, but she stopped me. "Lu-Lu's in the sitting room. Could you go talk to her, please?"

"Okay." Something was up. Louise appeared ill, worse than when I had left the apartment. It was as if she had reached the level where she couldn't cope with anything more. I felt sorry for her, and it was an odd sensation. She had always been so strong.

"You're back," Lu-Lu said to me. "That's good. I have something to ask you."

"What is it?" Because I was wet, I didn't sit next to her on the flowered sofa. As it was, the sand still clinging to my pant legs tumbled to the carpet. I grimaced.

"I want you to help me plan my wedding."

What! When she had talked about marriage the night before, I had assumed she meant months from now. "When are you planning it for?"

"Next week."

"What's the hurry? Are you pregnant?" I regretted the words immediately as I saw her eyes narrow defensively.

"Of course not!" Then more calmly she said, "Paulette's dying," as if that explained everything.

"So you have to get married now?"

She stood up and paced in front of the sofa. "She's going to die. It could be me. It could be Philippe. We have to use what time we have left." She sounded hysterical.

I stepped closer and put my hands on her shoulders, staring into her eyes. "Lu-Lu, you can't live in fear, none of us can. That's not the Lord's way. Fear is of the devil. Now, I'm not saying you shouldn't marry Philippe, but you need to give us all time. Especially your mother."

"She doesn't want me to get married."

"She's just had a severe shock. Her son and daughter-in-law are going to die within years, and possibly the baby, too. Besides us, you're all she has for certain, and by marrying out of the temple, you're going against everything she's ever believed is right. Look at her; she needs time. *You* need time. Don't rush the most important decision you will ever make."

"What if there is no tomorrow for Philippe and me?"

"That's what's so miraculous about marrying in the temple," I said. "Tomorrow will always be there for you, whether in this life or the next."

"So you won't help me?" she asked, her jaw tightening.

"Of course I will. But let's give it more time and do it right. Let your family get through this first crisis. You owe us that at least."

Her face wrinkled in sudden understanding. "Oh, Ari, I'm being selfish, aren't I?"

I smiled. "Yes, but I understand. I remember how I felt when I first thought I was in love."

"With your first husband?"

"Yes. It was a desperate sort of love—quite different from the stronger, more assured love I have for Jean-Marc. It's . . . well, it's eternal. It's hard to explain. Things aren't perfect, but I'll never give up."

Lu-Lu's expression was thoughtful. "I guess we could wait a few months. That would give Mother time to come around."

"And time for us to get to know Philippe. Perhaps we could even get him to listen to the missionary discussions."

"I'd never dare ask!"

That made me laugh. "Silly Lu-Lu! Here you are, all set to marry a man who doesn't even know what you believe in. Never mind—you forget that your family has three returned missionaries. We'll teach him ourselves."

She hugged me. "Thank you, Ari. I'm so glad I can count on you to be here for me."

"There's just one thing," I said. "I've noticed a change in you. Some of it I think is good, but some of it—" I didn't know how to continue, so I blurted it out. "Lu-Lu, are you taking drugs?"

Her gaze dropped to the floor. "I tried it," she said hesitantly. "But since I found out about Paulette . . . don't worry, I won't do it ever again."

I believed her. Relief hit me, clean and pure in the midst of turmoil. "I hope not," I said, just in case. "That's one thing none of us can tolerate. It's too dangerous."

"I know that now." Her voice was a whisper.

I left her and went to shower and change. In the bathroom, Louise was still washing the children's heads. "Well, did she tell you what she was planning?" she asked.

I nodded. "But she's agreed to wait for a few months."

Louise sighed. "Thank heaven!" Then she shook her head and blinked her eyes as if trying to keep the tears at bay. "I don't know what to do, Ari. It seems as if I'm losing everything. What am I going to do?"

I grabbed her soapy hands. "Believe, for one thing," I said. My own tears began in my sore eyes. "I don't know the answer to everything, like why Paulette and Pierre have HIV, but I do know God lives and that families are eternal. Let's just cling to that for now."

She held my hands tightly. "But what about Lu-Lu?"

I set my jaw as stubbornly as Lu-Lu had set hers. "We have to give Philippe a chance, for Lu-Lu's sake. We'll teach him so much that he'll be baptized or be scared away!"

Louise laughed through her tears. "Of course. Of course," she said.

The children laughed with us, without knowing why. All but Marie-Thérèse, who simply watched us. My heart ached for her, but I didn't know how to soothe her hurt.

After the bath, Louise and Lu-Lu took Marie-Thérèse for a short visit with her parents. I knew I should go, but I was afraid of seeing the death in Paulette's eyes, so I simply made the excuse of having no one to stay with the children. Louise and Marie-Thérèse returned in time for dinner. I served cake for dessert and was rewarded by a smile from my niece.

I had expected Jean-Marc to come home early that night, but he didn't. The children were long in bed, as were Louise and Lu-Lu, before he arrived. The rain had fallen steadily, sounding out a steady and comforting beat on the window. It washed the world clean, as it had me for a brief time that afternoon.

"Hi, Ari." Jean-Marc took me in his arms.

"How did work go?" I decided not to badger him about working late.

He was dealing with things in the way that fit him best. I could at least give him that much.

"Good, we settled the Augustin account. And you?"

Unbidden, tears came to my eyes. "We danced in the rain."

His gaze was tender. "You did? I wish I could have been there."

"Me too."

CHAPTER NINE

Twin shouts filled the silence of the early morning, awakening me from a sound sleep. I yawned and reached out to touch the space beside me. It was empty. The sound of water in the shower, echoing like a torrent of rain, came to my ears so I knew that Jean-Marc couldn't hear the twins' complaints. I stretched again and opened my eyes, squinting slightly against the white light streaming in from the curtained window. In the streets below, I could hear the occasional car passing our building.

It seemed too quiet outside, contrasting with the loud children's voices coming from the hall, and a shiver crept up my spine. I snuggled down in my soft blankets, but the warmth didn't take away the sinister chill that seemed to shroud my heart.

The screaming had diminished, but a loud bumping sound forced me out of bed and into the twins' room next door. What had they done now? I sighed when I saw that Marc had pulled the small bookcase down upon himself. Sometimes that child was impossible.

"Marc yelled at us," Josette said, holding tightly to Marie-Thérèse's hand. "And he threw books on the floor again."

I saw that he was unhurt. "Marc Perrault—" I began, but Louise came to his rescue.

"I have breakfast ready," she said, entering the room. "And Pierre's on the phone for you." She looked at the mess of books on the floor. "Don't worry, we'll take care of this right now." She stared at Marc purposefully, and his ever-ready grin vanished.

"But I hurt myself," he protested.

"You're really going to get hurt if you don't pick up those books," Louise threatened mildly. She was used to little boys' excuses, and didn't have memories of my brother to cloud her judgment. I tried to hide a smile as Marc quickly grabbed a handful of thin books.

I escaped down the hall and picked up the phone. "Hello?"

"Ariana, can you come to the hospital?" Pierre's voice was calm and oddly detached, yet I could tell he was agitated. There was a quiet desperation inside that rang out as clearly as if he had been screaming.

"What's wrong?" I felt the chill in my heart return.

"It's Paulette; she's taken a turn for the worse. Please, can you come? And bring Marie-Thérèse."

"We'll be right there," I said without hesitation. Paulette was my best friend, and she needed me.

I dressed hurriedly in the white dress of the day before, not stopping to shower or put on makeup. After a quick family prayer, I kissed the twins and André and left them with Louise. Marie-Thérèse held my hand, and with the other she carried the ever-present rag doll. On her face was a wistful smile.

Jean-Marc rode with me in the elevator. "Call if you need me," he said, kissing me goodbye.

"I will." But I completely dismissed the thought. Most likely I wouldn't be able to reach him.

When we entered Paulette's private room, I was sorry I had brought the child. Paulette's condition had noticeably worsened. She lay once more on her side, eyes clenched tight, breath rasping in and out in a grisly pattern, despite the oxygen tube. Marie-Thérèse's smile dimmed, and her large eyes became frightened again.

Pierre stood up and met us halfway across the room, swooping up his little daughter and hugging her. "I missed you," he said, rubbing his unshaven face against her cheek.

She didn't smile. "I missed you, too." She glanced over his shoulder at Paulette. "And Mommy. When is she coming home?"

Pierre sighed. "I don't know yet, honey."

"Is something different today?" I asked, choosing my words carefully so as not to frighten Marie-Thérèse any more than necessary.

Pierre didn't mince his words. "It's the baby. Dr. Medard thinks he could treat her much better if she weren't pregnant. He says her only chance might be to abort the baby. He thinks her life expectancy would be better."

I stared at him. *Abort the baby! How could it come to this?* "And if she doesn't?"

Pierre hugged his daughter close as he replied so softly I scarcely heard the words. "He's afraid she'll never recover from the pneumonia."

Before I could fully digest his words, a feeble voice came from the bed. "Marie-Thérèse?"

"Mommy!" The little girl wriggled from her father's grasp and ran to her mother. Paulette reached out her thin arms and hugged Marie-Thérèse the best she could in her reclining position, struggling to control her grimace of pain.

"How's my baby?" Paulette asked.

"I'm not a baby!"

Paulette smiled. "I can see that. Did you have fun at Aunt Ariana's?"

Marie-Thérèse nodded. "We played tiger with Uncle Jean-Marc yesterday, and last night we had cake and played princess. Do you think I'm pretty as a princess, Mommy?"

"No, you're much prettier than a princess."

Marie-Thérèse smiled, the first real one since we'd danced in the rain the day before. She climbed onto the chair and sat swinging her legs.

"Are you being a good girl?" Pierre asked.

Marie-Thérèse nodded. "I played in the rain, though. I forgot to tell you yesterday."

"If Aunt Ariana let you, then I'm sure it's all right," Paulette said.

Marie-Thérèse beamed. "I love you, Mommy." She leaned forward and touched her mother's lips with a tiny finger, then closed her fist and put it against her little chest.

"I love you, too. So much." Paulette touched Marie-Thérèse's lips and brought the hand to her heart.

Both smiled. I recognized this as a ritual they had done many times before, perhaps at bedtime. The twins had gone through a similar phase the year before, and it had intensified when André was born, as if they needed reassurance of my love. Marie-Thérèse needed such solace now.

"Hey, do you want to go get an ice cream with Daddy?" Pierre asked, patting his rounded belly. "There's a vendor on the corner, and I need to stretch my legs."

Marie-Thérèse nodded. "I'll be right back, Mommy. Don't worry," she said.

Paulette laughed weakly. "Okay, I won't. But don't be gone too long, or I'll miss you."

Marie-Thérèse's face crinkled in a wide smile. She waved and put her hand in her father's.

I walked to the bed and sank to the chair. Paulette looked at me as I took her hand. Thanks to Giselle and the booklet I had devoured over the past few days, I was not so fearful of contracting HIV. Casual touching would not pass the infection, only intimate contact. Not even tears or kissing had ever been traced to communicating the disease; I had been worried for nothing.

"Did Pierre tell you?" she asked.

"About the doctor wanting to abort the baby?"

She nodded. "How can I do something like that? The scriptures say 'Thou shalt not kill.' I feel this baby moving. I know she's alive. And I love her!"

"It sounds like you've made your decision."

Her face seemed more gray than white, as if she had aged in the past week. "I did a lot of things before I joined the Church, Ari. But never murder. I thought I had been forgiven—perhaps not, in light of this disease—but I know I could never be forgiven for killing my baby. I won't do it."

"Not even to save your life?"

She snorted. "I'm dying anyway, Ari. It's only a matter of time." She turned her face into the pillow and hiccupped softly. I smoothed her long hair, wishing I could soothe her pain instead.

"Pierre wants me to do it," she said.

I started. "What?"

"He wants me to abort the baby. He says I need to stay with him and Marie-Thérèse for as long as I can. How can he say that?" Her voice had tears in it, though her eyes were dry. "I don't want to leave them."

"He loves you. He's afraid of living without you."

She nodded slowly. "And perhaps of dying without me. I would be even more afraid if he weren't here." Her face had softened, but now it became resolute. "But he's not thinking about the baby. She deserves a chance to live. How can I take that away? Then they tell me the odds are high that she'll have HIV, and that I'll spare her the suffering later. That's what everybody says." She gave a short, bitter laugh. "Kill her now so she won't suffer later. It doesn't make much sense to me—especially because there is still a chance she won't be infected. I know they're afraid I'm going to die right away if I don't do this, but I can't kill her. I won't." She looked up, eyes pleading. "You'll support me, won't you? You understand."

And I did. "I think I might do the same thing," I said. But how hard it would be! To sacrifice some of my remaining time with my children and husband, on the chance of a new life that could be equally as damaged as my own! "It's the only choice you could make."

"That's what I think," she said. "And I've had a lot of time to consider it." She shifted her position slightly, grimacing, but staying on her side. I knew the doctor was worried about the blood supply to the baby, and had ordered Paulette off her back, but the side position was more painful for the pleurisy in her chest.

"You know, the irony of this whole situation would be that the baby will have HIV and I will have killed her anyway, as I have Pierre. In that light, I am already a murderer."

"No, Paulette. No!" I squeezed her hand tightly. "You didn't know you had AIDS; how could you? You wouldn't have infected any of your family if you'd had a choice. It's not the same as murder. Some things we simply can't change, and it's no one's fault. It just is. Like Antoine's death, and even Nette's. Nobody wanted it to happen."

"If I hadn't done drugs, none of this would be happening, would it?" Her voice was bitter. "And now it's too late." Tears slid down her cheeks, sluggishly, as if afraid to reach the sharp curve of her jaw. My own face was wet, though I didn't know when the tears had begun. "It's like the scriptures say," she added. "The sins of the parents will be visited upon the heads of the children. My poor baby!"

"I don't know what to tell you, Paulette. I wish I did. But one thing I know is that the Lord loves you. Can you try to hold on to that?"

She nodded. "I'll try. But I'm so afraid. Please," she tightened her grasp on my hand, "don't let me give in and agree to abort the baby! It's not worth it. Please talk to Pierre."

"I will. You just concentrate on making yourself well enough to go home. We're all here for you."

As if she hadn't heard me, Paulette lay with her eyes open, staring into space and saying nothing. Then she abruptly focused on my face. "Your tests. Louise told me they were negative. Were they really, or was she just trying to protect me?" Her voice held dread.

"They were all negative." I was afraid to show my happiness at the fact because it only seemed to emphasize her tragedy.

But Paulette gave a cry of relief, and a fresh batch of tears erupted. "Oh, thank God! Oh, thank you, God!" Her eyes shut tight in prayer, squeezing out more tears. Her reaction proved what kind of a person she was. In her position, I might feel embittered that my friend was free of the disease while I had to suffer. Paulette's honest face showed no such lowly emotion.

"I'm so sorry, Paulette," I said. "I wish more than anything that you wouldn't have to go through this."

The torrent of tears seemed to abate slightly. "I know, Ari. I know. I'm so grateful I won't have to do this alone. And that my little girl is taken care of and loved."

"She is, and always will be," I promised.

"Thank you."

"No, don't thank me. We are friends, sisters. There's nothing more to it."

I stayed with her until she drifted off to sleep, then went to find Pierre. I didn't know what I would say to him, but for Paulette, I had to try.

I found him on the sidewalk in front of the hospital. Both Marie-Thérèse and he were leaning against the rock and cast-iron fence surrounding the perimeter of the hospital grounds, finishing their ice cream. Pierre had only the sugar cone left, while Marie-Thérèse had nearly the whole thing, but worked at it steadily. She giggled at something her father said, and I smiled wistfully; she was too young to lose her mother and father both.

The afternoon sun was warm against my back, and the cloudless blue sky showed no sign of rain. The sidewalk had few people on it; most would be at their jobs. The traffic seemed heavy as usual, though without the intensity it usually projected. In all, it was a beautiful day in Paris. If only . . .

I shook away the yearning for what couldn't be and walked steadily toward them. "Didn't buy me one, huh?"

They turned. Pierre's smile subsided. "You left her alone?"

"She's asleep. But I made sure the nurse would check in on her. Giselle was coming on shift, and she assured me that Paulette is well monitored."

Pierre's face relaxed, but nevertheless he began walking toward the hospital. I stretched my legs to catch up to him, and Marie-Thérèse skipped on ahead. "She's a good one, Giselle is," he reflected. "We couldn't have asked for a better nurse. She really cares, and she can get Paulette to do things I can't."

"Like have an abortion?"

His face fell, and his lips twisted downward until I wondered if they would fall from his face completely. "She told you I wanted her to abort it, didn't she?"

"*Her*, " I emphasized mildly. "The ultrasound says the baby's a girl. And, yes, Paulette told me you wanted to abort her."

He stopped walking and faced me. Again, I was struck with the similarity between him and Jean-Marc. The eyes were brown, yes, and his voice deeper, but beneath the growing whiskers, he had the same curve of the face and similar expressions. "It's only to save her life. Or to extend it, at least. I don't want to be without her. And it's not fair to deprive the child we do have for one not yet born."

"What about the baby?"

"It's not real to me. Paulette is," he said brusquely.

"But she is real to Paulette. She's been hoping for this child for three years, and she already loves her. She feels her kicking and knows she trusts in her. You're asking Paulette to murder her baby. Don't you see, Pierre? This isn't about me, or you, or even Marie-Thérèse. This is about Paulette and the baby. And if you force her to do what she feels is wrong, then she will have no reason to fight for life, especially when she feels she's already killed you."

His jaw worked convulsively, and his eyes glistened with tears. "She said that?"

I nodded. "Yes. She needs you. And you've got to be there for her."

"How?" he croaked. "I can't let her die."

"It isn't in our hands, is it?"

His gaze was desolate, but I thought I saw a glimmer of acceptance. "And if the baby does come and is sick too?"

"Then we'll deal with it when the time comes. We're all here for you—your family, that is. But for now, let's concentrate on getting Paulette home and the baby here safely."

His eyes seemed to lose their wild look. I had done the best I knew how; I could only pray it was the right thing.

We began walking again, catching up to Marie-Thérèse, who waited at the hospital doors, finishing her ice cream. Pierre threw the rest of his away and faced me again. "I'd like to keep Marie-Thérèse here with me for a while. Do you think you could come pick her up before dinner?"

"Of course. Either I or your mother will come."

He nodded. "Thank you. The doctor said in the next twenty-four hours we should know what's going to happen one way or the other. She'll either start getting better or worse. I—I wanted Marie-Thérèse to spend some time with her in case—" He broke off.

"I understand. And plan on going home to shower or something when we come tonight. We'll sit with Paulette. You need a break."

He rubbed at his face. "I showered last night when Mom came, but I guess I could use a shave."

"Can't have you scaring the nurses now, can we?"

He smiled bleakly. "I guess not. Come on, Marie-Thérèse. Let's go see Mommy." He held out his hand, and she grabbed it trustingly. He took a few steps, then stopped and faced me again.

"Thanks, Ariana." He paused, gathering his thoughts. "You know, I think women must have a special way of seeing things. Giselle believes Paulette should fight for the baby as well, though she didn't say as much aloud. I felt it without her saying anything." He cocked his head back as if pondering something of great importance. When he spoke, his voice was rich and admiring, yet it also held a trace of stark torment. "What is it about women that they can risk their lives to have children? Even in a regular pregnancy, they spend so much time sick and uncomfortable, and then have to go through labor. What is it about women that makes them this special? What is it about my Paulette? She's closer to the Savior than I'll ever be. She's willing to die for this baby, as He died for us. I know it's not the same thing, but surely it's as close as a mortal could come." His voice cracked and the glistening in his eyes became large tears, dropping onto his cheeks. "She is one of the purest people I know, yet she is sure she deserves this disease because of her past. To her, it's the only explanation."

He looked at me, eyes beseeching. "You're good at helping me understand things; perhaps you can help Paulette understand the reason for the AIDS. Please."

I wanted to reassure him, but I couldn't understand it myself. It wasn't as if Paulette was someone who had refused the gospel and who continued joyfully in a contemptible lifestyle. While such people also didn't deserve an agonizing death, it was at least understandable. But she had repented, been married in the temple, and been faithful to all her covenants. Why her? The Lord had the power to save her; why didn't He?

"I'll try," I said woodenly. "I'll think of some way to explain."

Maybe then I would understand it myself.

CHAPTER TEN

I took a detour on the way home, stopping at the cafe to tell Marguerite and Jules about Paulette. I didn't admit to myself that the reason I was going was to find comfort, and perhaps an answer to my question about why Paulette had contracted AIDS.

"I know about the AIDS," Marguerite said. "Your mother called me last Sunday. I haven't told anyone else. I don't really know what to say. It's just like what happened to Michelle."

"Michelle had AIDS?" It seemed that each time we talked about her daughter, I learned something new, something she had held back from me.

Marguerite nodded grimly and leaned over the counter closer to me. "Her body was unable to fight the pneumonia, and she died. It's the most common killer of AIDS patients."

It wasn't what I had come to hear.

Marguerite sighed. "Oh, I'm sorry, Ariana. You didn't want to know that, did you? I'm sorry. It's just such a shock." She came from behind the counter and hugged me. I laid my head on her ample shoulder, fighting tears.

"I want to know why," I murmured. "Why?"

She shook her head, and a few more wisps of gray hair strayed from her bun. "I wonder if we will ever fully understand until we are resurrected."

The bell hanging over the door tinkled, and a group of young people entered. I recognized most of them as youth from our ward. School must have let out, and Marguerite's place was their hangout.

"Hi, Sister Perrault!" they called out as they crowded around the counter, gazing hungrily down at the array of breads and confections. I had been the Young Women's president for over four years before being released after having André, so I knew most of them by name.

As I greeted them, I couldn't help thinking how different Paulette's life would be if she had been raised in the Church. They appeared so clean, happy, radiant. They knew why they were on earth and where they were going. Maybe faithful parents could have taught Paulette the dangers of drugs. Maybe she wouldn't have AIDS now. She was every bit as worthy as these young people; why didn't she have a chance?

"I've got to get back to the children," I said abruptly.

Marguerite nodded. "Let me know if I can do anything."

"I will." I turned to go, but her voice stopped me.

"Uh, Ariana?"

"Yes?"

"Do you think she'd like a visit? We didn't know with Michelle until it was too late. I'd like to be there for Paulette."

I smiled. There had been a time, long before either Marguerite or Paulette had been baptized, that Marguerite hadn't approved of Paulette. Yet in the last year or so, they had become good friends. "Of course. She'd love to have you. I think it would mean something to her for you to visit."

There was a flurry of queries from the group surrounding the counter, but I escaped and left Marguerite to deal with it. I had told enough people about Paulette's AIDS already, and each time brought the painful questions.

Next I drove to the cemetery. It was the fourth Wednesday of the month and around my usual time of visiting, but my father was nowhere in sight.

"Paulette's dying," I whispered into the air. The sun shone through the leaves of the large trees lining the cobblestone pathway, leaving a dappled design on the tombstones. The pattern changed as a light wind rippled through the leaves, making it seem to dance across the stones and the short-cropped grass.

Today the cemetery held no answers for me, standing only as a bitter reminder that Paulette's body would soon be resting here. As usual, I knelt down and traced Antoinette's name with a light finger.

"I love you, Nette," I said softly. With a quick wave at my brother's stone, I abandoned the suddenly oppressive silence, leaving the dead to their rest.

Once again I didn't go home. The Seine seemed to call to me, and I drove to near the Quai de Montebello and the booksellers' stalls. Leaving the car, I crossed the quay and walked through the crowd. I paused, looking over some of the wares: magazines, old prints, engravings, maps, and, of course, books. They sold a variety of other items, some simply junk. The tourists ate it up, but I could also spot a serious collector or two among the crowd, scrutinizing each box for the treasures they might occasionally contain.

Turning my back on the stalls, I stood staring down at the water from the stone wall rising far above the bank. The waves crashed against the sides as a huge boat passed by.

"The water is us," said a voice beside me.

I jerked my head up to see Paulette's mother. On her thin figure she wore a sleeveless summer dress of fluorescent yellow, and her face was painted with more makeup than necessary. Her dark-blonde hair wasn't greasy today; in fact, it looked to have just been washed. But her eyes still had the unfocused stare I knew to be related to drugs. Anger bubbled inside my heart. This woman should have taught Paulette better. It was her fault that Paulette was dying.

"How's that?" My voice was clipped, my face stony.

"The water is us," she repeated. "We're helpless against the trials that come. We can't push them away; we can only go where we're pushed. What good is life when we can't control anythin'?" The desperation in her voice softened my anger, but then she fumbled in a worn brown bag she had slung over her shoulder and grasped a few thin cigarettes. She shoved one into her mouth and drew a great breath, holding it inside for a while before expelling the smoke through her nose. It was an appalling sight, and my heart hardened once again.

"Paulette has AIDS," I said without preamble.

I saw the pain etched on her face and immediately felt sorry, but her response surprised me. "I know." She gazed at the water, and tears trickled down her worn cheeks.

"How?"

"I went to see her. She was sleepin', but a man was there. Her husband, I guess. I didn't go in, but I talked to a nurse—Giselle, I think. Nice girl. When I said who I was, she told me about Paulette."

Now I understood the remark Simone had made about the water. We were all helpless to change Paulette's condition. My estimation of Simone had changed; she did care about Paulette, despite the apathy she had shown when I first went to visit.

"When did you go?"

"Tuesday. Yesterday." She flicked ashes from the cigarette. A few pieces wafted below to the walkway next to the river, some landed on the stone wall. She brushed them off nervously.

"She's become worse," I said. "They want her to abort the baby."

Simone became more agitated. "Is she goin' to do it?"

"No. But Pierre is afraid she may die sooner because of it."

She closed her eyes. "Some things are worth dyin' fer."

I believed that, but it seemed odd coming from this woman whose lifestyle was so utterly different from mine.

"Are you going to see her again?" I asked to cover my surprise.

"What would I say?"

In her eyes I saw guilt; she knew she was partly at fault. With this insight, my anger dissipated completely. I turned to her. "We can't change this situation, we can only be there for her. For the time she has left."

A flash of gratitude sparked in her eyes. "The nurse said Pierre has it too, but my granddaughter don't. What will happen to her?"

"Pierre may not get sick for a while, but when he does, she'll have a home with me, if that's what Paulette and Pierre want."

"Good. Yer the best one fer the job. You was always good to Paulette, Ariana. Even when ya had a right not to be. I thank ya fer that."

I felt uncomfortable with her thanks. Besides, I wasn't the best one for the job of Marie-Thérèse's mother; Paulette was.

"What about the baby?" Simone said.

"What about her?"

"Will ya take her, too?"

I wanted to say yes, but in reality my decision would depend on if the baby was sick or not. How could I risk an HIV-positive baby constantly around my other children? A simple cut could pass the virus on. It was too much risk. Besides, how could I take care of a sick child without neglecting the others? Jean-Marc certainly was not around to help, and even when he was, I took care of them during the times they were sick or cranky. With four small children to care for, I couldn't do any more. I couldn't.

"It depends on a lot of things," I said ambiguously. "Louise, Pierre's mother, might be able to help take care of her, especially if she has the virus."

"Maybe I can help too, if ya want," Simone said almost eagerly. "I have two days off from waitin' at the bar. Each week, I mean."

Could she be trying to atone for her mistakes? "It's all really up to Paulette," I said. "And she could have years left to decide. We need to pray for her to get well. Regardless, you need to go see her."

"Maybe." Simone turned her face away and leaned partially over the stone wall. I followed suit. We stood in silence as a fresh breeze drifted up from the water and whispered through our hair. My white dress swirled around my knees.

"How do ya watch yer daughter die?" Simone said, her voice so soft I barely heard the words.

I understood too well what she was saying. Every time I saw Paulette, I wanted to run away and hide. But another experience kept me coming to visit her. I hadn't been there when Nette died, and the guilt I felt at not being with her had been overwhelming. At least I would be there for Paulette as I hadn't been for Nette.

"Better to be there than not," I replied. "How do you forgive yourself for not holding her during her last moments and saying how much you love her? You have the chance to help your daughter into the next world, as I didn't. Don't miss it, Simone."

Her light eyes met mine, watery but decided. "Yer right, Ariana."

She left me then and I wandered back to my car. I had already been gone much longer than I had planned, but I didn't hurry. For me everything seemed to slow down, though logically I knew it was probably my own wish to stop Paulette from dying that made each moment stand alone. If only I could stop time!

When I returned to the house, Louise went to visit Paulette and pick up Marie-Thérèse. I began dinner early, with the twins dancing around my feet. Even the normally self-sufficient André played with his toys in front of the stove, wanting to be near me, and I tripped on them each time I passed. Finally, I'd had enough. "Go to your room!" I shouted. "I'm trying to make dinner."

Marc stared at me, and tears welled up in Josette's eyes. André ignored me completely.

"Mommy, are you mad at us? Don't you love us anymore?" my daughter asked.

"Are you going to the hospital again? Can we go next time?" Marc added.

I sighed and sank to the floor to put my arms around them. *How did they always know how to get my attention?*

"The hospital is not really a place for children," I explained.

Josette sniffed. "But Marie-Thérèse goes every day."

"She has to visit her mother."

"What do you do there?" Marc asked.

"Well, what do you think I'm doing?"

"Getting more tests like when the nurse took our blood. Are you sick?" he asked.

I thought I was getting to the bottom of the twins' concern. "Are you afraid Mommy's going into the hospital to stay like Aunt Paulette?" Both nodded, and I hugged them tightly. "Well, I'm not. I promise." I had thought the twins were too young and too removed from the situation to really understand it. I believed their innocence would protect them, but it seemed I was wrong. They could feel pain and worry. It wasn't only Marie-Thérèse we had to safeguard, but the twins as well.

I let the dinner sit and went with them to their room, where we played prince and princess. Only occasionally did I find myself losing concentration and wondering how Paulette was doing. I wished Jean-Marc was home to talk things out with me. I almost went to the phone to call, but it wouldn't do any good. They never seemed to know where he was these days.

Louise came home with Marie-Thérèse barely an hour after we had eaten dinner. Her eyes were red and swollen, her face drawn with anxiety. She waited until Marie-Thérèse was playing with the twins before motioning to me. I scooped up André and the pajamas I was putting on him and followed. Louise's steps dragged in the hall, her shoulders hunched like a woman with a massive weight pressing down on her. Paulette's sickness was taking its toll on everyone.

"Paulette's getting worse," she said when we reached the sitting room. "Pierre's beside himself. He doesn't look good."

I paused with André's shirt half over his head. He struggled, and I finished pulling it down quickly. Before I could speak, the apartment door opened.

"Ari?"

"In here, Jean-Marc."

At least he is home in time to kiss the children goodnight. The thought was cynical and struck me by surprise. I thought I had begun to accept the situation with his work. *Change yourself,* I thought, remembering my father's words. *You can't change other people.*

Jean-Marc kissed me, taking stock of our glum faces. "What's wrong?"

Louise explained while I pulled on André's pajama bottoms. Jean-Marc slumped to the couch beside me. "Why didn't you call me at work?"

I wrinkled my face at him. "What for? They never know where you are."

A shadow passed over his face and I could feel his defenses going up. "I was at my desk all day," he said.

Louise coughed. "What are we going to do about Paulette?"

"What can we do?" I asked. "I've been praying, but—"

"Let's begin a family and ward fast," Jean-Marc said. "We can't save Paulette's life in the long run, but she doesn't have to die now. We'll call the bishop and home teachers and go bless her. Maybe together we'll have enough faith."

Is that what this was all about? Faith? If so, then my attitude needed changing. I was too busy questioning the Lord for allowing Paulette to have AIDS to have time to pray with faith.

"But she's had a blessing," I said. "Pierre gave her one."

"Then she needs another one," my husband said. "I remember reading that in the early days of the Church, when the elders went to preach the gospel, it was sometimes necessary for them to have blessings each hour to help them through the heavy blizzards. It's no different with Paulette. The first blessing got her through a few days, and now she needs another one for this new ordeal."

Within minutes we were on the phone with the bishop, and then with the home teachers and visiting teachers who would get the message out to the ward. While Jean-Marc finished calling, I read the children a story and put them to bed. Then I called my mother to come and baby-sit while we went to the hospital. Lu-Lu, with her new fiancé tagging along, arrived in the midst of our departure.

Jean-Marc put his arm around the taller Philippe and propelled him back to the door. "So glad you could come, Philippe. And of course we want you to come to the hospital with us. It's about time you met the rest of our family." Philippe started to protest, but Jean-Marc continued, "No, I insist. Don't be shy. If you and Lu-Lu are going to be married, you might as well see how we Mormons operate. We're going to give Paulette a blessing right now."

I had told him my idea of either baptizing Philippe or scaring him away, but I thought he might be overdoing it. Still, Lu-Lu was his sister; he would fight for her as he saw fit.

As Lu-Lu watched Jean-Marc with Philippe, a smile covered her face. "See? I told you my family would try to accept this, Philippe. Let's go with them to the hospital." Under so much pressure, he had no choice but to agree.

I was about to follow them out the door when I remembered Paulette's mother. I went to the phone and called information for her number, then placed the call. I didn't have much hope of reaching her, since her phone had been disconnected, but I prayed silently.

The phone rang, and before it chimed a second time, Simone picked it up. "Hello?" Her voice sounded perplexed.

"It's me, Ariana. Paulette's worsened again, and we're going to the hospital to give her a blessing from the elders in our church. Please, will you meet us there?"

"I don't know."

"It might be the last time you see her," I said bluntly.

"I didn't know my phone was workin' again," she said, as if talking to herself.

"Well?" I waited impatiently. Already the others were in the hall, holding the elevator for me.

"I'll be there." She sounded surprised even as she spoke.

"Good." I hung up the phone and ran out the door. I stepped inside the elevator, waving a farewell to my mother who stood watching. My hand paused at seeing her face, but my momentum forced me into the elevator with the others, and the door closed. What had I seen on her face? She had appeared drawn and tired, but there was something more—a haunting sadness that had nothing to do with Paulette.

We arrived at the hospital at nearly eight-thirty. A nurse with a wide nose and chipmunk cheeks barred the entrance to Paulette's room. "Not so many people tonight. She's in a bad way. Besides, visiting hours are almost over."

"But we have to see her," Jean-Marc said.

"All of you?" The nurse's eyes widened as she saw our bishop and Paulette's home teachers come up behind us. They nodded and smiled their greetings.

"All of us," Jean-Marc said. "These are our ecclesiastical leaders, and we've come to give her a blessing."

"I don't know," the plump nurse said hesitantly. She plucked nervously at the dark hairs escaping from under her nurse's cap. "Does the husband know you're here?"

"No, but—"

"Then I'm afraid you'll have to leave."

"I'm his brother!"

"Well, maybe just you can enter."

"What's the problem?" a familiar voice said behind the big nurse. She turned, revealing Giselle in the quiet light of the hall.

"They all want to see Madame Perrault. I told them it's too risky, that she's weak, but they are insisting." Her nostrils flared at our audacity.

"I'll take care of it," Giselle said to the older woman.

"But—"

"Paulette is my patient. I'll take care of it." Giselle's voice was firm and unyielding, yet somehow sensitive as well. The other nurse nodded and retreated, a relieved expression dominating her stocky features.

"Well?" Giselle asked.

"We've come to bless her," I said before Jean-Marc could respond. His normally cheerful face had darkened, and I worried about what he would say. I wanted the nurse to be on our side. "In our church, some of the men hold the priesthood. Paulette may not live through the night, or the baby either. So we wanted to let the Lord have a chance."

"A blessing," she mused aloud. "Is it done by the laying on of hands?"

I was surprised at the question. "Yes. May we, please?"

Giselle nodded slowly. "But could I . . . Do you mind if I . . ."

"Of course you can stay," I said. "One only needs to have faith in God." I thought perhaps Giselle had more than I did right then.

Jean-Marc knocked softly on the door, and at Pierre's call, he entered. A sad smile creased Pierre's white cheeks as he saw the large group. Silently we filed in, barely fitting in the small room. Philippe stood closest to the door, and beside him Lu-Lu clutched at his hand.

"We've come to bless Paulette," Jean-Marc said softly. "And the bishop has called a ward fast."

Pierre hugged his brother. "I'm so afraid. I can't lose her."

Jean-Marc didn't bother to wipe the tears springing from his eyes. I hadn't seen him cry so earnestly since I was in labor with the twins. "It's going to be all right," he murmured.

The bishop, home teachers, Pierre, and Jean-Marc crowded around the bed. Paulette had been sleeping, but her eyes flew open. Fear glared in her eyes before she recognized the people. Her gaze rested on the bishop. "Am I going to die now?" she asked. Her voice was aloof, her expression detached, as if she didn't really care about the possible response.

He stared a moment before replying. "Are you ready to die?"

"No." But again she spoke with the same lethargy she had shown before. Her despondent manner beckoned to me like a silent appeal. Even her smell reminded me of death.

"Then let's have faith."

She nodded and struggled to sit up. The blips and beeps on the monitors quickened, and Giselle stepped forward. "You need to stay down, Paulette." I watched, feeling helpless, as Giselle pushed her gently back. Once more Paulette's stomach dominated the scene, and for a moment I was angry at the baby who was causing me to lose my friend sooner than was necessary.

Jean-Marc took out the consecrated oil he always carried with him in a small vial. "Who will do the anointing?"

Pierre gazed at the bishop. "Will you?"

He nodded. "And you will bless her."

Pierre shook his head almost violently. "I gave her one before. I—I think my faith is lacking in this." I knew he was talking about the baby. He had wanted Paulette to abort her; he couldn't pray to save her now. Pierre turned to Jean-Marc. "Will you do it? You know how much I love her. And you have always had much more faith than I."

"I learned from you," Jean-Marc said, clasping his brother's shoulder. "But I will do it gladly."

The bishop placed a drop of oil on Paulette's scalp. We bowed our heads. Before he could begin, Philippe catapulted forward as the door opened, pushing him further into the room. Simone stood there in the open space, looking awkward in the same bright summer dress I had seen her in that afternoon. Her hair was drawn back into a short ponytail and her heavy, blood-red lipstick emphasized her thin face.

"Momma!" Paulette gasped.

"I'll leave, if ya want." The vulnerability in Simone was unmistakable.

For the first time, Paulette let her indifferent facade slip, revealing a scared little girl. "I need you to stay," Paulette said succinctly. "Please don't leave."

Simone smiled. "I won't."

The men placed their hands on Paulette's head again, and we bowed our heads. All but Philippe, whose full lips were twisted into an angry frown.

I had never heard such a blessing. The Spirit seemed to pervade the room, filling in the cracks the fear had left in our hearts. "Your sins are forgiven you," Jean-Marc said near the end. "And I command you to become well from the pneumonia in order to deliver your baby in due time." His voice shook as he completed the blessing in the name of Jesus Christ. I heard a strangled cry and opened my eyes. The person making the sound was Philippe, who was standing by the door. He was pale and shaky.

"My sins are forgiven?" Paulette whispered, as if not quite believing. "What does this mean? How can he say that?"

Her question was addressed to no one, but the bishop picked up a set of scriptures from the small bedside table where Pierre had laid them earlier. "Forgiveness with a healing blessing is not new," he said. "In James, chapter five, verses fourteen and fifteen, it says this: 'Is any sick among you? let him call for the elders of the church and let them pray over him, anointing him with oil in the name of the Lord: And the prayer of faith shall save the sick, and the Lord shall raise him up; and if he have committed sins, they shall be forgiven him.'"

Philippe snorted, opened the door, and fled, as if escaping something evil. Lu-Lu ran after him, but the rest of us ignored the interruption.

"It wasn't me, Paulette," Jean-Marc said. "I didn't choose the words."

Paulette looked away. "Thank you, Jean-Marc. Thank you all for coming." She didn't sound convinced. Her eyes closed and she lay still. Only her rasping breath and the monitor showed she still lived.

"It was beautiful. Thank you for letting me stay," Giselle said. She had tears on her dark face and an unfeigned smile on her red lips. With a final glance at the monitor, she turned to the door. "Five minutes," she said. "Then she really needs to rest."

The bishop and home teachers said their goodbyes. Pierre thanked them again, but Paulette didn't open her eyes.

"Can I talk to my daughter?" Simone asked. Pierre nodded, though his expression was doubtful. We turned to leave. "Stay, Ariana," Simone said. "I want ya to hear this."

Paulette opened her eyes as Simone and I approached the bed. Again she had the appearance of a small child. "Am I doing right, Momma?" she asked. "Would you abort your baby to live a little longer?"

"I aborted a baby once," Simone said. "I wasn't married and my father made me go to the clinic. We were poor, but my father somehow got the money. They said after it was over, I'd forget it and go on. But I never forgot. It ruined my life—and yers."

"How?"

"I felt guilty about killin' that baby. I left home shortly after, and got into drugs. It helped me forget. When I got pregnant again, I didn't abort ya, but I was never able to give ya a chance at a good life. Every time I tried to get away from drugs, the guilt wouldn't let me. I'm so sorry!"

"It's not your fault, Momma."

"If I hadn't killed that baby, maybe I would have done somethin' with my life, maybe even gotten married to yer father. He wanted to, but I wasn't willin' to give up the drugs, 'cause then I'd have to face my guilt." She paused and reach out a tentative hand to her daughter. "I'm proud of ya, Paulette. Yer brave enough to stand up and do what I never could."

"The situation is different," Paulette said. "You were just a child."

"Maybe. But it don't make what I did right."

A hush fell over the room. Then, "I thought you rejected me," Paulette said with the emotionless voice she had used earlier.

"Never. I just didn't want my life to affect yer bein' happy."

"You won't leave?" The hope was clearly written on my friend's face.

"I'll be here for as long as ya want me." Mother and daughter hugged. I felt out of place and drifted to the door.

"Ariana, don't leave," Paulette said. "I have to ask you something." I stopped and retraced my steps.

"Will you take care of Marie-Thérèse? Pierre will have to work and won't be able to be with her all the time."

"You're not going to die now!" I said. "Didn't you listen to the blessing?"

She nodded. "I heard, but I know it is based on my faithfulness. And since I was never forgiven for my sins from before, I can't believe it now." She stared into my eyes, entreating me. "Do you believe it? Do you believe God could forgive my sins and still let me get AIDS?"

"Lots of worthy people die."

"That's not an answer. I need to understand." Paulette's face collapsed into pathetic resignation.

I backed away. "I do believe in the blessing," I whispered fiercely. "I do." I practically ran from the room. I didn't know what to tell Paulette. She needed something from me, and I couldn't give it to her.

CHAPTER ELEVEN

"He felt something, I know he did," Lu-Lu said jubilantly in the car. Philippe had left the hospital alone, but she had waited to ride home with us.

"He didn't seem impressed," Jean-Marc commented.

"But he felt something." Lu-Lu sounded less sure.

I watched the lights from the oncoming cars and said nothing, playing with the gauzy folds of my white dress, now wrinkled from the long day. Philippe had seemed more scared than anything to me. I dismissed him almost immediately; I was more worried about Paulette. I knew she was supposed to get well, at least temporarily, but somehow I didn't feel she would. I silently berated myself for my lack of faith, and for lying to Paulette by telling her I believed in the blessing.

We arrived home well after ten. My mother was up and waiting. Louise told her about the blessing, her face full of hope, but again I said nothing. Leaving the others, I went to check on the children. All were sleeping soundly, even Marie-Thérèse. The rag doll had fallen to the side of the bed, and I picked it up and tucked it next to her small body.

Next, I made my way into the kitchen to clean the dishes I had left after dinner, but my mother must have washed them. I slumped to the table and laid my head on my folded arms. *What's wrong with me, Father?* I prayed silently. *Please help me. Please send an answer so I can help Paulette.* Despite my apparent lack of faith, I did believe my Father loved both me and Paulette.

"What's wrong?" my mother asked from the doorway.

I lifted my head. "I could ask you the same thing."

She sighed. "It seems rather petty compared to Paulette's problems." She sank into a chair.

"Well?"

"This evening, right before you called me to baby-sit, I told your father I was going to be baptized no matter what he said. He claimed I loved the Church more than him, and that no true God would come between a man and his wife. Then you called and I left. It's the first time I ever left without telling him where I was going. He was very angry, so angry he couldn't talk. He just stared at me with his mouth working, up and down. It was awful."

"So what are you going to do?" I asked.

"Can I stay here tonight?"

"It won't help things."

"I know, but I have to think about what I'm going to do. I can't think of living my life without the gospel, and I can't imagine leaving Géralde. I love him. Oh, why does he have to be so stubborn? I'm not asking him to be baptized, just to support my decision." She laid her head down on her arms and sobbed.

It seemed, of late, that people were asking me a lot of questions to which I didn't know the answers. *What should I do?* I asked instinctively of my Heavenly Father, as I had learned to do through the years since I had became a member.

"Would you talk to him?" my mother asked, wiping her face with both hands.

"Now?"

She nodded. "I'll stay here with the children."

"But what will I say?"

Her slender shoulders lifted in a helpless shrug. "I don't know, Ariana. But you always seem to find a way. Please try." I didn't understand what she was talking about, but because of her pleading expression, I had to agree.

In the sitting room, I took Jean-Marc aside. "I'm going to visit my father."

"Now?"

"It's important. My mother wants to be baptized, and they had a fight about it."

"I'll go with you," he said immediately.

"I think I should talk to him alone."

"At least let me drive."

I hugged him, touched that he wanted to be there for me. "Thanks. I think I'm tired of being alone."

"Alone?"

My eyes watered. "I've missed you."

"But I'm right here," he said, pulling me close with a smile.

He didn't understand my reference to the many evenings I had already spent alone. I smiled wistfully and turned to grab my white sweater.

We drove the few minutes to my parents' home in comfortable silence. He walked me up the cement steps to the outside door, where I rang the black buzzer. The night was quiet and tranquil, and not another person was in sight. Stars overhead shone brightly, hovering in their constant vigil.

"Yes?" my father's voice responded quickly, as if he had been waiting.

"It's me, Ariana. May I come up?" The buzzer sounded, and Jean-Marc pulled open the heavy door.

"I'll wait down here," he said, jabbing a finger at the elevator button.

"I won't be long." At least I hoped I wouldn't.

As I rode in the elevator, I wondered what I was doing. It had been a long time since I had been a fearless missionary, accustomed to rejection. "But he's your father," I said aloud. "He can't reject you." But he had once before, when Antoine died.

My father opened the door before I rang the bell. He had his keys in his hand and was pulling on a sweater. For the first time I noticed the wrinkles around his eyes.

"Going somewhere?"

"To find your mother," he said curtly. "She left. Since you are here, I suppose she's not at your house."

"You suppose wrong," I said lightly.

"Is she okay?" His tone reprimanded my frivolity.

I sighed. "May I come in? She's the reason I'm here."

He stood aside and ushered me into their spacious entryway. I led the way down the short corridor past the kitchen and into their oversized sitting room. I knew each step well, as I had grown up in this apartment; even the faint smell of spice my mother used to freshen the air was familiar. As always when coming to my parents' house, pleasant memories of Antoine filtered through my mind.

Mother had changed the sitting room since I had been here last, as she occasionally did. A new picture of the Christ in Gethsemane had a dominant place over the hearth, and another of the Swiss Temple was positioned in the corner by the window where my mother usually sat reading. The couches had been arranged to one side to allow space for a new easy chair, and on the coffee table in front of this chair, a statue of Christ with two children on his lap sat next to a copy of the Ensign and my mother's scriptures. I observed all this with some portion of my brain; there had been a time when my mother hadn't dared bring any of her new beliefs into the house.

"She's not okay," I said, settling myself in the easy chair.

My father didn't sit. "What do you mean?"

"Oh, Father, she's torn between her love for you and her beliefs. What does it matter if she's baptized? I am, and it has only changed me for the better. Has it ruined our relationship?"

"You are not my wife."

"But I am your daughter. The gospel makes Mother happy; it doesn't take away from your love."

"She'll want me to change—eventually. It'll tear us apart."

I felt my face flush with anger. "Has it torn us apart, Father? No. It was what brought us back together!"

"You're not my wife," he repeated stubbornly.

I stood up. "This is ridiculous. I shouldn't have come. You don't want to listen!" Then I saw it clearly. "You're afraid, aren't you? Afraid that if you let Mother be baptized, you will have to find the truth for yourself. That's it, isn't it? You're afraid!" The idea seemed ludicrous, but there it was. My father was frightened of the truth. For over seven years since I had made up with my parents, I had hoped for their conversion. Now my mother was ready, but fear stood in her way.

I suddenly felt very tired. "I can't do this! You and Mother will just have to work it out. I can't be caught between you. Paulette's dying, and I don't understand why. And all you can think of is your fear of change. You won't even try to learn the truth." I shut my eyes, feeling dizzy. When was the last time I had actually eaten? I had fed the children, but I had not been hungry when we had begun our new fast. "I have to leave."

"Wait!" My father put his hand on my shoulder. "What's wrong, Ari? Tell me."

The anger left me as quickly as it had come, leaving me weak. I sagged, and my father caught me.

"Tell me," he repeated, holding me close like he had when I was a child.

"It's Paulette," I said through my tears. "She's looking to me for the answer, but I don't know why this is happening to her, especially after she's worked so hard for forgiveness. I can understand trials, but death? And Pierre too? And possibly the baby? She was forgiven for her sins, but now they've come back to torment her. She feels her sins are being visited upon her innocent family. What kind of forgiveness is that?"

I felt guilty even as I spoke. My father was an unbeliever, and certainly not the one I should speak to about my doubts. Belatedly, I realized I should be talking with Jean-Marc. We might have our troubles, but he was a priesthood holder and well-versed in the scriptures. Of course, he hadn't been around much lately. When could I have asked? The thought was caustic, but I didn't fight it. It was the truth. Maybe he was trying to escape the situation with Paulette altogether; I certainly wished I could. And now here I was talking with my father, the biggest church critic I had ever known besides my former self. He would surely point out the fruitlessness of my faith.

His next words filled me with astonishment. "It's more complex than that, Ari," he said. "I'm surprised you don't know."

I blinked at him. "What?"

"Your church teaches that when a person repents, forgiveness is complete; but repentance doesn't negate the consequences of previous actions. If it did, people could simply repent at the last moment and be cured of anything. For instance, a person who has committed adultery could immediately have the consequences removed. Like a resulting pregnancy could disappear, or the spouse would never leave and sue for divorce. Or perhaps a man caught embezzling would retain his job. Doesn't that sound preposterous? Of course it does. No, the consequences have to be in place; they are unchangeable, and they actually serve as an example to others. Meanwhile, the trial itself refines the person even more. What use is faith if there are no tests? God sent us here to be tested, and what better way for a person to be tested than this? It doesn't mean Paulette was never forgiven, or that God is at fault and has abandoned her. There are rules in the universe, and He follows them. Yes, He has the power to change things, but how much more will we learn if we go through it? And those around us?"

My father's speech sounded strangely Mormonized, and I wondered if he had been reading Mother's *Ensigns*. I smiled inwardly at the thought. "But the baby—"

"She is an innocent, to be sure, but any religion in the world will tell you that her innocence makes it a much more potent test. Some of the innocent are sacrificed to stand as witnesses against those who wrong them, but others simply stand as complications to whatever trials are sent to the faithful. It is much easier to suffer yourself than to see someone else suffer for your mistakes—especially in a case like Paulette's, where such a drastic repentance has occurred."

My father's words were difficult to understand. "Are you saying God didn't change the consequences of Paulette's drug use because He wants to test her?"

"Like He tested you." My father's words were gentle. "Your Nette died through no fault of yours, yet had you chosen another path, she wouldn't have died. But does it mean you are to blame? Or that any forgiveness you obtained was tainted? I think not."

I was beginning to understand. "Regardless, Nette still died."

"And Paulette still has AIDS, as she would have had she not repented," my father continued. "We always have a choice in life, but we can't choose the consequences. Those won't change simply because we repent."

I nodded and stepped away from him. "I don't understand it," I said. "You talk like a bishop or something. I never knew you understood the scriptures so well."

He laughed. "Not only members of your church read the scriptures."

"When did you start reading them?"

He appeared startled at my question. "About a year ago," he said.

I smiled. That was about the time my mother had begun attending church regularly. "So Mother's church activity has influenced you." I picked up my mother's scriptures from the table and thumbed through them until I found what I wanted. "And whatsoever thing persuadeth men to do good is of me; for good cometh of none save it be of me." As I quoted the scripture in Ether, my father's eyebrows drew together tightly.

"That has nothing to do with it." His voice was clipped.

"Yes, it does. Father, I really appreciate what you said to me tonight. It really helped. But I have to point something out. *You* are at a crisis point in your life. *You* have a decision to make, and like Paulette, you can't choose the consequences. Mother loves you more than anything. She also loves the Lord. Please work this out with her." I kissed his cheek and ruffled the top of his hair, as I had as a child when he tucked me into my bed each night. "I love you."

He didn't follow me, but stood staring after me as I left. My own heart was much lighter. I knew my parents still had a long way to go, but whether my father knew it or not, he was on the right path. And, strangely, the Lord had helped *me* by sending me to him. My father had given me at least part of the answer to Paulette's dilemma. Now I would follow up on my earlier feelings and talk to Jean-Marc.

When I stepped off the elevator, Jean-Marc stood up from his seat on the cool marble stair. "How'd it go?" he asked.

"All right, I think." I settled on the stair and patted the place beside me. He sat again, looking at me questioningly.

"My father helped me understand something," I said. I noticed my mother's scriptures then. I had forgotten to return them to the table in her sitting room. I let them slide to my lap.

Jean-Marc's face appeared bemused. "And I thought you came to teach him."

I laughed. "Well, we've heard time and time again how the Lord works in mysterious ways. I think my father has been studying religion. Not ours in particular, perhaps, but in general."

He smiled. "So what happened?"

I bit my lower lip. "Well, I couldn't seem to understand why Paulette has AIDS. I mean, I know she did drugs, but she has repented, and it doesn't seem fair for the Lord to let her die like this. She doesn't understand it either."

He shook his head. "The same question has been plaguing me. Pierre has never done anything wrong in his life, and now he's got it and eventually he's going to die." His voice was low as he added, "Like my dad."

"My father said these things happen because of consequences, and we can choose our course but not the results." I explained by using the examples my father had given. "But when it comes right down to it, the whole thing is a test, to refine not only Paulette but the rest of us."

Jean-Marc put his arm around me. "I only hope we all pass it."

"We won't have to do it alone. We have each other and the Lord." I stared at the swirling patterns in the marble floor. "But I doubted His wisdom," I whispered.

Jean-Marc's hand gently touched my chin and brought my face around to meet his gaze. "We all do it. It's a part of learning. And if we don't keep on learning, we forget."

I knew what he was saying. At the time it had happened, Nette's tragic death had crushed me; but after becoming a member, I had never questioned the Lord about it or anything else He had sent my way. Until now.

"Yet Paulette believes her family is being punished for her sins," I said. "She even quoted scripture to me."

Jean-Marc fingered the scriptures I had taken from my mother's table. "I know where that scripture is—we just had a lesson on it last week in elders quorum. It's in Exodus and again in Numbers. But she has misunderstood it. It is only if a person doesn't repent that the punishments will fall upon their children. Look, here in the Doctrine and Covenants it explains it better."

I read the scripture eagerly. "This is it!" I said.

"What?"

I kissed his mouth. "The rest of the answer!" I stuffed the scriptures in my sweater pocket and stood up. Grabbing his hands, I pulled him to his feet. "Come on."

His green-brown eyes sparkled. "You're up to something. Where are we going?"

"To the hospital." My voice was determined.

He grinned. "Right now? What if they don't let us in?"

"They will."

Twenty minutes later, we walked into the hospital and rode up the elevator to the third floor in the wing where the AIDS patients were located. Jean-Marc kept trying to duck into deserted corridors when people passed, but I strode ahead without looking around. "You've seen too many American films," I said to him. "The trick is to look like you belong." If my white dress was a bit fuller in the skirt and more gauzy than the nurses' uniforms, such a thing went unnoticed this late at night, especially because of my white nurse-like sweater. For his part, Jean-Marc stood out in his dark suit.

We made it to Paulette's door without being challenged and slipped inside. The room was dark. "You keep watch," I said to Jean-Marc, "and I'll talk with her."

The only light came from blinking machines and through a crack in the heavy curtains. Labored breathing came from the bed. In the dim light I could see the chair next to the bed; it was empty. *Where was Pierre?*

"It's Ariana," I whispered, touching Paulette's shoulder. "Are you awake?"

"Yes." The voice was low and unrecognizable. "I've just been lying here waiting for you."

"How did you know I was coming?"

The thin figure shifted slightly. "If not today, then tomorrow."

I took her hand. It seemed so incredibly fragile, the skin paper-thin and dry like old parchment. "I came to tell you I've found the answer. God *has* forgiven you and loves you! But you see, the consequences can't be changed simply because you repent." Again I explained about the adulterous man and the one who had embezzled, silently thanking my father for his clear examples. "So you see, the Lord didn't let you have AIDS because He didn't forgive you, but because He can't go against His own rules and change the outcome. When Nette died, a missionary told me God loves those He tests. He loves you so much!"

"You really think so?" The rasping voice had a touch of wonder.

I nodded, though Paulette could not see me in the dark. "He knew you would stay faithful, no matter what. And when you stand before Him, you can know for a surety the Savior has made your robes white before Him through His sacrifice, and through your own faithful endurance. Remember, this life is but a blink in the eternity of things."

I wasn't sure if I was explaining it correctly, but her frail grasp tightened on my hand.

"Thank you! Oh, thank you. And to Him who sent you."

This was my first inkling that I wasn't talking to Paulette. I held the hand for a long time, wondering what to do. Finally, I reached out to the curtain with my free hand and parted it further. Rays from the outside lights surrounding the hospital shone down on the figure in the bed—an old woman, impossibly thin and wrinkled-looking. She was sound asleep, a slight smile on her pale lips.

I grimaced. This wasn't Paulette at all! I let the curtain drop and crept to the door.

"Finished already?"

"It's not Paulette!"

"In that case, what took you so long?"

He grabbed me with one hand, the other opening the door. I stared at the number outside the room: 301. Paulette was in 307, three doors down. In my hurry, and with the muted light in the hospital corridor, I had made a mistake.

We glanced up and down the hall. Several nurses passed, but none looked our way. Jean-Marc sprinted down the hall, pulling me with him. He opened Paulette's door.

"Who's there?" Pierre s voice came from the dark.

"It's me, Jean-Marc, and Ariana."

"What are you doing here?" We heard a click, and a soft glow appeared on the headboard of Paulette's bed. Pierre blinked at his watch. "It's nearly midnight."

"I needed to talk to Paulette," I said, feeling suddenly absurd. It could have waited until tomorrow.

"How is she?" Jean-Marc asked.

Pierre frowned. "Not well. I mean, her body is responding to the drugs, but she's not getting better. It's like she's given up." His voice hardened. "Tomorrow, I'm telling the doctor to take the baby, regardless. Either way it will die."

She! my mind shouted.

"But the blessing," Jean-Marc said. "I felt it. I don't understand."

"I do," I said. I crossed to the bed, and despite Pierre's objections, I shook Paulette's shoulder.

"Huh? What?" she said. Her eyes fluttered open and tried to focus on me. "An angel?" she asked. "Oh, it's you, Ariana."

I sat on Pierre's vacated chair. "Having AIDS doesn't mean you aren't forgiven for the past," I began for the third time that evening.

"I've been thinking about it," she said. "My grandfather forced my mother to have an abortion when she was young, and she never recovered. She raised me with drugs, and because of that I am passing this disease to my family. It is the sins of the parents being passed to the third and fourth generations, just as I thought." Her face was glum, her voice hopeless.

I pulled out my mother's scriptures and turned to Doctrine and Covenants 124:52. "And I will answer judgment, wrath, and indignation, wailing, and anguish, and gnashing of teeth upon their heads, unto the third and fourth generation, so long as they repent not, and hate me, saith the Lord your God." I paused to let it sink in. "You see, Paulette, you're not in that category. You love the Lord. You have repented, and He has accepted your repentance. But that doesn't mean He will change the consequences." I launched into my examples, and then reminded her of what Elder Tarr had told me so long ago: "The Lord loves those whom He tests. If He didn't, why bother?"

Paulette was crying. "But this is too hard!"

"So was losing Nette and Antoine."

She blinked twice, causing large tears to slide down her face in rivulets, and her mouth trembled as she caught her lip in her teeth, biting until the blood came as she had on the night Nette died. "He knew *you* could do it," she said dismally.

"As can you," I responded softly.

"How?" The question came out as a cry.

"One day at a time. And we'll be here for you."

"He loves me," she whispered fiercely. "He loves me."

I nodded. "He does."

"I can do it!" Her voice was stronger, though still filled with an aching sadness.

I glanced over to the door, where our husbands stood watching us. Their faces were full of heartache, yet the pain had been changed by hope.

Paulette sat up alone and hugged me tightly, until my ribs begged for breath. "I love you," she said.

"Then get well. You have a little girl who needs you, and a baby to help grow."

We left Paulette and Pierre, feeling we had done something good. Both Paulette and I had the faith we had lacked earlier, and already she was feeling stronger. The priesthood was healing her body, but my words—no, my father's and Jean-Marc's—had healed her mind and her heart.

The day had been a long one for me, both physically and mentally. I drifted to sleep in the car and almost didn't wake when Jean-Marc parked the car. He helped me to the apartment, undressed me, then tucked me into bed tenderly. I felt his love, strong and sure.

"Check the kids?" I asked.

"They're fine," he said, snuggling in beside me.

I knew they were, and that my mother was curled up with Josette in her bed as she often was when sleeping over. But knowing and seeing didn't mean the same thing to a mother. I slipped out of the warm bed and went to check on my children and Marie-Thérèse, leaving Jean-Marc to fall asleep.

As he predicted, all the children were covered and slumbering with the peaceful abandon of the innocent. I kissed their rosy cheeks, feeling grateful I would be there tomorrow to see them wake. I considered Paulette one of the most righteous people I knew, but I didn't want her trial, not even to become as close to God as she would be. I remembered all too vividly how savagely the refining fires burned. Even now, as I watched from a distance, my skin felt scorched by the blaze.

CHAPTER TWELVE

Jean-Marc was in the kitchen when I awoke. My mother and Louise were serving a breakfast of juice and hot mush to the twins and Marie-Thérèse, who were seated at the table. The women's eyes were tinged with red and swollen from yesterday's crying, but today both looked happy. Lu-Lu had André on her lap and was spooning in his customary baby cereal.

"Oh, Ariana, the blessing worked!" Louise said.

"What?"

"Pierre called this morning, nearly an hour ago. You got in so late, we didn't want to wake you," she explained. "Now we can finish our fast in thanksgiving, instead of asking for something."

André held out his arms for me, and I leaned down and kissed his cheek. At the table, the twins played a peculiar game with their hot cereal as Marie-Thérèse watched.

"Pierre said Paulette looks much better this morning. They've taken her off the oxygen and everything. He says she got up to use the bathroom and announced she's going home. They're waiting for the doctor to come in this afternoon to see if he'll release her."

Jean-Marc put his arms around me and gave me a kiss. "See what a little faith and fasting can do?"

"Will you take me to the hospital?" Marie-Thérèse asked me.

"Of course I will."

"I want to go!" the twins said in unison.

"But then you won't get to go to the park with me," Lu-Lu said. "I've got suckers," she added enticingly. The twins cheered.

"I wish you could live with us always," Marc said.

"I do too," Lu-Lu said.

Louise watched her. "I've been thinking of moving here myself. I think Paulette will need us."

Jean-Marc and I glanced at each other. For years we had been trying to get Louise to move to Paris, but she had always refused.

"If you're serious about moving here, Lu-Lu," Louise continued,

"Pierre said he could get you a job with his company. He said they could always use a good manager, and you have the training for it, having grown up working in our store."

"What, nepotism?" Lu-Lu said dryly. She sounded far more grown up than I had ever seen her.

"Why not?" Jean-Marc said. "It worked for me." We all laughed. "As for that, I could get you a job at the bank, especially since you've had a few years of college. We have a teller job open."

Lu-Lu appeared thoughtful. "Maybe I'll take you up on that. After all, this is the famous city of love, and I'm certainly ready for some excitement."

Louise frowned, but I was the only one who noticed.

"What about Philippe?" Lu-Lu asked.

Jean-Marc's jaw tightened momentarily. "Him too," he conceded. "I have a job lined up for him, if he wants it. He'll have to cut his hair, shave, and wear a suit, but I'll give him a shot."

Gratitude filled Lu-Lu's face. "Thank you, Jean-Marc. I really think we'll accept. I mean, I'll have to talk with him, but we wanted to move here anyway. This will be the perfect opportunity. I can't wait to tell him!" She stood and handed André to me. "May I use the telephone in the sitting room?"

"Of course," I said.

Jean-Marc smiled, and I knew he was grateful he had supported his sister, despite his disaffection for her fiancé. "Don't worry," he said to Louise. "It's nothing with money, if that's what you're worried about. Philippe will be doing something with the paperwork after the tellers are finished with it."

She sighed. "I just wish I could get her away from him for a few months. That's all it would take, I'm sure."

"How long have you been planning on moving to Paris?" I asked. I knew Louise wouldn't have said anything if the decision hadn't already been made.

"Since I talked to Pierre this morning," she said. "I'm going to give up my apartment in Bordeaux and live with Pierre and Paulette until an apartment in their building opens up. That way I'll be close enough to help when—" she broke off, and I understood why. Now that Paulette was feeling better, it seemed like bad luck to talk about her dying. "I'm going back to Bordeaux today to arrange things, if Lu-Lu will come. I'd better go talk with her."

"But she's taking us to the park," Josette protested as Louise left. The children had been monitoring the conversation without much interest until their outing had been threatened.

"I'll take you," my mother said.

"Do you have suckers?" asked Marc.

My mother smiled. "I can buy some."

"All right then," he agreed.

The buzzer in the hallway rang. "I'll get it," Jean-Marc said.

"Go get dressed," I told the children, seeing that they weren't going to eat any more. "Make sure it matches. Marie-Thérèse, you help them decide what to wear, okay?" They scrambled from their chairs and ran down the hall.

I grinned at my mother. "You've been watching my children so much, you might as well move in."

She grimaced and said softly, "I may have to."

"Nonsense. Father may be stubborn, but he's not stupid."

"I hope you're right," she said, heaving a sigh. André held out his arms for her, and she took him from me and held him tightly against her chest. "He certainly is a sensitive child." My mother kissed his soft cheek. I agreed. I didn't know what I had done to deserve such a compassionate little boy, but I was grateful.

"Josephine," my father's voice came from the kitchen doorway. Behind him I saw Jean-Marc's hesitant grin. I knew he had planned this meeting. I only hoped it worked out.

"Géralde." Surprise tinged with hope covered my mother's face. She held André tighter.

My father glanced briefly at me, then back at my mother. "I love you, Josephine. Please come back home." He took the few steps between them and reached for her hands. She shifted André to her hip and let him lift her free hand between his. "I'm sorry for the way I acted," he said. "I had no right to treat you that way."

I started to edge past him to join Jean-Marc in the hallway, but my father stopped me. "No. Ari, Jean-Marc, I want you both to hear this." He turned back to my mother. "I had no right to treat you that way, Josephine," he repeated, "but I do have the right to take steps to protect my family. I don't want to lose you, and I feel that I will if you join this church. It will separate us. Please, come home and reconsider. Attend all you want, but don't consent to baptism. Remember, I love you. Isn't that what's important?"

My mother let André slide to the floor. In her eyes, I thought I saw all of the things she would like to say, but she knew they were things my father wasn't ready to hear. "I love you," she whispered, "and yes, I'll come home."

They held each other in a close embrace, with my father leaning over to bury his face in her neck. I took André's hand and left the room.

"You planned this," I accused Jean-Marc in the hall.

He shrugged. "It worked, didn't it?"

"For now." I knew that the issue had been shelved, not settled. Just as Jean-Marc and I had done to our own problems. Perhaps it was good enough.

Marie-Thérèse and I arrived at the hospital shortly before lunch. Pierre was in the hall, and he picked up Marie-Thérèse and whirled her around. "We're taking Mommy home," he said.

She giggled. "I know!"

He set her down and she ran into her mother's room. Paulette was standing, pacing the floor. Pierre grinned at me. "I can't get her to rest. She's like her old self again."

"Then maybe now *you* can get back to your normal self." I patted his belly, which had shrunk noticeably in the week Paulette had been in the hospital.

He grinned. "I'm looking forward to it," he said. "Getting back to normal life, I mean. In fact, I'm going to have to go in to work for a while this afternoon. I've already taken three full days off as it is. I'm not worried about vacation time—I still have nearly my whole month's annual vacation to take—but I left some important things unfinished."

"Why don't you go ahead, and I'll take Paulette home?" I said. "Then you can take care of whatever and meet us at your house."

"Would you?"

I nodded, and he turned into the room to tell Paulette. I was about to follow when I noticed several nurses and doctors emerging from a room down the hall. Two of the nurses pushed a bed with a still figure on it, a blanket drawn up to obscure the features. I took a few steps down the hall to check the number on the door: room 301. The woman I had talked with last night was dead.

"She died just a few minutes ago," Giselle said, separating herself from the other nurses coming from the room. Her dark cheeks had tears on them, yet her eyes were happy.

"She had AIDS?"

The nurse nodded. "For three years now, she's been fighting for life, though sometimes I wondered why. She was a mean, bitter lady. I often found it hard to take care of her."

"She was your patient then?"

"Yes. But today she was different. This morning when she called for me, I thought she was going to complain about breakfast as she usually did. Instead, she told me she had seen an angel during the night."

I gulped. "An angel?"

Giselle nodded. "At first she thought it was Death come to take her, but then she saw an angel with a flowing white robe who held her hand and told her God had forgiven her and loved her."

"Do you believe her?"

Giselle's even gaze met mine. "Paulette is better today after your husband's blessing, almost miraculously so. It is easier for me to believe in an angel than to see her recover so quickly."

I opened my mouth to confess, but she shook her head. "Angels come in all forms, Ariana, both heavenly and earthly. Sometimes one doesn't know when she will be someone else's angel."

I knew then she or one of the other nurses had somehow seen me the night before, coming from the dead woman's room. "What was her name?" I asked.

"Madeleine. And she died happy, with a smile on her face. I had never seen her smile." Giselle walked away.

When I pushed open the door to Paulette's room, she was waiting for me in the chair beside her bed, an unfinished blessing gown in her hands. It still made me smile in wonder at the idea of Paulette embroidering. It was an art I still had not grasped, though not for lack of diligence on the part of certain sisters from our ward.

Pierre was nowhere in sight, but Marie-Thérèse stared out the window. The thick brown curtains had been drawn back to let in the warm sun. I focused on Paulette. She was still too thin, but her light-brown eyes glistened with life.

She nearly bounced from her chair. "Oh, Ariana, thank you so much! Because of you, I'm going home today. At least I will if the doctor ever gets here."

I thought of telling her about the lady in room 301, but decided against it. "It wasn't me, it was the blessing," I said.

"Yes," she agreed, "but you returned my faith to me." She hugged me, and this time I no longer smelled death. She really was going to be okay—for now. I sighed in relief.

"There now, Ari." She patted my back, misconstruing my emotion. "Everything's all right."

"I've missed you. I've been lonely. I don't know what I'd do without you."

"Survive," she said. "You're good at that. We both are."

The door opened and our conversation died. "Dr. Medard," Paulette said.

This was the AIDS specialist, my first time meeting him. He was a relatively young man of average height, and his face was plain. Nothing to set him apart from a million other faces in the world, except perhaps for his moustache and the compassion in his light-brown eyes.

Those eyes now stared at Paulette. "Back in the world of the living, are we?" he asked. He came closer to the bed, and I saw that his moustache hid a cleft lip, repaired in the days before such surgeries had been perfected. Somehow the defect seemed to give him a sense of presence, something that arrested the attention and made me understand he was a man to be admired.

"I feel good," Paulette said. "I'm tired and my chest still hurts a bit, but I'm well enough to go home."

He frowned. "So it seems. I'm frankly astonished, but from all the tests and from the way you look and feel, I must say there's no reason to keep you here. But I'm a little worried you'll overdo things. Do you have someone to help you?"

She nodded. "My husband's sister and mother are coming to stay with me for a time. And even now, the sisters from my church are lining up at my door to bring meals and do laundry."

The doctor chuckled. "Good, very good. You have to take care of yourself. The next infection you get may be your last. I'll want to see you every few weeks, of course, to make sure you and the baby are progressing well. At any hint of sickness at all, you must come in."

"Okay, okay," Paulette said.

"In that case, you can leave." He smiled again and left the room.

"What happened to your regular doctor?" I asked, remembering the man who resembled a basset hound.

She shook her head. "He's not equipped to deal with AIDS. I'm seeing Dr. Medard permanently now. He's one of the best, and the only doctor around who takes care of pregnant women with AIDS or HIV."

"But he wanted to abort your baby," I protested.

"He wanted to do what was best for me," she said. "Once I explained how important she is to me, he didn't push. It was mostly Pierre."

"Love is an odd thing. Sometimes I don't understand it."

"Me either," she agreed, picking up a sturdy plastic sack packed with her things. She carefully folded the blessing gown and tucked it inside. "Shall we?"

I proffered my arm. "Yes, we shall."

We sauntered out the door and down the hall, with Marie-Thérèse hopping after us. Under her breath, she hummed a melody as she moved from square to square on the linoleum lining the hall. Unlike the other floors, this one had carpet only in the waiting room.

"Marguerite!" Paulette exclaimed.

I looked to see the robust woman striding down the hall. "But you're all better," she said, staring at Paulette in surprise.

Paulette laughed. "Yes, I am." There was a note of determination in her voice.

Marguerite hugged her. "I'm so glad. Want to celebrate? I'll buy lunch." She glanced at me. "You're still fasting, aren't you? We can break our fast together."

Paulette shook her head. "No offense, Marguerite, but I just want to go home."

The older lady chuckled. "I understand completely."

"But since you're here, there's someone I want you to meet." We were approaching the nurses' station. Giselle stood near it, eyes fastened on a report in her strong hands.

"I'm leaving," Paulette said. "I've come to say goodbye."

"I've never seen anyone recover so quickly," Giselle said to us.

"I'm not surprised," said Marguerite. "Ever since I joined the Church, I've seen many miracles. Why, the fact Paulette is alive today is proof enough."

"You're a member of their church?" the nurse asked. Marguerite nodded. "But I wasn't always."

"Giselle, this is our good friend, Marguerite Geoffrin," I said. "She owns several cafes here in town." As I introduced her, I exchanged knowing glances with Paulette. Marguerite had recently been made a stake missionary, and there was nothing she liked so much as a serious investigator.

"Why don't you two come to the house, and we can talk about it?" Paulette said.

"I wouldn't want to intrude. You need your rest," Giselle said. But the words seemed reluctant.

"Nonsense," Paulette dismissed the thought. "I've done nothing but rest for days. Besides, as my friend, you should come and make sure I'm settled in bed, right?"

"Well, I am getting off now," Giselle said, her black eyes sparkling with amusement. "I'm tired since I've just finished a double shift, but I guess I could come for a while."

"I'll stop off for lunch at the cafe," Marguerite said. "No sense in going hungry." She turned to Giselle. "Want to come along to help me choose the food?"

"Why not?" Giselle said. "Just let me get my things."

We left the two of them talking like old friends and made our way to the parking lot. I could hear honking in the distance and sounds of traffic. Nearby, a woman getting into a car talked excitedly, and the man with her laughed. They were the usual noises, but each seemed precious. Paulette lived, and I was taking her home!

When we arrived at Paulette's apartment, I called my mother to tell her I wouldn't be home for a while longer. "I don't want to leave Paulette, at least until Marguerite gets here. She shouldn't be alone at all this first little while."

"We're fine here," my mother said. "We went to the park."

"Did Marc make it to the bottom of the sandbox?"

She chuckled. "No, not yet. In another year or so, perhaps."

I hung up and went to where Paulette was settled on the couch. Marie-Thérèse had covered her mother with a light blanket and now lay cuddled beside her.

"How're you doing?" I asked.

Paulette sighed contently. "Good. Tired, but good." The hoarse voice of previous days had all but disappeared. She motioned to her chest. "The pain here is gone, all gone. It's a miracle!"

"I agree."

"Will you hand me the phone? I'd like to call my mother at work." There was a sense of pride as she said the words. "I called her earlier, but she wasn't in. I want her to know that I'm all right."

I did as she asked, then went to the kitchen to make myself scarce.

Paulette has her mother back, I thought as I took dishes out of the cupboard on which to place the lunch Marguerite would bring. *Something good has come out of this whole mess.*

The buzzer in the hall rang, signaling Marguerite and Giselle's arrival downstairs. I went to let them in. When they stepped out of the elevator, they were smiling—a good sign. "We're eating in the sitting room," I said. I led the way to where Paulette was resting. The apartment had the same basic layout as mine, except the entryway was three times the size and floored with warm wood strips instead of cold ceramic tile. Paulette also had two balconies, one off the kitchen and one off the sitting room, whereas I had none.

Marguerite had spared no expense, bringing a variety of food, from soup to pastries, that she or her husband had made themselves.

As we set it out, the phone rang. It was the Relief Society president with a list of sisters who had called to help out by bringing meals or staying with Paulette while Pierre was at work. Paulette hadn't been joking when she told the doctor about the lines of people waiting to help. I hung up and relayed the information.

"The members of your church are doing that?" Giselle asked, her eyebrows rising. "But they just found out about Paulette being released today."

"Oh, we have a sort of network." Marguerite explained about the visiting teachers. "And they probably passed a sheet around on Sunday, asking who would like to help out."

"Can we pray?" Marie-Thérèse now sat on the floor near me, eyeing the meat pastries Marguerite had brought. The others had settled themselves on two comfortable chairs opposite the sofa. "I'm hungry."

"Would you like to offer it?" Paulette asked.

The child shrugged. "Okay." We bowed our heads and folded our arms. Giselle did the same. "Heavenly Father, thank you so much for making Mommy better. I knew You could do it. And thank you for Marguerite bringing the food, especially the pastries. Please bless them and the meat and rice, too. Help us to know if someone needs us so we can help them." She closed in the name of Jesus Christ, and we all said amen.

We began to serve ourselves from the food loaded on the coffee table, but Giselle sat without moving. "How does she know how to pray like that?" she asked.

Paulette looked at Giselle in mild surprise. "We taught her, I guess."

"But she talks to God, not at Him. Like she knows Him."

"I do," said Marie-Thérèse. "He's my Father, and Jesus is my Brother. I learned that in Primary."

A sensation of wonder passed over Giselle's face. "I have always believed God was my Father," she said slowly, "and I have always prayed to him as such. Other people I have met have similar beliefs, yet never have I felt it as now. How can that be?"

I stopped with a piece of bread halfway to my mouth. Paulette lay on the couch in perplexed silence; Marguerite had her mouth full. It was up to me to answer.

"Do you feel warm inside?" I asked.

Giselle nodded. "Tingly. Almost like when your foot goes to sleep, except it feels good."

"That's the Spirit," I said. "Sometimes it comes as a warm feeling or a tingling. Sometimes it's simply a certainty, or even like a hug. It's hard to describe, but once you feel it, you can never forget."

Giselle nodded. "I felt it last night when your husband blessed Paulette," she said. "And it is this that interests me. He did it by laying his hands on her head, but where did he get the power? I've never seen anyone recover so quickly. It wasn't possible, and yet," she glanced at Paulette, "there she is. Is your husband a prophet?"

The question startled me until I remembered that she had seen a miracle. "No. But he has received the power of God to heal and to bless. Every worthy male member in our church has this ability."

"Oh." Giselle seemed disappointed. "Then you don't believe in prophets."

"Yes, we do," Marguerite said. "We believe the priesthood was restored to the earth by a latter-day prophet who, like those of old, receives the word of God and passes it to the whole church."

"Marie-Thérèse, go in my bedroom and get the *Ensign* on the table by my Book of Mormon," Paulette said. "It's the conference issue."

"We believe that the Lord always reveals things to prophets," Marguerite continued. "Just like in the Bible times. You see, when Jesus was on the earth, He established his church." She took a blue book from her purse, one with a gold angel on the cover, and grabbed it firmly between the fingers and thumbs of both hands. "Pretend my fingers are Jesus' disciples, and this book is the church. When Jesus died, the Church remained, guided by apostles and a prophet. But eventually wicked people killed the apostles, one by one." One at a time, Marguerite began lifting her fingers from the book as we watched in fascination. "Until at last, the Church fell." She let the book plummet to her lap. "It broke into many different pieces, as shown by the many different religions of today. Each had a part of the truth, but none held the truth in its entirety. Thus began the dark age of apostasy from the Church of Christ. And so it remained until the Lord decided the time had come to restore His Church." Marguerite stopped like a good missionary did, to give her companions a chance to speak. There was only Paulette or me.

I picked up where Marguerite had left off. "In eighteen twenty a four-teen-year-old boy, Joseph Smith, was searching for the true church. His family visited various churches and each chose one to attend, but Joseph couldn't decide which one was true. One day while reading in the Bible, he came across a scripture in James that said, 'If any of you lack wisdom, let him ask of God.' When Joseph read those words, he knew what he had to do." I explained how young Joseph had gone to the woods alone to pray, and how he had been answered. Everyone was quiet and intent on my words—even Marie-Thérèse, who had returned with the *Ensign*.

"He saw God the Father and Jesus," I said with quiet conviction. "And through him they restored the true Church to the face of the earth, never to be taken away again. Later Joseph was given the priesthood, and since then it has been passed down through the members of our church."

Marie-Thérèse handed the *Ensign* to Giselle, opened to the page with the General Authorities. "See, that's our prophet," she said. "And those are the 'postles."

Giselle took the magazine gingerly in her hands. "A prophet and twelve apostles," she mused. "And who are these?"

Marguerite explained about the Seventies while Paulette's eyes met mine. I saw a contentment there, and instinctively I knew it was because of Giselle's interest in the Church.

"My grandfather always said that Jesus' true Church would have a prophet and twelve apostles," Giselle murmured, as to herself. "He said they would have the power of God. But he never found a church like that." She touched the picture of our prophet with a brown finger. "A real prophet of God? Could it be true?" I could actually feel the hope and longing in her voice, and for the first time in a week the tears springing to my eyes were from joy, not from sorrow.

"I want to know more," she said. "Please teach me."

"Gladly," Marguerite said. "We'll set up an appointment for you to talk with our missionaries. But for now, take this." She gave the Book of Mormon in her lap to Giselle.

"What is this?" Giselle asked.

"It's a book that the Prophet Joseph Smith translated," Paulette answered, her uncertainty about teaching overcome in her eagerness to share the knowledge. "It's a second witness of Jesus Christ. Part of it tells the story of when Jesus visited the people on the American continent. It is the most beautiful book I've ever read. It was what first made me believe in God's love." Her face shone with the strength of her belief.

Giselle stared at the book in awe. "Thank you. I'll be very careful with it."

"Keep it as a gift," Marguerite said. "There are some passages marked, and a study guide. Read those first, if you will, and then the missionaries will begin from there."

"May I bring some of my family to listen to the missionaries?" Giselle asked.

Marguerite smiled. "Of course."

Giselle stood abruptly, clutching the book to her chest. "Thank you. I really must be going now."

"But we haven't eaten," Marguerite protested.

"Suddenly, I'm not hungry." In Giselle's eyes I saw a hunger that had nothing to do with food.

"Let her go," I said to Marguerite, then to Giselle, "But leave us your number so we can arrange the discussion with the missionaries."

Giselle pulled a card from her purse and handed it to Marguerite. "Any time in the afternoon is best," she said, "since I normally work the night shift—twelve hours, four days a week. Or I sometimes have the weekend off. Just let me know."

"You can take this, too." Marie-Thérèse picked up the Ensign from the table where Giselle had left it. Giselle glanced at Paulette, who nodded.

With her treasures, Giselle went to the door. "Thank you," she said as I walked with her.

When I returned to the others, everyone had begun eating except Paulette. "To think what life would be like without the gospel," she murmured. "I'd quite forgotten. What a wonderful feeling!" She turned to me. "Ariana, will you help me with my mother? I want her to understand how much God loves her."

"Of course," I said automatically. I didn't know how Simone would take to the gospel, but I would do anything to help her.

During the rest of lunch, Paulette and Marie-Thérèse chatted happily about the new baby. Marguerite and I had everything cleared away when Pierre walked in the door. He settled on the floor near his wife, and they exchanged a loving glance.

"I'd better get home," I said, taking the cue.

Marguerite rose. "Me too."

I kissed Paulette on the cheek and hugged Marie-Thérèse. "Call me if you need anything."

The Lord's love radiated in the room. They looked so happy sitting there as a family, and my heart filled with thanksgiving for this time they had together. The priesthood of God had surely worked a miracle.

CHAPTER THIRTEEN

The summer days slipped away like rats scurrying out of sight behind the garbage bins in the basement parking lot. As Paulette continued to mend, everyone relaxed and began to treat her as they had before we knew she had AIDS. Only I seemed to hold my breath, as if waiting for something dreadful to happen.

Nothing did. My parents had called an unspoken truce and settled again into their lives without discussing the gospel. Neither appeared extremely happy, but at least they were together.

Louise returned from Bordeaux and set about taking care of Paulette while she waited for an apartment to open up in Paulette's building. Lu-Lu stayed with us; I suspected she wanted some time away from her mother.

To our dismay, my sister-in-law persisted with the idea of marrying Philippe, and we had no choice but to go along with it. We tried to fit him into our family, but he mocked our beliefs at every turn. "Crazy. Your family is crazy," I heard him say to her several weeks after Paulette was released from the hospital.

"They are not!" They were out in the hallway near the elevator, but Lu-Lu had left the door ajar as she bid him farewell for the evening.

"If they think a little prayer is going to save your sister-in-law from AIDS, they are crazy. It's incurable, and nearly everyone dies within three years of coming down with the symptoms of AIDS. Three years!" he repeated. "That's not a long time. And your brother has been infected with HIV; it's only a matter of time before he gets AIDS and dies, too. No olive oil and prayer will help him then."

"Philippe!" Lu-Lu chided. "Miracles do happen. I'm not saying Paulette is going to be cured, but I'm telling you she was made well this time by the power of the priesthood."

He snorted derisively. "The doctor's drugs made her well. I tell you, as soon as you are out from under your family's influence, the better I will feel. I love you, Lu-Lu. I'll take care of you." His voice lowered, and I couldn't hear any more from the sitting room where I had been reading before their arrival. I supposed he was kissing her. At first, I hadn't understood her attraction to the man, but once he had cut his shaggy hair and shaved his scruffy beard, he had uncovered a genuinely handsome person. To make things worse, in our view at least, he was succeeding so well in his job at the bank that he was already being considered for a promotion.

"I don't know if I like the way he does things," Jean-Marc said to me late one evening when he had returned home from work. "But it's always done on time and correctly."

"What's wrong with the way he does it?" I asked.

He shook his head. "I don't know exactly. People seem to jump when he calls. He has a sort of magnetism or something. The other workers seem to be in awe, or maybe even afraid of him."

"That's not good."

"No, it's not. But I don't know what to do about it. I hoped he'd fail and Lu-Lu would see what a loser he is."

"Is he really a loser? Or is it because he's not a member? Lu-Lu loves him so much. Can she be so blind?"

Jean-Marc didn't have an answer, nor did I. Once I had been blinded by the man I thought I loved—my first husband, Jacques. I knew it was all too easy to get caught up in the emotion. Was it true love, or simply the dream of love, that held Lu-Lu in its grip?

"I think she's tired of being alone," Paulette said. It was Sunday and Paulette's first day back at church. In her arms she carried an array of projects and lesson aids for her Primary class.

"Marrying the wrong person is a heavy price to pay for companionship," I countered. "It's worse than being alone."

Paulette sighed. "I know. But we can't expect her to realize that."

"So what do we do?"

"I don't know. Just keep on like we are, I guess."

"Maybe she'll come to her senses in time." My voice didn't hold much hope.

"I'm praying," she said.

Since the onset of her illness, Paulette had changed. She had always been good, but now she seemed more centered somehow, and more patient. I guess looking at life from her perspective made a difference. It wasn't something I wanted to think about.

We had arrived in Primary opening exercises, and I said goodbye to the twins. They were jumping with excitement at having Paulette back after two weeks of substitutes. "I hope they're not too wild for you," I said.

Paulette smiled. "They won't be." She sat down with the twins near her, but not one of the other class members appeared. I saw several parents peek into the room, but when they saw Paulette they hurried their children away. At first I didn't want to believe it, but when Primary started, only one out of the other five children appeared. Children in the other classes stared at Paulette with open curiosity.

Time showed that many of the parents with children in Paulette's class had withdrawn them from Primary when they learned of her illness. They felt it was one thing to let someone with AIDS in the church house, but quite another to expose their precious children to the risk at close range. The bishop refused to succumb to pressure to release Paulette, and worked to educate the ward members and calm their fears. In the end, his effort was in vain, and Paulette decided to resign rather than see the ward divided into two warring factions.

"What hurts most," she said to me, "is that they can think I would actually expose their children to such a grave danger. If there were any risk at all of them getting AIDS—any at all—I wouldn't even *want* to teach."

Part of me carried a heavy guilt because I remembered too well how I had felt upon learning of her AIDS—especially the uncontrollable fear. If I, who loved her so deeply, could feel such a thing, how much more anxiety would accost those who were more distanced?

Marie-Thérèse's Primary teacher was one of the few parents who had backed Paulette, and she treated Marie-Thérèse the same as the other children in her class, never recoiling from her embraces or her outstretched hands. She had calmed the other parents enough so that they hadn't ostracized the little girl because she had infected parents. Her influence had healed my breaking confidence in the members of our ward in general. She reminded me the Church was still true, even when sometimes the members didn't act accordingly.

That same first Sunday back also brought another surprise to our lives—one that gave us unexpected joy.

"I would like you two to stay," Marguerite said to us after church. "Giselle is coming here after work with a few members of her family for her first discussion with the missionaries."

I glanced at Jean-Marc. "What do you think?"

"I guess we can stay," he said.

"I meant for you to take the children home," I clarified. "You can take the car and drop Pierre and Marie-Thérèse off, and Paulette and I will use her car. A missionary discussion is no place for children."

He made a face. "Baby-sitting, huh?"

I laughed. "No. It's not baby-sitting when they're your own children. Besides, they need to spend some time with you."

He appeared disconcerted, almost fearful, but he agreed.

The missionaries showed up—two young French elders. We waited outside in the warmth of the summer sun until Giselle arrived. With her were four other people, each with skin as dark as hers. One was older than the rest, and his hair was almost completely white. He had a benevolence about him that made me want to be his friend.

"My grandfather," Giselle said as she introduced the old man—no, not old. Though he was aged, he would never seem old.

I held out my hand. "Nice to meet you." But I was more surprised than anything. From the reverent way Giselle had talked about him, I had the impression he was already deceased.

"The pleasure is mine." His deep voice was rich and flavorful, his smile warm and sincere. "Please call me Grandfather," he said when I asked his name. "I've been called that so long that I don't remember any other."

"Shall we go in?" the missionaries asked. "Can we wait a bit?" asked Giselle.

"We have a few more of our family coming," Grandfather explained.

Another car drove up, and three people emerged. The missionaries greeted them and started to lead the way up the walk.

Grandfather held up a dark finger. "Just a moment more, if you would," he said politely. He turned to welcome another handful of people, who piled out of a station wagon. The missionaries' jaws dropped.

Our surprise deepened as several more cars drove up to the church to let out people of all ages, dressed in their Sunday best. The skin tones were varied, but all could clearly trace their heritage to Africa.

Next to me Paulette breathed in amazement, and I heard the missionaries make quick arrangements for a larger room. I counted silently; in all, Giselle had brought us twenty-three investigators.

Grandfather noted our astonishment. "I have raised my family to believe in God," he said. "We are searching anxiously for Christ's Church. I have faith that one day my search will come to an end." He held up the Book of Mormon Marguerite had given to Giselle. "This, I believe, is true. Now I want to hear the rest."

The missionaries appeared dazed for a few moments, and having served a mission myself, I understood their feelings. In France, most missionaries were lucky to have this many investigators during the whole two years they served, much less in one day.

"Working through the members really works," I heard one elder say quietly, almost under his breath. He was a new missionary, a greenie, and I knew this was a day he would never forget. Nor would I.

We went to the Relief Society room and talked about Heavenly Father and Jesus and the coming forth of the Book of Mormon. Grandfather sat in full patriarchal authority and watched as his family responded to the missionaries, their faces eager. I had a feeling he understood the principles on a level that could only be achieved by one who was already close to the Lord. These people were obviously elect.

Paulette turned to me. "I feel so strange," she whispered. "I love them so much, and I don't even know their names!" She brought her hand to her chest. "I'm so happy." Aside from her own conversion, her experience with Giselle was her first close-up view of missionary work.

"I know," I whispered back. It was the same way I had felt on the day she was baptized. I reached out and held her hand.

At the end of June, a month after Paulette's hospital stay, Louise and Lu-Lu settled into a two-bedroom apartment next to Paulette's. They both seemed content and happy with their move to Paris, and it made me feel easier to know they were near enough to check on Paulette during the day.

Not that she had needed it. She had recuperated quickly, though she didn't gain additional weight as her pregnancy progressed. She faithfully visited Dr. Medard, and aside from a few odd tumor-like growths on her neck, which he was able to remove, and her lack of weight gain, her AIDS seemed to be temporarily arrested. She spent her days with Marie-Thérèse, and in anticipation of the baby, together they busily decorated the third room in their apartment. I often joined them, and we talked for long hours about everything—except her AIDS. By unspoken agreement, it was the one subject we held as taboo.

Mid-July found us in Paulette's sitting room working on new curtains for the baby's room. Paulette fingered the fabric she had purchased six and a half months earlier, when she first found out she was pregnant. It had a charming array of clowns and balloons in pastel colors, with solid stripes setting off the different sections. Because of the design, it had to be arranged just so. It was all too complicated for me, but Paulette had taken to sewing and worked what I considered miracles before my very eyes. I was there more to give support than for anything else, but at least I could cut where she told me, saving her the problem of working around her large belly.

As she smoothed the material out over the floor, I videotaped her with the new camera she had made Pierre buy. She wanted to record what moments she could to leave for her children. Her baby might not remember her, but at least she would understand how much Paulette had loved and wanted her.

"There'll be enough for a baby quilt too, I think," Paulette said, smiling up at me.

I was glad the videotape recorder hid my expression. She looked so happy, and yet . . . sick. Though Paulette had gained no weight since her hospital stay, the baby had grown. This meant Paulette was thinner than ever, and her bones seemed to stick out awkwardly. The skin on her face stretched tight, and was so dry it looked almost brittle. I didn't know what was going on inside of her, but obviously her body wasn't taking care of itself as it once had. Each time the thought came, a wave of dread assaulted me until I pushed it somewhere into the back of my mind, firmly out of awareness.

"Mom!" Josette's wail came from Marie-Thérèse's bedroom. "We're trying to dress up and Marc won't leave!"

"I want to play too," he said.

I walked down the corridor and to the bedroom door. "You all need to play together," I said.

"We are," Josette said. "We just want him to leave until we get our princess dresses on. Boys aren't 'posed to see girls naked!"

I sighed. I appreciated my daughter's modesty, but lately it had been causing problems between the twins.

"She's not naked, she has underwear," Marc protested, pushing his dark locks out of his eyes. It was long past time for a haircut.

I grabbed him and tossed him into the air, catching him in a tight hug. It took all of my strength, but it got his attention temporarily away from the problem.

He laughed. "Do it again!"

"Me too!" chorused the girls.

I gave them each a turn, then knelt down in front of Marc. "Why don't you come outside the door and knock on it? You can be the visiting prince. Then you get to come in and see the beautiful princesses all ready for the ball."

He thought about this for a moment. "Okay. But why does André get to stay?"

"He's just a baby," Marie-Thérèse said. "He doesn't know any better."

"Oh."

I took Marc's hand and led him out the door. The girls slammed it. "You'd better be ready soon," I yelled through the door, "or the prince won't dance with either of you!"

"I'm going to huff and puff and blow the door down!" Marc howled like a wolf, and behind the door the girls screamed with laughter.

I returned to Paulette. She was scrunched down, trying to cut the material. "I'll do it," I said, taking the scissors from her. I sighed. "Sometimes I don't know what to do with those two."

"You're very good with them," she said. "It's a talent I admire."

"What do you mean? You're good with Marie-Thérèse."

"It's not that hard to take care of one," she said.

"What about your Primary class? You handled them pretty well." I knew the minute the words escaped me that it was the wrong thing to say. Paulette's face turned despondent, and a strong feeling of heartache emanated from her body.

"I'm sorry," I said quickly, dropping the scissors and crawling across the floor to sit beside her.

"It's not your fault," she said. "You couldn't help their reaction."

I knew that, but I could have kept my tongue from reopening barely-closing wounds.

"At least Marie-Thérèse's Primary teacher understands," Paulette said, her pain eased by the memory. She found the good in even this woeful situation.

"Yeah, I guess."

"So what was the problem?" Paulette asked.

"What?"

"In the bedroom with the children."

I snorted. "Josette and her suddenly discovered modesty. Ever since that TV show last month, she won't dress in front of Marc. It's getting so bad I'm thinking about moving her into her own room and letting the boys share. The only problem is that Josette gets scared at night. And besides, André sleeps great by himself."

"Too bad she doesn't have a sister," Paulette said mildly.

"Oh, no. I don't know where I'd fit another child in at this point. Maybe in a few years." I stopped cutting and added, "Maybe when Jean-Marc isn't so busy."

"He's still working late?"

"Every night. He's so good about most things, and I love him more than ever, but . . ." My voice trailed off. I had thought Paulette's illness might make him change his devotion to work, but I guess my father was right when he had said that change had to come from within.

"It's more than work," I said suddenly. "It's like he's afraid of something, but I don't know what. Something that prevents him from opening up completely. I don't know, maybe I'm making it up."

"Give him time," she said. "Men usually need more of it than we do to get things straight." She lifted her shoulders and let them fall again with an exaggerated sigh. "It's in their nature."

I laughed. That was one thing I could certainly agree with.

The doorbell rang, and Paulette opened it to Louise. She carried a huge box of wedding invitations. "Well, here they are," she said unhappily.

I took one. "They turned out nice."

Louise grimaced. "Unfortunately. And now I have no choice but to address them. Will you help? I wanted to mail them this week. Oh, I can't believe she's going to marry him in less than a month!" She groaned and slumped into a chair opposite the couch. Paulette and I exchanged understanding looks. Lu-Lu was heading straight over a cliff, and there was nothing any of us could do to save her.

As we commiserated together, another visitor came. Simone. Two good things had come out of Paulette's illness: Giselle's introduction to the gospel, and then Paulette's reconciliation with her mother. Simone now visited frequently at Paulette's apartment—on the condition that she didn't swear, drink, smoke, or use drugs around Marie-Thérèse. Simone obeyed strictly, but had been unable to completely conquer her addictions. Occasionally, she wouldn't appear at Paulette's for a few days.

During these times, Paulette had learned to leave her alone. For her part, Marie-Thérèse loved her grandmother and no longer complained about the smell of smoke lingering on her clothing and breath.

After greeting everyone and spending a short time with the children, Simone settled on the sofa to watch Paulette with the curtains. "Them are lookin' real nice," she said. "Ain't no talent ya got from me, that's fer sure."

Paulette looked up. "The women at the church taught me. They could teach you, too, if you wanted."

Simone seemed to bristle without provocation. "Ain't good 'nough fer ya, am I?"

"That's not what I meant." Paulette came to sit with her mother on the sofa. "I just meant that if you wanted to learn, they could teach you. They did me. I've learned so much since I've joined the Church." Louise and I watched, unable to stop what would happen next.

"Well, can they teach ya not to die?" Simone said, lurching to her feet. The careless way she spoke made me wonder if she had been to a bar for a drink before coming here. Or perhaps she had recognized the sickness eating away at her daughter, as I had earlier.

Paulette stared up at her mother calmly. "I'm not afraid to die," she said, lifting her chin slightly. "I'm going to be with Jesus and my Heavenly Father. That's what's so wonderful about the gospel; you don't have to be afraid anymore."

"But what if it ain't true? Did ya ever think of that? What if ya die and that's it? Poof!"

"I know the Church is true, Mother. I know it with my whole being!" Paulette's simple testimony was potent, but it didn't stop the fear in Simone.

"I wish I didn't see ya again. It ain't worth it." Without another word, Simone fled from the room.

"Go after her, Ariana," Paulette pleaded. In her eyes there was no hurt, only compassion for her mother. "She won't listen to me. Please!"

I glanced at Louise, and her face told me she would take care of Paulette, if needed. I hurried to follow Simone, but the elevator had already closed. Throwing open the door to the stairs, I practically plunged down the five flights to the bottom. Simone was just leaving the building, head bowed and shoulders hunched, when I arrived.

What should I say? My thought was a silent prayer.

Down the cement sidewalk she went, then across the street and a half
block more until she turned on a side road. I followed from a distance,
recognizing the path to the store near Paulette's. To my left there were
more apartments, to my right a small forest-like strip of undeveloped land
that had a path of logs leading down the gentle slope to the store. It was
the only green for miles around, and the children loved to come here,
where they were free to romp at will.

Simone stopped halfway down the slope, clutching the remains of a
wooden railing that had once run the length of the path. "Go away," she
muttered.

"What's really wrong?" I asked. "You picked a fight on purpose."

She stared at her foot as it systematically ground a fallen twig into the
dirt. "It ain't true, that bunk about yer church, and I don't like to see my
daughter trustin' in stuff that's only goin' to let her down. She's dyin', and
that's it." Her despair was easy for me to understand. Not so many years
ago, I had been in her position.

I put a gentle hand on her shoulder and said with all the emotion I
could muster, "I *know* the gospel's true! Look around you. The very
beauty of the world, the exactness of the universe—everything testifies of
God, of His love for us! Every blade of grass, every bird that flies, every
idea that man has! This is no random accident we see, this is the loving
creation of a Supreme Being, a God! It's perfect, and all made for us."

"A perfect world wouldn't have no people dyin' like Paulette,"
Simone retorted. For the first time her colorless eyes met mine. "What's
perfect about that?"

"That wasn't God's fault and you know it, Simone! Heavenly Father
must let people suffer the consequences of their actions, or no one would
learn anything. If He came down and solved all our problems for us, we
would never grow. We would never develop faith, because He'd be right
there in front of us. Our Father gave us our free agency because He knew
it was best for us. What would life be like if we were forced to do right
all the time? Don't you see? Sometimes the innocent have to suffer, but
it's not God's fault. It's ours, because of our free agency."

"I wish it was true," Simone said. "I really do. And ya know, if it is
true, I hope ya can make me believe. Or maybe Paulette."

"Oh no," I said, pulling back from her. "Wait a minute. It's not my
responsibility to make you believe. Or Paulette's. It's yours to seek out

the truth. Everyone is responsible for their own salvation. You can't put that burden on someone else."

She stared. "Am I doin' that?" Her voice was low, and I knew it wasn't directed at me. "How can I know?" she asked.

"You could pray."

"Me?" The word came as a snort. "He won't tell me."

On my mission, I had always been taught to use the Book of Mormon because it would bring the Spirit. I knew it wasn't coincidence that only the day before, my study with the children had led me to 1 Nephi 15.

"There's a story in the scriptures about a man named Nephi," I began. "He was a good man and obeyed the Lord's commandments. But two of his older brothers were wicked, and they complained because they thought the Lord's words, given to them through their prophet father, were difficult to understand. Nephi asked why they hadn't asked the Lord, as he had done, for understanding, and the brothers said they hadn't asked because the Lord wouldn't answer. This makes me assume that perhaps they had tried at some point in their lives and didn't receive an answer." My words seemed to strike a cord in Simone, and she listened intently. "Nephi's response to his brothers was to ask why they did not obey the Lord's commandments. You see, the Lord will not answer those who have hardened their hearts through sin."

"You mean the drugs," Simone said. "He won't answer me while I'm doin' stuff like that."

I nearly smiled. Simone had once again proved how agile her mind was. "Well, you know it's wrong. Your body is a temple, the Lord's temple, His gift to you. He has commanded us to take care of it. I know that if you obey his commandments and ask him with your whole heart, he will respond."

Her face crumpled. "I can't do it! I can't stop. I've been tryin' real hard, but I can't."

"It's not easy. Drugs are addicting. The Lord knows that. You just need to do your best. It won't happen overnight."

"Paulette quit."

"Not alone."

"No?"

"The ward members helped her."

"But I thought ya couldn't join the Church if you was—I mean, why would they help her?"

"Because she's a child of God, like you are."

"If that's true, I'll go to hell anyway 'cause I can't stop." She gazed into the canopy of green above us. "I want to believe that Paulette will go to heaven, and that I'll see her again like she says. But even if it's true, I won't make it there to be with her 'cause of the drugs."

"You're right."

Her eyes flew to mine in surprise. "What?"

"Not without help. But if you want to, you can beat it."

"I do want to! I do!" There was no doubting the fervent emotion in her words.

"There are programs—" I began.

"Too expensive." She dismissed them with a wave of her hand.

"Not for your family and those who love you," I said. "We can help, if you'll let us."

"I can't let ya do that."

"Why? Because you don't really want to be free?"

"No, I do! But—"

I took her hands in mine. "I love Paulette. She's my best friend, like the sister I never had. To see you freed of drugs would be the greatest gift ever. Can you deny her that joy? Or me?"

"What if I fail?" she murmured.

"If you don't try, you have already failed." It was a quote I had heard somewhere, and it seemed to fit.

Calm determination filled Simone. "I want to do it," she said. "Please help me."

We walked back to the apartment, and I called a friend from my days working with the Anti-Drug Coalition. The next day, Paulette and I checked Simone into a six-month program with constant supervision for the first few weeks and varying stages thereafter. Any setback would return her to constant supervision. If all went well, Simone could gain a work release in two weeks, providing she found a new job; her old one as a barmaid was too tempting. Pierre took care of that, setting her up as a clerk in one of the grocery stores he oversaw.

"You can do it, Mother," Paulette encouraged. Her face shone with happiness.

"I think maybe I can."

Before we turned to leave, Paulette pressed a small package into her mother's hands. I knew it was the Book of Mormon. "Read a chapter a day, it'll help," she said. They hugged as well as they could with Paulette's huge stomach, and the glow of their love warmed me.

"Try first Nephi, chapter fifteen," I said. "You might recognize the story."

CHAPTER FOURTEEN

The next week, Paulette came down with a severe cold. The doctor, fearing another bout of pneumonia and an early delivery, ordered her to bed, and Louise once again took over running her household. But Paulette seemed to be recovering nicely.

The end of July found me alone in my sitting room, wondering where the days had gone. Lu-Lu's wedding was to be held in a mere two weeks; we had still found no way to stop it. I sighed and gazed out the window into the dark night. My reflection stared back at me, my eyes seeming to fill my whole face, large and pensive. I glanced hurriedly away.

It was Monday, and I had hoped Jean-Marc would come home for family night, which I always held after dinner; but he didn't. I had put the children to bed at their usual time, after reading a Book of Mormon story and singing to them in the dark.

I missed Jean-Marc. A feeling of melancholy settled over me as I thought about our relationship. *How could I reach the part of him that was holding back? And why was he holding back?* I needed to ask him, but I was apprehensive of his reaction. I didn't want him to retreat from me to think things over. *Is this how life is supposed to be?* I wondered. The burdens seemed much heavier than they should have been. I put my head into my hands and sighed.

"Mommy?" Marc and Josette stood in the doorway.

"Is something wrong?" I asked. They nodded and ran to me, burrowing their faces into my body.

"I'm scared," Josette said. "The closet was open and I could see a man in it."

"Why didn't you shut it?" I asked Marc. He shrugged.

"He was afraid, too."

"Was not!"

"Was too!"

"That's enough!" I hugged them both tightly. "I guess I'll go take care of the man in the closet."

Amidst the giggles, I heard someone at the front door.

"Daddy!" The children ran to the hall and smothered him with chubby arms and wet kisses.

Jean-Marc smiled wearily, but returned their embraces. "What? Still awake? I guess the tiger will have to eat you up. Grrr!"

They screamed in delight. Now it would take even longer for them to settle down and sleep. But I forced a smile; at least they were able to spend some time with their father. The wrestling continued until Marc hit his head on the coffee table. He screeched in exaggerated agony.

"Big baby!" Josette taunted.

"It hurts!"

Their argument began in earnest, but it was only a shadow of what I faced daily alone. At least now my husband was here to take care of it. He would sit them down and discuss why they shouldn't argue, and how the Lord expected them to act. I turned to face Jean-Marc, but his expression frightened me.

"Go to bed now!" he said. His face wore an ugly frown. "I have enough problems at work; I can't deal with this petty bickering!"

"But I can't go—" Josette began.

"Now!"

"But the closet," Marc wailed.

"One, two, three," Jean-Marc said. Before he had finished counting, the twins were out the door, crying loudly about the monster.

"What was that all about?" I said stiffly. "You didn't even listen to them. They're scared to death because of something they saw in the closet, but you're so busy being sick of their arguing that you don't hear them when they really need you!"

"They were arguing about something stupid," he said. "I just stopped them."

I wondered if he thought I should be grateful. "By yelling at them and not listening? Is that what you want to be to them—someone who comes home at night, just to yell when the mildest of arguments break out?"

"Mildest?"

I nodded, and he gave me a sheepish grin. "I'm sorry. I just got angry. Sometimes I forget they're only four. I'm not with them all day, so I don't have as much patience as you do."

"That's exactly why you should have *more* patience," I retorted. "You haven't had to listen to it all day."

We stared at each other in silence. "Is something else wrong?" he asked. Beneath his calm exterior, I sensed an odd fear.

"It's Monday. Tonight was family night."

He slapped his hand against his forehead. "I forgot."

That's what I thought was so strange. His forgetting didn't go with his character. Something—perhaps fear?—was causing him to act this way.

"They're only four," he said. "It's not like they really need family night."

"Don't they? Wouldn't a lesson on fighting come in handy?" I purposely made my voice light. I turned to leave.

"Where are you going?" he asked.

"To get the man out of the closet."

Jean-Marc followed me to the twins' dark bedroom, where we found them huddled together on Josette's bed. Jean-Marc's face was full of remorse. He strode across the room and swept both children into his arms. "I'm sorry, kids. I didn't know you had a monster in here."

"He's in the closet." Marc wrapped his arms around his father in forgiveness, but Josette pouted a few more seconds before giving in.

I turned on the light and went to open the free-standing closet in the corner. There was nothing but clothes. "See? He's gone."

"Your arguing must have scared him away," Jean-Marc said. The twins laughed.

"Maybe he heard you come home, Daddy," Marc said. He scratched his eyebrow. "Why did you miss family night again? We ate cake."

Jean-Marc's eyes met mine. "I don't know." His voice seemed puzzled. "I had to work."

I shrugged and left him with the twins. There was no telling how long he would stay with them now. He was a good man, he just didn't know his children well.

Or know how much I missed him.

André had slept through the entire commotion. As I kissed his little cheek, I marveled again at how good he was. The compelling desire for another child entered my heart, one with Jean-Marc's green-brown eyes, but I pushed it away. I couldn't handle another child, not now.

An hour later, Jean-Marc came to our room. He undressed quickly and climbed into bed, reaching out his arms for me. I moved closer and curled my body into his. I tried to sleep, but Jean-Marc's breathing told me he was wide awake.

"What's wrong?" I asked.

"I was thinking about my father," he said softly. "Why can't I remember him? All I can recall is his voice, not his face."

"What brought this on?"

He sighed. "Something you said earlier. When I was there, with the twins, it came back to me. I began wondering how they would remember me when they got older."

"They'll remember playing tiger," I said, trying to cheer him. Whatever had brought this mood, I welcomed it. If change could only begin within, perhaps it had started tonight.

"I hope so," he said.

So did I.

The phone rang in the middle of the night, its tone loud and piercing. Thinking it was the smoke alarm, I jerked to a sitting position. "Wake up, Jean-Marc!" I shook him briefly and ran into the hall before realizing it was only the phone. Dread rose within me. A phone ringing in the night only bode ill for those it reached.

"Hello?"

"The baby's coming now!" Pierre blurted out the instant I spoke. I almost cried with relief. At least no one had been killed in a sudden accident. The baby was early, nearly two months, but the doctor had warned us it might happen. In fact, he had even given Paulette drugs to help the baby's lungs develop faster in the event of an early birth.

"Can you come? She wants you here. Louise is staying with Marie-Thérèse."

"I'll be right there!"

Jean-Marc had appeared in the kitchen. "What's up?" He trailed after me as I returned to our room and began dressing.

"The baby's coming. I've got to be there with her."

He sat on the bed, watching me sleepily. "How long will you be?"

"There's no telling. I'll call when she's born."

He nodded. I ran a quick hand through my hair. "You look beautiful," he said.

I could tell he meant it, but I had no time for sentiment. "Now, please," I said, holding his gaze with my own. "If the children cry, get up with them. And don't be upset." Sometimes he could become annoyed if awakened from a sound sleep. I didn't blame him exactly because I got angry too, but as parents we had to contain our irritation at things that in twenty years wouldn't make any difference.

"Of course," he said, sounding offended.

I kissed him and literally ran out the door.

I was out of breath when I arrived at the hospital. A nurse made me scrub my hands with a sterile brush and special soap, wrapped me in a white gown, and hustled me into the delivery room before I had a chance to think. They were taking every precaution to prevent germs from infecting the premature baby. Paulette lay on the bed heaving, rivulets of perspiration streaming from her forehead. Pierre held her hand, coaching her. Two doctors and three nurses surrounded the bed. One of the doctors was Medard. Each member of the medical staff wore thick rubber gloves, reaching past the elbow, presumably a safeguard against their becoming infected with HIV. I thought I caught a glimpse of plastic lining under their white coats as well.

"I'm here, Paulette," I said.

"Thank you, Ari." She reached out her other hand and grasped mine. Then the contraction began again, and her face contorted in pain.

"Push, Paulette!" the doctor said.

"Oh, it hurts," she moaned. "I can't!"

Seeing her pain, I remembered the experience all too well. "It'll be over soon," I murmured. "And you'll have your little girl."

Paulette glanced at me gratefully. She let go of our hands and grabbed her own legs, bearing down.

"Good! She's coming!"

We watched as the head eased out and Dr. Medard checked for a cord. "Okay, now push again, Paulette," he said. With a final effort, the baby was free.

"You have a girl," someone said.

"A girl!" Paulette sighed. We had already known from the ultrasound, but they had been known to be wrong.

I saw only a glimpse of a tiny baby with dark hair before the second doctor picked her up and carried her to the table and equipment at the side of the room. Only a few inches of scrawny legs hung over his cupped hands. How can such a tiny thing be alive at all? I wondered. The doctor set her down and two of the nurses crowded around him, working quickly. What was wrong? I couldn't see what they were doing, and it scared me that I couldn't hear the baby. I wanted to rush over and see for myself what was happening, but Paulette reached out for my hand, squeezing it tightly. At last we heard a tiny cry.

"Is she all right?" Pierre asked.

"They're stabilizing her," said Dr. Medard. "And cleaning off any blood. Then Dr. Orlan will take her to run more tests since she's so early."

At the words, Dr. Orlan glanced over his shoulder at us. He was part Oriental, by the slant of his dark eyes, and it made him seem mysterious in the midst of the more common French features. "She looks good and is breathing well with the oxygen," he said. "I think she'll be fine."

Paulette sobbed her relief, but apparently not all was right. Dr. Medard had continued to work with Paulette, and was now asking the nurse for drugs whose names I didn't recognize.

"What's wrong?" Pierre asked with a hint of hysteria in his voice.

"She's hemorrhaging a little, but we'll get it under control," Dr. Medard said. It seemed like long minutes until the man heaved a sigh and stepped back from the bed. He looked up at Paulette and Pierre. "It's stopping now."

"We're taking the baby," Dr. Orlan said. He looked at Pierre.

"You can go with the baby, or you can stay with your wife." Paulette shook her head. "You go with her, Ariana."

I nodded and stood up, but the doctor hesitated. "We usually only let parents come when the babies are so early. It's important for the baby not to be exposed to too many different people at this stage."

Paulette glared at him. "There's nothing usual about my situation," she said. "I've got AIDS, and my husband is HIV positive. Who do you think is going to raise this child?"

Pierre nodded. "My sister-in-law is closer than family," he said.

Dr. Orlan appeared to make a quick decision. "Okay, then, come on."

I followed them as they whisked the baby from the room in a warmer, and down the hall to the other side of the floor, opposite the delivery rooms. The doctor and nurses paused to open a door with a sign reading *Intensive Care Nursery*. The quiet in the room was relieved by the hum and beeping of the equipment, and occasionally one heard soft human voices or a weak baby's cry. Incubators were spaced at regular intervals; about ten of the forty box-like chambers were empty. The rest held tiny babies, some much smaller than Paulette's daughter, all watched over by attentive nurses or parents. There were no windows as in the regular nursery, where parents, friends, and family could peer at the babies. They wanted to keep this nursery as germ-free as possible, and no windows meant fewer people in the area. The array of equipment and the number of personnel, even this early in the morning, was impressive. I was beginning to appreciate the large and varied nature of this hospital.

They took the new baby to a corner and continued to work with her, taking all kinds of tests before bathing her, putting on a miniature diaper, and taping on numerous thin wires that connected to nearby monitors. Through it all she whimpered softly, sometimes even crying loudly. I felt my heart go out to her, as any mother's would at the sound of a newborn's cry. In between tests, one of the nurses rocked the baby close to her chest. I was grateful that she could do for the child what Paulette could not.

"How is she?" I asked when they seemed to be finished. Even to me, my voice sounded distant.

"Thanks to the drugs Dr. Medard gave the mother, the baby's lungs are pretty well developed," said the doctor. "She seems to be breathing better now. We only had to give her oxygen for a short time, and that's pretty unusual this early."

"How much does she weigh?" I asked.

"One point seven kilograms. And she's thirty-six centimeters long." That was much shorter than André had been, and only half of what he'd weighed.

I watched with detached interest, trying to tell myself this tiny, two-hour-old baby with the numerous white wires trailing from her body had nothing to do with me. Yet with her dark hair and enormous brown eyes, she reminded me of my own twins, who had been born three weeks early and had weighed less than two and a half kilograms each. They had been so small and yet so perfect. My earlier desire to have another child returned swiftly and unexpectedly. I stared at my niece, forcing myself to notice how small she really was. If not for the diaper, it would seem she had no bottom at all, just legs that began at the base of a too-slender back.

"Would you like to hold her?" the doctor asked. I didn't—it wouldn't pay to become attached until we knew about the HIV. But he wrapped her body, bare except for the diaper, in a pink blanket which covered all the wires attached to her, and placed her in my arms before I could protest. "It helps to have someone who loves them to cuddle them, if only for a while," he added. "And the blanket will help keep the wires in place."

One of the nurses handed me a bottle of warm milk with a minuscule nipple on the end. It had been a long time since I had used a bottle. André had never taken one, and the twins had only needed one extra a day to supplement my milk until they were old enough for cereal. I was out of practice and my hand shook. The nurse helped me guide the nipple into the baby's mouth. She sucked and the whimpering stopped, but almost immediately she choked. I glanced at the nurse anxiously.

"It's all right," she said. "Babies born this early have a problem swallowing and breathing at the same time. She'll receive most of her food for the time being through a tube in her nose. Each day we'll give her the bottle, and gradually increase the feedings until we can take the tube off completely."

"When will that be?"

"It depends. It's usually about the time they go home," she said. "Try to give her a little more. The faster she learns, the sooner she'll go home.

I did as she asked, but the baby didn't seem happy about it. At last, I handed the bottle back to the nurse and simply rocked her. Soon she closed her eyes, which seemed overly large in her small face, and slept. I gazed at the precious newborn, thinking how cruel life could be, even at the same time a miracle was happening. Had this little baby come from heaven only to go back so soon? We wouldn't know until later in the afternoon if she had HIV.

Despite my determination to the contrary, I felt an immediate and distinct bond with my niece. Was this what Paulette had planned? What did it mean? *Nonsense*, I told myself. *I would feel the same for any newborn who was also a relative. It meant nothing.*

I cuddled her gently for a moment more, until the nurse told me it was time to leave. She placed the infant carefully in an incubator with warm air circulating inside, removing the soft blanket. She checked all the wires while my niece slept peacefully on.

"Don't worry. I'll watch over her," she said kindly. For the first time, I noticed the nurse's features. She was older than I, near fifty by the looks of her. She had a liberal sprinkling of gray in her dark hair and heavy lines around her eyes and mouth, as if she'd done a lot of laughing. "I'm a mother of six, and a grandmother too," she added.

"Thank you," I said. I felt comforted to know she would be there. Paulette would also be grateful.

As I turned to leave, she continued, "Only parents and grandparents are allowed to visit here. And you, of course. Are there any siblings?"

"A sister. Four years old," I said.

"She can come in a few days to see the baby," the nurse said.

I nodded. "How long will the baby be here?"

She smiled. "It really depends. Some are here for a week, others months. But I would say about a month, give or take a little. Provided, of course, there are no complications."

I retraced my steps to find Paulette, but they had already moved her to a room. When I found her, she glanced up anxiously.

"She's fine," I assured her. "She's breathing on her own, and she looks good."

"Thank heaven!" Paulette said. "They won't let me see her until later. They're worried about how much I bled."

"Why don't you go see her?" I suggested to Pierre.

"Will you stay with Paulette?"

"Of course." I settled in the chair next to her bed.

He left, and Paulette stared after him. "He doesn't look good," she said.

I started. "He's been worried, that's all."

She didn't reply, but turned to face me. "How long before we know?" She didn't need to explain further. We all ached to know if this new little baby had HIV.

"This afternoon," I said.

She bit her lip. "I can't nurse her, you know. They won't let me because of the virus—even if she already has it. In many ways, I feel I'm not her mother at all." There was a touching sadness in her voice.

"She's here because of you," I said. "And tomorrow, when you hold her in your arms, you'll know you're her mother."

"Thank you, Ari. I'm so glad you're here."

"I'll always be here for you, Paulette. Always."

There were tears on her lashes as her eyes drooped and closed. In a short time, her steady breathing told me she slept.

I let my head drop into my hands, shielding my tired eyes from the bright morning light coming through the blinds. My head ached from lack of sleep, and my heart from something else. There was a hope, an aching, torturous kind of yearning inside me.

I began to pray.

CHAPTER FIFTEEN

"Ariana, wake up," a voice said softly. A gentle hand nudged my shoulder.

My eyes flew open. "Oh, Pierre. Did you see her?" I stretched and yawned.

He nodded. "I'd like to give her a blessing. I've called Jean-Marc. He's waiting for you to come home, then he'll stop by on his way to work. I've gotten it approved with Dr. Orlan."

"She's okay, isn't she?" I asked quickly.

"Yes. She's having a little trouble breathing now—they're giving her oxygen again—and her heart rate is slower than it should be. But she's got a strong spirit. I think she'll be all right." I noticed he didn't mention the HIV virus. The omission was all too obvious.

"What time is it?" I asked.

"Seven."

"I'll go home. Jean-Marc will be here soon."

Pierre's nod was absent-minded. His gaze was already focused on Paulette, a tender expression filling his face. With a light hand, he touched her cheek as she slept.

I left them and wandered down the hall to the elevator. I didn't notice anyone as I found my way to the car. When I arrived home, the house was bustling. The children were at the table, and Jean-Marc was ready to leave.

"Are you all right?" he asked.

"Yes. I'm just tired."

He kissed me, and we had a family prayer before he hurried out the door. I sank to a kitchen chair and concentrated on answering the children's questions.

Paulette slept the morning and part of the afternoon away. Near three, Louise took Marie-Thérèse to the hospital to see her mother. Afterwards she came to my apartment. I was shocked at how old Louise looked. She walked slowly, hobbling, her face contorting at each step.

"My arthritis is acting up," she said. I helped her sit on the couch.

"I have a baby sister," Marie-Thérèse was saying importantly to the twins. "Only the doctor said I can't see her till tomorrow."

"What's her name?" the twins wanted to know.

"We don't know yet." Marie-Thérèse's voice was matter-of-fact. "We weren't expecting her so soon. But I want to call her Marie."

"That's your name," Marc protested.

She shrugged. "Mommy likes my name."

"Why don't you go to your room to play for a while?" suggested Louise. "I want to talk to your mommy." When the children left, she turned to me, her face grave. "The baby has HIV."

I felt as if someone had kicked me in the stomach. I had been so sure she would be healthy, especially since Paulette had been so willing to sacrifice her life to save the baby.

"I have to go to Paulette," I said.

Louise nodded. "I'll stay with the children. I'll walk them over to the park."

"But your arthritis . . ."

She waved it aside. "I'll sit on the bench and watch them. A little walking will do me some good."

When I told the children about going to the park, they nearly broke the door down in their hurry to leave the apartment. "I like it when people have babies," Josette confided to Marie-Thérèse. "We get to play a lot more."

Jean-Marc had taken our car, but Louise gave me the keys to hers. I drove numbly to the hospital, wondering what I would say to my friend.

Paulette wasn't in her room. The doctor had let Pierre wheel her into the ICU to see the new baby. I waited until she came out. Her eyes were wet, but strangely elated.

"I held my baby," she said when she saw me.

"How is she?" I glanced at Pierre, but his face was impervious to my scrutiny.

"Better since the blessing," Paulette said. "She doesn't need the oxygen anymore. The doctor seems encouraged—except for the HIV. . ."

I knelt in front of her wheelchair. "I'm sorry," I said. My voice sounded like I might cry at any moment—exactly how I felt.

"She's an angel," Paulette whispered to me, looking more beautiful than I had ever seen her, despite the emaciation of her body. "I'm so grateful to have her any way she is." She held out her arms and we cried together. Only Pierre's eyes were dry, his dark orbs standing out against the odd pallor of his face.

That night Jean-Marc came home early, after I had visited Paulette at the hospital. Carrying a bouquet of white roses and a box of fresh pastries, he announced a second family night. I was baffled and the children were ecstatic, but we all accepted his presence gratefully, without asking why. The lesson he gave was on fighting. I decided my husband still felt guilty for the night before, and I wondered how long it might last. Despite my cynicism, his presence lifted the somber mood that had overcome me since learning the baby was HIV positive.

The next day, when I took Marie-Thérèse to the hospital to see her sister, the feeling of optimism remained. Before taking Marie-Thérèse to the nursery, we stopped to talk with Paulette. She lay listlessly on the bed, staring into space. Her breathing seemed labored, and her eyes had lost a bit of their light.

"Where's Pierre?" I asked. I knew he had taken a week off from work to be with her and the new baby.

"He went to see the doctor."

"Are you all right?"

"I've got pneumonia again," she said, frowning. "My body's weak now, I guess. But I'll be okay."

"Does it hurt, Mommy?" Marie-Thérèse asked. She gripped her doll so firmly that her little fingers were turning white.

"Not much, honey. I feel much better seeing my princess."

Marie-Thérèse relaxed and smiled. She climbed onto the bed and lay next to her mother, giving her a full-body hug. Paulette sighed contently, the light coming back to her eyes. I wondered if her arms felt empty without her new baby.

Marie-Thérèse's patience didn't last long. "I'm going to see the baby now," she declared, sliding off the bed. "But what are we going to name her? She has to have a name."

We hadn't told her the baby had HIV, that it might be as little as six months before she contracted AIDS. I understood Paulette's dilemma; it was hard to name a child who was almost a part of heaven already.

"You're right," Paulette said. "What should we name her?"

"Marie?"

"That's a wonderful name, but it might get a little confusing, don't you think?"

"Well, Mommy, what do you want to call her?"

Paulette glanced up at me quickly, penetratingly, then away again. "I once knew a baby named Antoinette. She was very pretty."

"Where is she now?"

"She's in heaven with the angels."

"Is that Josette's sister you're talking about?"

Paulette nodded. I stared at her, but she refused to meet my gaze.

"I like that name," Marie-Thérèse said.

"No," I whispered with an intensity that frightened me. "People with that name never live very long." I had named my daughter after my dead brother Antoine and after Queen Marie-Antoinette, who had been beheaded during the French Revolution. Naming this new little life Antoinette would be paramount to burying her early.

"Let's think about it some more," Paulette said. "We'll talk to Daddy, okay?"

Marie-Thérèse nodded. She turned to me. "Can we go see her now?"

As we left the room, we ran into Simone. She was dressed as usual in a summer dress, but today her dark-blonde hair was swept up into a bun and little tendrils of hair fell in wisps against her cheek and neck. It was flattering, and for the first time she almost looked the forty-five she was instead of the sixty most people took her to be. The heavy wrinkles on her face were still there, but her expression was less tense, more content somehow.

"Grandma!" Marie-Thérèse held out her arms and hugged her. "You look different today," Marie-Thérèse said. For the first time I noticed Simone wasn't wearing heavy makeup, probably the reason for her more youthful appearance.

"You look great, Simone," I said. I had only seen her twice since her admission to the drug and alcohol program two weeks before, but she had always seemed the same.

She smiled. "Thanks. I been experimentin' with my hair and makeup. They teach a lot of stuff at the clinic. Today's my first day out alone. They let me come a day early, seein' as Paulette had her baby and all. I have two hours before I have to go back."

"Did you come to see me?" Paulette said weakly from the bed.

Simone pushed past us. "Of course—and my new granddaughter, if they'll let me."

"Oh, they'll probably let you in, but they may not let you hold her," Paulette said. "Though she's stronger today."

"We're going to the nursery now. Would you like to come?" I asked.

Simone shook her head. "I'll catch up with ya. I want to visit with Paulette fer a while first."

We said goodbye and went toward the nursery. Marie-Thérèse nearly danced with excitement. "My very own sister," she said over and over. "I can't believe it!" Her enthusiasm was catching, and soon I had overcome my dread at seeing the new baby again.

After scrubbing our hands and arms and putting on white robes, we were admitted to the nursery. They almost didn't let Marie-Thérèse bring her doll, but the child insisted. The older nurse who had been there the day before watched over the baby. "You must be the big sister," she said brightly.

The brightness made me wonder if the baby's condition was worsening. "Is she all right?" I asked.

She smiled. "Better than all right. She's doing so wonderfully, you can hold her for a few minutes, if you'd like."

"I . . . uh . . ." I couldn't explain it, but the last thing I wanted was to feel again that strong bond with the baby.

"Oh, goody!" Marie-Thérèse said. "I was hoping I could hold her. You know, I brought my favorite doll to show her." She held her worn rag doll up for the nurse to see. "My mommy made it," she said proudly.

"It's very pretty," the nurse said. "I'm sure your sister will love it. But let's not get it too close to her yet. Only things that have been sterilized—that means scrubbed clean with special soap—can touch your sister right now because she's so little." She opened the incubator and lifted the baby out. "Have you decided on a name?"

"Probably Antoinette, but we still have to talk with Daddy," Marie-Thérèse said. "Antoinette is Josette's sister who lives in heaven now. Mommy says she was pretty."

The nurse glanced at me questioningly, but I looked away, feeling my face tighten. From the corner of my eye, I saw her wrap the baby in the pink blanket, once again covering the wires.

"Here, honey," the nurse said to Marie-Thérèse. "Sit right here, and I'll help you hold the baby. We have to be very careful because she's so tiny."

"I will." Marie-Thérèse climbed onto the chair. She handed me her doll. "You hold it up so she can see it."

So I held the doll up as Marie-Thérèse gazed down into her sister's face for the first time. "You are so beautiful," she cooed. "Why are you so beautiful? I just can't believe how perfect you are. See?" She motioned toward the doll with her head. "That's Dolly. When you are older, maybe Mommy will make you one, too." I had never known the doll had a name, but then I had never dreamed Marie-Thérèse would take so quickly to mothering her little sister, either. I hoped it would be a long time before she would have to take on that role.

"Why does she have the little tube in her nose?" Marie-Thérèse asked. The nurse launched into a simple yet thorough explanation, ending with a promise to let Marie-Thérèse help feed the baby a bottle before we left. I wondered if my niece might drop the baby in her excitement, but the nurse didn't take her gentle hands away for an instant.

"What are all these white strings on her?" Marie-Thérèse asked.

"They're wires. They go to these machines right here. They listen to the baby's heartbeat and stuff to make sure she's okay."

"What does that other baby have in its mouth?" Marie-Thérèse tried to point, but remembered the baby in her arms.

The nurse motioned to a baby across from us who was being gently cradled by a young mother. "You mean that baby?" Marie-Thérèse nodded and the nurse explained. "She has a mouthpiece to stop her mouth from being deformed because of the respirator. The respirator helps her breathe."

"But my baby's breathing."

"She sure is. She's very lucky. Some babies are born so early they can't even be held. They have to lie under a heat lamp, and the first thing their mothers can do for them is to lightly wet their mouth with a soft sponge."

It seemed Paulette's baby was very lucky indeed. I knew some of the babies now fighting for their lives in the ICU nursery would never go home with their parents. At least my new niece and her mother would share some time together.

After a while, a second nurse came with a warm bottle for the baby. "Good, the family's here," she said. "It's feeding time." She handed the bottle to our nurse, then went on to the next baby.

Marie-Thérèse grasped the bottle tightly and the nurse helped her put it into the baby's mouth. "What kind of milk is this?" As with most children, Marie-Thérèse's curiosity knew no bounds.

"Formula," I said.

"Actually," the nurse explained, "it's mother's milk—a donation from some of the mothers whose babies are here. They usually express much more than their babies can eat, so they donate it to the babies whose mothers are unable to nurse for one reason or another. The milk is the best thing we can give them; it will help them grow strong faster."

As she had the day before, the baby had problems drinking the milk, but she got some of it down. Marie-Thérèse's face glowed with happiness, and I also felt proud of the effort the baby put out. She seemed strong and willing to try.

"We'd better put her back now," the nurse said when she was asleep. "She hasn't any fat to keep her warm." She laid the baby in the warm incubator.

Marie-Thérèse stood on the chair to better see the baby. "I'll be back, Antoinette," she whispered so softly that I almost didn't understand the words. "I'll be back as soon as they let me." She helped Dolly wave goodbye to the baby.

We made our way back to Paulette's room, only to find Simone pacing outside.

"Mommy?" Marie-Thérèse walked to the door, but no one was inside.

"What happened?" I asked Simone in a hushed tone.

Her eyes held fear. "Paulette stopped breathin'," she whispered urgently. "I called the nurse and they worked on her. She's breathin' again, but that's all they'll tell me. They're takin' her to ICU. I waited here to tell you." Tears welled up in her eyes. "Oh, Ariana, I'm afraid."

So was I.

Marie-Thérèse had satisfied herself the room was empty and returned to my side. "They've taken her to another room," I said, "to watch over her better."

"I want to see her." Marie-Thérèse held her doll tightly in her arms. I wondered if she could feel our fear.

"We will, honey," I said.

Her lips trembled. "Is she going to die?"

She had asked me that question once two months before, and I had said no. Then I found out about Paulette's AIDS and knew she *would* die. I knew Marie-Thérèse's parents had explained about the AIDS then, but two months was a long time in the eyes of a child. To her, everything had been all right again. What should I tell her now?

"No," I found myself saying. "Don't you worry, she's going to be fine."

We made our way to the ICU waiting room, where we talked to several nurses. No one would tell us anything, except that Pierre had been found and was now with Paulette. Simone paced the floor while I called Louise at home. I also called my mother. "I can't leave until I know," I said.

"Everything's fine here," she replied. "Take as long as you'd like. I'll call Jean-Marc at work and put him on alert."

"Good luck," I said.

As I hung up, Giselle, the nurse who had taken care of Paulette before, came into the room. I was relieved to see a familiar face. "Ariana?" she said.

"What's going on?" I asked.

She put her arm around me and drew me away from Simone and Marie-Thérèse. "Paulette's dying. Dr. Medard doesn't think she'll make it through the night. It's not a gradual decline like it was last time, but a sudden one. It's time to call your family and say goodbye."

I felt shock on my face, and tears rolled unbidden down my cheeks even as I fought them back. I had known this day would come, but never had I been prepared for it to come so soon. "No! Not yet." I stared at Giselle, begging her to refute her words, but she only nodded gently.

"She died once already, but we brought her back. She seems determined to live, but I don't see how she can hold on. It's a miracle she's alive at all. She's still too weak from having the baby to be able to fight the pneumonia. If it weren't for the AIDS . . ."

"Not now. Oh, please, dear Lord, not now," I murmured.

Giselle squeezed my shoulder. "She keeps asking for you."

"I have to call my mother."

She nodded. "I'll take the others back for a while, and then you can come when I bring them out. We want to keep the excitement down; we never give up hope completely that they'll recover."

Her comment sparked some hope within me. She *had* recovered once. It was still possible for her to do so again—if we could get her another blessing.

I returned to the phone while Giselle led Marie-Thérèse and Simone into the back room. Both looked frightened. I could barely speak as I told my mother what was happening.

"I'll call Louise and Jean-Marc," she said. "We'll all be right there."

Minutes ticked slowly by as I sat alone in the waiting room. The harsh glare of the fluorescent lights made my eyes ache. The now-familiar smell of the hospital—somehow formal and removed from real life—seemed stronger than ever. Yet this was life—and death.

My mother and the children arrived first, followed almost immediately by Louise. Saying nothing, my mother enfolded me in her arms, and I burst into tears. My children crowded around my knees anxiously.

"Is Aunt Paulette going to heaven?" Marc asked.

I nodded. It seemed my mother had prepared them on the drive over.

"Can I say goodbye?" Josette was crying. The large teardrops spilled from her eyes and onto her face.

"Yes. But just for a minute, then Grandma will stay with you out here." I looked at my mother, who had André in her arms, and she nodded.

A few moments later, Giselle came back with Simone and a tearful Marie-Thérèse. "Who's next?" she asked somberly.

I stood up, taking the twins by the hands. "Can they come? They want to say goodbye."

Giselle hesitated only a moment. "Of course. Come along."

We followed her along the silent corridor. The shiny linoleum squeaked beneath our feet, giving the silence its only relief. The twins clung to my hands tightly. Giselle stopped at a sink, and we had to scrub our hands thoroughly as we had when visiting the baby. Then she brought us to a door, motioned us inside, and continued down the hall alone.

Pierre sat by the bed, holding his wife's limp hand. I was appalled at Paulette's condition. There was pain etched on her face. I could hear her breathing, ragged and harsh, and an oxygen tube dangled from her nose.

"I'm dying," she said when she saw me.

I shook my head. "You can't give up."

"It isn't a question of giving up," she said. "It's time."

"Aunt Paulette?" Josette whispered, stepping closer to the bed. "I love you." Tears fell to her cheeks.

"I love you, too."

"I wish you didn't have to go." Marc stood by his sister bravely, but his lower lip quivered and his eyelashes glinted with moisture. I felt terrible exposing them to death at such a young age, but I knew it would be better for them later on, after Paulette's death. This way there would be closure.

"I'll miss you, too, but I'm going to heaven. I'm not going to be suffering or sick anymore. And we'll see each other soon. You see, Jesus is going to take me in his arms and hug me. Do you know how happy I will be?" Paulette spoke to the children, but her words were for me. I wanted her to cling to life, but at the same time I knew that to waste painfully away, as many AIDS patients did, was not a pleasant way to die. Paulette was trying to tell me that at least she would go quickly, and also to remind me of the beauty awaiting her in heaven.

"Could you say hi to Antoinette for me?" Josette said. Her words startled me. I knew she was talking about her sister, but I had already begun to think of Paulette's baby as Antoinette.

Paulette nodded, a faint smile touching her lips. "I will. And I'll tell her all about you and Marc."

"And André," Marc added. "But she probably already knows. She looks down on us, you know."

"Will you look down on Marie-Thérèse?" Josette asked.

"Every day."

Josette nodded in satisfaction. "I'll tell her."

"It's time to go now, children." Taking turns, the children kissed Paulette's cheek. Then they buried their faces into my body. I knew they didn't understand death yet, that over the months to come I would have to help them cope with their aunt's death. I was more grateful than I could express for the wonderful plan of salvation that made eternal families possible. Because of the gospel, I would have answers to their questions.

"Don't go yet, Ariana. I need to talk to you."

"I'll take them back to the waiting room. I'll be right back."

When I arrived in the waiting room, Jean-Marc was with the others. I was surprised; it seemed my mother had been able to reach him. I took his hand gratefully. "How is she?" everyone asked at once. I shook my head and bit my lip to keep it still.

"I have to go back in," I said, trying to keep the dread from my voice. "She wants to talk to me."

"Jean-Marc, go with her," Louise said. "You and Pierre need to give her a blessing. I'll go afterwards."

Yes! A blessing. It had worked the last time. Hope flared in my breast.

"I want to go, too," Marie-Thérèse said. Her face drooped in a frightened frown. I understood her need to be with her mother and I reached for her hand, feeling her small fingers close around mine. I led them back to the room, stepping more confidently. As we were about to go in, Giselle appeared.

"Going to give her a blessing?" she asked. We nodded. "Good," she said.

"How is it that you're here, instead of in the other wing where you worked before?" Jean-Marc asked. "Not that we aren't glad to have you." I had wondered too, but hadn't the presence of mind to ask.

"When an AIDS patient becomes critical and needs the additional care they can only give here, we like to have someone specifically trained in AIDS to come over. When I learned it was Paulette, I volunteered. I'm sort of on loan, you might say. I've worked here enough to know my way around. Besides," her voice lowered, "even here people are afraid of getting HIV. It helps to have someone who is used to working with AIDS patients."

"We appreciate you," I said.

We turned into the room. Giselle entered and stood near the door. Marie-Thérèse ran across the room and scrambled up onto the bed as she had earlier in the day. Paulette's frail arms went around her. The scene was poignant, tugging at my heart until I thought it would burst.

Jean-Marc greeted his brother with a hug, then pulled out his oil. "I'll anoint her," he said. "But you need to bless your wife."

"Yes, please," Paulette rasped. "It will make my passing easier."

"You can't die, Paulette," Pierre pleaded. His voice sounded nearly as bad as hers.

Marie-Thérèse buried her face in her mother's body, and I coughed gently, reminding them of the child's presence. I moved closer to the bed to stroke Paulette's leg beneath the blanket. She smiled fleetingly.

The brothers placed their hands on her, and we bowed our heads. After Jean-Marc finished the anointing, Pierre began the blessing. Among other things, he blessed Paulette with courage and with a knowledge of her Father's love. Nowhere did he mention her regaining her health.

"Thank you," Paulette said when it was over, reaching up to grasp her husband's hands.

Pierre smiled at her tenderly, but I could see the seething anger in his eyes. He squeezed her hands, then backed away from the bed. "I need a breath of air," he said. Without explaining further, he stalked from the room.

"Go after him," Paulette pleaded.

Jean-Marc and I ran out the door, leaving Giselle and Marie-Thérèse alone with Paulette.

Pierre was out in the hall with his forehead resting against the wall, and his fists beating uselessly at the stretch of white.

Jean-Marc grabbed his shoulder, bringing him around to face us. "I could have healed her!" Pierre said, gazing at us with fury. "I could have! I felt the power of God within me. It was right there within my grasp." He held out his hand, palm up, and clenched it as he spoke. "I could have made her well, gotten rid of the AIDS completely."

Jean-Marc and I exchanged looks, not knowing what to say. "Then why didn't you?" I asked. More than anything I wanted Paulette to be cured, as impossible as it seemed.

With one hand he wiped tears from his cheeks. "It wasn't right," he whispered hoarsely. "It just wasn't right. I had the power, but I couldn't do it. She isn't going to live. Paulette is supposed to die!"

I shivered at his words, despite the warmth of the corridor. He stared at us defiantly, then his shoulders crumpled and he began to sob, racked with a torment I remembered so well.

Jean-Marc threw his arms around his brother, but Pierre shrugged him aside. "I should have healed her," he said. "It's my fault she's going to die." He turned on his heel and fled down the hall, leaving us to gaze helplessly after him.

CHAPTER SIXTEEN

Jean-Marc stared in the direction his brother had gone. His normally cheerful features were drawn with anxiety, the ever-ready grin replaced by a worried frown. He turned to me without speaking, eyes apologizing for what he wanted to do: leave me and go after his brother.

"Go," I said. "Go after him. He needs you. I'll be fine." He smiled slightly and leaned forward to hug me. "I'll be back as soon as possible." He sprinted down the hail, and I smiled after him wistfully. I felt a great loss at his leaving because I would have to face Paulette alone, but I knew he had to follow his brother. I was losing my best friend; Pierre was losing his wife. There was no comparison.

Reluctantly, I returned to Paulette's room. She looked up as I entered. "Jean-Marc's with him," I said. "He'll be fine."

Paulette appeared relieved. "In some ways this is harder for him," she said.

Giselle nodded. "It really is."

"But there's one thing I have to know." Paulette's gaze met mine and dread washed over me. I had known all along this moment would come.

"Why don't I take Marie-Thérèse back to her grandmothers for a while?" Giselle said.

Marie-Thérèse slid off the bed. "I'll be back, Mommy." She held her finger to her mother's lips, then to her heart.

From somewhere, Paulette found the strength to copy the motion. Her eyes fixed on Marie-Thérèse's as if never wanting to let her go. "I love you more than anything," she said.

"I'll be right back." Giselle led Marie-Thérèse from the room. Paulette and I watched each other, and I wondered what would come next. But my friend lay silently on the bed, saying nothing until Giselle came back into the room and stood on Paulette's other side near the monitors.

"I want to know if you'll take care of my daughters when I'm gone," Paulette said.

"No, you need to fight!" My head spun, and I wondered if I was hyperventilating. Violent sobs racked my body.

She closed her eyes, as if fighting and gathering strength. "Don't you think I want to stay?" she croaked. "I have just given birth to a beautiful new baby, and I can't even hold her and help her to become strong. Do you know how that feels? I'm going to leave her, and I won't be around to explain why—not to her or to Marie-Thérèse. Who's going to tuck them in each night? Who's going to take care of them? Who will answer their questions in ten years?"

She began to plead in earnest. "And when the time comes, who is going to help my baby understand why she's dying? Who's going to teach her to love God and to find peace in Him, despite the trials? Only *you* can do that."

"But Pierre—"

"Is HIV positive," Giselle said calmly. I turned to her, for the first time feeling resentment against the nurse. This was a private conversation.

My feelings must have shown in my face, because Paulette said, "Giselle is more than a nurse, she's my friend. I asked her to be here when I talked with you." I knew Giselle was still taking the missionary discussions and that Paulette had kept in touch with her. I myself had great hopes for the conversion of her family, but that all seemed far removed in this clinical situation.

"But he will be around a long time," I said. "A person can be HIV positive for up to eleven years without showing any signs of AIDS. It says so in the booklet you gave me."

Paulette looked at Giselle and nodded, as if telling her to go ahead. Giselle's eyes fixed on me. They were a deep brown, filled with love and compassion. "Pierre has cancer, inoperable. It's one of the opportunistic cancers that attack AIDS patients."

I turned my face to Paulette. "When did you find out?" I couldn't believe she hadn't told me.

"Only last week," she said wearily. "We were deciding how to tell everyone when the baby came. We didn't have time."

"Well, isn't there something they can do?" I questioned Giselle.

"It's a non-Hodgkin's lymphoma," she said, "called Burkitt's-type. These tumors are unusually aggressive, and they don't respond well to chemotherapy."

"So what are you telling me?"

"It's pretty progressed, but the doctor thinks he should have a year, maybe more, depending. But he'll become very sick. He won't be capable of taking care of two small children."

"Even if he was and could work," Paulette added, "I want my daughters to have a mother during the day, not a baby-sitter."

"But Pierre's their father! You can't expect Marie-Thérèse to cope with losing both of you at once."

Paulette shook her head. "You're right. But we've given this a lot of thought, and we came up with an idea, even before we knew about the cancer. The wall between our apartment and Louise's could be removed, and you could change apartments with her. With the joined apartments you would have five bedrooms—as good as any house in the country."

What she said made sense. As in any big city, houses were a scarce commodity. Most people bought apartments instead, and two linked together was not uncommon, especially for those who were well off.

"You've been saying you wanted to put your boys in a room together," she continued, "but you were afraid Josette would be scared alone. Well, now she can share with Marie-Thérèse. With you and Jean-Marc in one room, and Pierre in ours, you'll still have an extra room for the baby." Her voice dwindled to a whisper. "Or for a nurse, if Pierre needs one. We've got pretty good insurance to pay for a lot of it. Plus our savings."

I shrugged the last bit of information aside. If there was one thing Jean-Marc seemed to be good at, it was making money. My father was also wealthy, and the bank was always giving charitable contributions of some sort. To me, money was the last thing to worry about. Paulette had obviously been doing a lot of thinking. Belatedly, I wondered if I wouldn't have done the same thing in her situation. Knowing you were dying had certain advantages over the sudden deaths people hoped for.

"I'll understand if you don't want to do it. And I won't hold it against you. It's a risk having an HIV baby around your other children, and a lot of extra work." Paulette closed her eyes again. She lay motionless; only her rasping breath told me she still lived. Then her eyes opened. "Louise said she would move in with Pierre, and take care of him and the girls until—" She broke off. "I know she means well, but it's not the same thing as having a mom and a dad, and it's not really fair to her. Her health isn't too good."

I knew exactly what she was saying. Louise would do her best, but she couldn't play ball with the children, or take them camping or to the beach on vacation. It would be too strenuous for her.

"My mother also volunteered to raise the baby," Paulette continued. "But how, when she works so much? And she couldn't teach her about the gospel."

That was another point well taken. In similar circumstances, I would have chosen Paulette over my parents to raise my children. Being firmly entrenched in the gospel was all-important to me.

"Think about it and tell me later." Paulette seemed to be gasping for breath.

I glanced at Giselle anxiously, but she smiled. "She just needs to rest."

I stared at my friend, lying so helplessly on the bed. I wanted to reassure her, to tell her I would love her babies as my own, but something inside me wouldn't allow me to lie. If I told Paulette I would do it, then I would have no choice but to follow through. I couldn't say the words. Marie-Thérèse I would accept gladly, but the baby? She had HIV and would develop AIDS; with that came all the opportunistic illnesses. I had learned enough to know this was no small favor she asked of me.

"Give me a little time," I said. "I need a little time."

Paulette's eyes drooped. "I'm not going anywhere," she said. I wasn't too sure she spoke the truth, but I nodded and left the room.

Louise and Simone still sat in the waiting room, but Pierre and Jean-Marc were nowhere to be found. My mother and the children, including Marie-Thérèse, were also gone. "Josephine took them for a snack," Louise said when I asked. "They were getting restless."

"How is she?" Simone motioned to the door with her hand.

I gazed at the ceiling, blinking back the tears. "Not good." I paused and then continued, still not meeting their eyes. "She said she wants me to take care of the girls—to adopt them, so to speak."

"What about Pierre?" asked Louise.

Now I had to look at her, but it made me angry. I shouldn't be the one to tell this woman her son would be dead in a year. "Pierre has cancer," I began tightly, steeling myself against Louise's pain. I repeated what Giselle had told me, and then described Paulette's idea for me to move into the apartment. "I can see why she wants this," I said. "But I don't know if I'm able."

"You don't have to do it alone," Simone said. "We'll all take turns. I can take the baby two days a week."

Louise nodded. "And I'll take her two. Lu-Lu can take her part of the time, and that will only leave a day or so for you."

I felt relieved at their words, but inside something asked me what kind of a life the baby would have. Four homes instead of one? And all because she had HIV—something that wasn't her fault to begin with. Didn't the child need a stable home?

"I'm going for a walk." I pushed past them and their plans and ran for the elevator. I thought fleetingly of trying to find my children, but my mother had taken them often enough so I knew they were all right.

I didn't realize where I was going until I ended up at the ICU nursery. Silently, I studied the baby inside the incubator to be sure she was only sleeping and not dead. But her little chest rose and fell at a regular rate—still without the help of an oxygen tube. She seemed so vulnerable, so unprotected with all those wires coming from her, dressed in nothing but a diaper and a small crocheted hat.

Even as I looked at her, I knew I wasn't capable of taking care of her alone. I couldn't even consider having a healthy baby yet, with all the other responsibilities I shouldered alone. I just couldn't.

Maybe it was better for her to die.

I practically fled from the nursery and my macabre thoughts. Before I knew it, I was in my car, driving to the cemetery. Making my way to Nette's grave, I knelt there, crying and wondering how I could tell Paulette I couldn't submit to her dying wish.

I prayed long and earnestly, ignoring the few people in the graveyard who glanced curiously in my direction. Over and over I relived the pain of my daughter's death, remembering how empty my arms had felt then.

I don't know how long I had knelt there when I heard footsteps behind me on the path. *Could it be my father?*

"I thought I might find you here," Jean-Marc said as I looked up at him. He had André in his arms and the twins by his side. André held out his chubby arms for me, and Jean-Marc let him down. All three children greeted me with wet kisses and warm hugs before wandering off to play by the trees. Instinctively I scanned the area for the caretaker, but he was nowhere to be seen.

"They told me what Paulette wanted," he said, sitting beside me.

I said nothing for a moment, but gazed at the pattern the sun, filtered by the leaves, displayed on the gravestones. "And?" I finally prompted.

"I think it's a good idea. For the children, I mean. Less of an adjustment in the end. And Pierre will need someone to look out for him when he's no longer able."

Anger flared to life at the comment. "And who will that be?" I said vehemently. "Me? Is that before or after I take care of all the needs of five small children under the age of four? And one with HIV? All by myself? And is that before or after I go crazy?"

"But I'll help you!"

I didn't doubt his sincerity, but the idea made me laugh. "You aren't even home for family night! No." I held up my hand to stop him from speaking. "Don't give me that story about how it is all for us. We don't need more money, we need you! By the time you have finished building your empire, the children will be gone and it will be too late. And you and I will be too far apart to do more than say hello."

He stared at me and I watched anger, fear, and disbelief wrestle for dominance.

"Your priorities are turned around," I continued, standing up and brushing my hands on my pants to clean off the stray pieces of grass clinging to them. "We were supposed to do this together, but who gets up at night when the children need something? Who can calm them when they're upset? Me, that's who. We had the children together, but I'm raising them alone! The fact remains that they are just small children who need to be taught how to act, how to become big people. You must be patient and enter their world, to try to understand them, even if you think their logic is stupid."

"You always take them from me," he rejoined hotly. "Every time they cry or need something. You won't let me take care of them, even when I *am* home."

His words hit me like a bucket of cold water to my face. Was it possible that I was partly responsible for his alienation of the children? I thought back, and yes, I did take them from him when they were upset. But it was only because if I didn't, the crying would go on and Jean-Marc would become impatient. What he needed was to spend more time with them, to understand them, and to grow to love them through service.

My own thoughts condemned me. Perhaps if I had given him more practice during the brief times he was home, he would have learned to be better with them, as I had. Maybe he would have realized how much we all needed him.

"You're a good mother, Ari," Jean-Marc said. "Sometimes I'm jealous because you're so much better with the children than I am." He put his arms around me tentatively. "The point is, I recognize we have a problem, and that I'm a big part of it. Can't we work things out? I want you to be happy, and the children, more than anything else. I want to be a good father."

It seemed we were finished blaming each other; now we could take responsibility for our happiness and not leave it to chance. "I need you to help out more," I said. "That's all." It seemed so simple, yet it wasn't.

He smiled. "That's what Paulette said to me."

"What?"

"Yesterday morning. When I came by to give the baby a blessing. Paulette looked straight into my eyes and asked me what I would be doing if it were you who had AIDS, or me, or one of the children. At first I couldn't believe she'd ask me such a thing, but then I thought about it. And I realized that I certainly wouldn't be working. I'd spend every second with you and the kids, making memories to last long after I was gone. Then it hit me. There are no guarantees in life. We may not have AIDS, but anything could happen to separate us—an accident, another illness, who knows? Life is too short; we never know when it will be taken away. Paulette made me see it's *now* that counts. You're right about my needing to get my priorities straight." He pulled me close and nuzzled my neck with his nose. I hugged him back, wanting to believe.

"Like my father." He spoke softly, but his mouth was so close to my ear that I couldn't mistake the words.

I drew back and stared at him. "Your father?"

He nodded, and when he spoke his voice sounded strangled. "When I went to bless the baby, I had a strange experience—two, really. As Pierre asked me to do the blessing, I suddenly remembered being with my father in the hospital when two missionaries gave him a blessing." Jean-Marc's eyes became unfocused as he remembered. "We were all there: Mom, Pierre, me, and even Lu-Lu. She was almost one—just a baby, really."

"After the blessing, Dad looked solemnly at Pierre and me. I remember what he said, word for word. He said, 'Sons, I'm sorry I haven't been with you more. I've put far too much effort into the store. I thought I was building a secure future for you, but now we'll never have the time to get to know one another. May the Lord forgive my error.' He sighed and shut his eyes, and I remember wanting to run and get the doctor. I was so scared. But then he spoke again. 'At least I have found the true gospel for you. Now use it. Follow the Church programs. Don't neglect your families until it's too late—like I did.' He held out his arms to hug and kiss us. When it was my turn, I ran away. I just ran. I didn't want to kiss him, to feel his tears on my cheeks. I didn't want to smell the death. It was the last time I saw my father alive."

"You remembered all that?"

"Yes. It came back in an instant, like I was seeing it in fast motion on a movie screen. Suddenly I could remember the late nights when he would come home and was too tired to do anything with us—play, I mean. Then I realized the real reason I couldn't remember my father was because we had made no memories I wanted to hold on to. I didn't *want* to remember him the way he was." His shoulders shook with emotion. "Isn't that horrible?"

I held his face between my hands. "No. You were only seven. You didn't understand what it was to be a father, to be responsible for supporting a family. That's a heavy burden. Now you know and can forgive him."

"I do understand him," he said. "And I am just like him." His words were desolate.

"Yes," I said. "You love your family as much as he loved you."

"But I ran, Ari. I ran." He gritted his teeth. "Just like I did before our wedding, when I realized how strong and good you were and how weak I was in comparison, and just like I did when you challenged me about my neglecting you and the children. I ran from my father, and I haven't stopped running since. I finally understand that all these months I've been afraid of being close to the children because I'm afraid they'll feel about me the same way I felt about my own father."

"A vicious cycle. The lucky thing is you've realized your error before it's too late."

He hugged me again, squeezing me tightly as if he would never let me go. "I love you so much, Ari. It scares me to think of losing you."

"I love you, too. But why didn't you tell me this last night?" At least I knew why he had come home early.

"I wanted to surprise you today when I showed you this." He reached into his suit pocket and pulled out an object.

"It's a cellular phone," he said. "I made the company buy it today. In fact, I went straight to the owner—your father." His grin was back. "Now we'll never be more than a phone call apart, wherever I am."

I took the black object and flipped open the plastic part covering buttons with white numbers written on them. I smiled. "This is exactly what we need."

"I know," he said. "It was how the secretary reached me today when your mother called." I handed back the phone, but he grabbed my hand. "I want you to call me whenever you need me. Whenever you feel I'm neglecting you or the children. Whatever it is, I'll come. I want to make it work between us. I'm through running, forever. You are the most important thing to me, and I want us to be best friends again." His expression was so utterly sincere and full of love that it brought a strange emotion to my breast. I couldn't identify it, except that it was akin to love, only much, much deeper.

"And I promise never to abuse it," I said.

He shrugged and put the phone into his pocket. "Of course you won't." He pulled me close and kissed me, running a gentle hand through my short hair. A little shiver surged down my spine, making me laugh with the exhilaration it brought to my body.

"So this is what the extra family night was about?" I asked gruffly. He could always bring out that special feeling in me.

"It was our first one in a long time," he said. "Oh, I know you always do it with them, but you can't have a real family night without the head of the family." His face was pensive. "The strange thing is that I knew all along what I should be doing. The Church has the plan, and of course it's inspired. I figured the children were too young, that it wouldn't make a difference yet. I was wrong."

"There's nothing wrong with making mistakes," I said.

He nodded. "As long as we learn from them."

We stood without speaking for a time, linked together and feeling the strength of our love. Our children had drifted from the trees and were ducking behind some of the tombstones. The caretaker hated it when they played with such abandon; he didn't think they were getting a proper, reserved French upbringing. But the man was nowhere to be seen, and we had more important things to worry about.

"So what are we going to do?" He didn't have to spell it out for me; I knew he was talking about taking care of the baby and Pierre. "He's my brother, and I'm willing to do the work, or hire a nurse if it becomes necessary. But regardless, I can't abandon him now."

"Of course we're not going to abandon him. I just don't know if I'm able to do as Paulette asks."

"Don't you think her idea is best for the children?"

I chewed on my lower lip. "I don't know. It would be if I could handle it. I'm not worried about Marie-Thérèse; she's already like one of ours. But the baby—she's going to get AIDS."

"Yes, but maybe not for ten years, and there may be a cure by then. Meanwhile, she needs a real home. I promise I'll be there every night to help; I promise on the strength of my love for you. I will be there. And if I forget, you call me." He touched his breast pocket, where I could see the slight bulge of the phone.

"Aren't you worried our children might get HIV?" I protested. "Certainly our first responsibility is to our own children."

"We can educate ourselves, and we can teach them," Jean-Marc said. "The biggest problem with HIV or AIDS is the fear it brings; that much I'm learning. As long as we are careful, nothing will happen."

"It's not going to be easy."

"But worth it in the end."

His words reminded me of how I had visited my ex-husband in prison after my mission, to forgive him for causing our daughter's death. I had told him something then, when he had wished aloud that he had not hurt me so terribly; and now, nearly six years later, the words echoed in my mind. "But Jacques," I had said, "the making of a queen or a king is never easy, you know, though terribly worth it in the end."

It had been true then, and nothing had changed since. Still, I fought against the inevitable. "Your mother and Simone said they would take her a few days each week."

"You mean we should shuffle her about? What kind of life is that for a child?" Jean-Marc put his hands on my shoulders and gazed earnestly into my eyes. "I said two things happened when I went to the hospital yesterday. The first was remembering about my father's death; the second was the strange sensation I had when I placed my hands on the baby's head to bless her."

I tore my gaze away from his. Behind him, I saw the oh-so-cold stone marking my daughter's grave. I wanted to cry.

There was a sudden intake of breath. "You felt it too, didn't you, Ari?" Jean-Marc said, moving into my line of sight. His eyes probed my face. "You felt the connection to the baby. Tell me!"

Then I knew the truth. It entered my heart like a sword, stabbing deep and bringing excruciating pain. I was afraid to take care of Paulette's baby—not because the other children might contract HIV or because of the additional burden, but because I would grow to love her. It would not be just the love of an aunt for a niece, but the stronger, more profound love only a mother could feel for her baby. And when the time came, I would have to say goodbye as I had with Nette. Grief flooded my entire being. How could I watch this new Antoinette die? How could I lose another innocent baby to drugs?

Jean-Marc's face was obscured by my tears. "We can do it," he said softly.

I nodded mutely, and he held me while I cried. I didn't know if he completely understood my fear, but there was time enough to explain later. For now, it was enough to know we loved each other and would face the coming tragedies together.

"Let's go back to the hospital," I said. "We need to talk with Paulette before—" I broke off, unable to complete the sentence.

"Before it's too late," Jean-Marc said.

He rounded up the children while I stepped closer to Nette's grave. As usual, I ran my hand over her name. The sun still played across the gray stone, and I touched the place where the light danced.

I gasped. The stone wasn't cold; it was warm from the sun's light. Or was it from the Son's light? Maybe it was the same thing. The Son of God had given life to the whole world, and all light stemmed from Him—from the Light of Christ.

It was this Light that would sustain me, this Light that would give me the courage to persevere—and to love.

CHAPTER SEVENTEEN

I drove back to the hospital in our car with the twins, while André rode with Jean-Marc in my mother's car. I wondered idly where my mother was and how she would get home. My nose twitched at the smells of the hospital, but the twins skipped to the elevator, unmindful, where Jean-Marc and André waited. I felt a twinge of guilt as I noticed my little boy sleeping in his father's arms. He had obviously missed his nap earlier.

To my surprise, my father was in the ICU waiting room. "I called him to come and get me," my mother said. "I didn't know when you would be back." My father always had use of a company car, and since my mother hated the metro, it was logical for her to call him.

"Has there been any change?" I asked.

She shook her head. "Simone and Louise went to ask the doctor if there's any way Paulette can see the baby. She's very upset."

I knew it was my fault for not being able to give her what she wanted. I sank to the brown floral couch and let my head drop to my hands. "I don't know if I can handle this," I muttered. Jean-Marc passed André to my mother and sat beside me, rubbing my back.

"You can," my mother said. "The Lord will give you the strength."

"We need to fast," I said. I hadn't eaten anything since lunch anyway, and didn't feel like I would ever be hungry again.

"We already are," my father said quietly.

For no reason I could define, his comment made me angry. "You're fasting? Like you did when you thought we might have the virus?" I glared at him. "That's great, Father, but when will you realize that even if Paulette does die right now, she'll be better off than you? When you die, you won't be anywhere near us because you are too proud to accept the truth. You said no one could change another person, and you were right. I'm tired of trying. Only you can change yourself. So do it! I don't want you to fast for Paulette, I want you to fast for yourself. You need to know the truth, or we'll never be an eternal family. You're the only one who is standing in our way!"

Hurt and outrage played on his face, but he kept his temper as I hadn't mine. "We'll take the children home," he said. "We'll feed them dinner and they can have a sleep-over."

I dropped my gaze and nodded, once more feeling guilt. I shouldn't have treated my father badly when he was trying so hard to help.

Jean-Marc clapped him on the back. "Thanks, Géralde. We appreciate it."

"You'll let us know?" my mother said.

Jean-Marc kissed her cheek. "Of course."

We kissed the twins and the still-sleeping André goodbye. As they turned to leave, I hugged my father, trying to make amends. "I love you," I whispered past the lump in my throat.

"I know," he said. "I love you, too."

After they left, we tried to see Paulette but weren't allowed. "The doctor's with her. We'll let you know," the nurse on duty told us.

The bishop, our home teachers, and several of the ward members, including Marguerite, stopped by, but we sent them home, promising to call when we had more news. We alternately paced the brown carpet or sat on the ugly couches. It was a relief when the elevator opened to reveal Louise and Simone.

"The baby specialist says she can see the baby," Simone said. "They're arrangin' to roll the incubator into her room."

"Luckily, they have Paulette isolated enough so they feel there's no danger to the baby from the other patients," Louise added.

I knew luck had nothing to do with it, but I didn't feel like speaking.

"How's Pierre?" Jean-Marc asked.

"He seems a little better since you talked with him," Louise said. "But he's still pretty angry. He tries to hide it from Paulette, though."

"This is harder on him than on anyone," Jean-Marc said.

The women nodded at his words. Simone opened her mouth to speak, but the elevator chimed. A second later, Lu-Lu, with Philippe in tow, burst through the double doors.

"I just got your note!" she said, rushing to where we stood. She hugged each of us. "I came home from work and saw the note. I made Philippe bring me immediately."

I glanced at Philippe, whose lank figure leaned nonchalantly against the wall near the elevator. Dressed in a business suit, he stared at his fingernails, as if trying to distance himself from the rest of us.

"Can I see her?" Lu-Lu asked.

"Probably in a while," I said. "The doctor is with her. The nurse won't let anyone in except Pierre and Marie-Thérèse right now."

She nodded. "At least I'm in time to—" She abruptly dropped her head and brought a hand to her face. Her hair tumbled forward and sobs shook her shoulders. Philippe made no move to comfort her.

"But there's something else we have to tell you," Louise began. Her voice sounded determined. I turned away as she told Lu-Lu about Pierre's cancer. I couldn't bear to see any more pain. I pretended interest in a painting across the room, but I couldn't shut out the sharp gasp and muffled cries behind me. When Lu-Lu was calmer, I returned to stand beside Jean-Marc.

Louise hugged her daughter. "It's going to be all right."

"But the baby! Pierre can't possibly take care of her alone now. What's going to happen to her?" Lu-Lu hadn't yet been allowed to see the baby—only parents, grandparents, and siblings were allowed in the ICU nursery—but her concern for her niece was touching.

"We can take turns," Simone said. "Together we can do it."

"Yes. It's the only way," Louise agreed.

I watched them talking about the baby, feeling as though things were moving in slow motion, as if in a dream. I knew they meant well, but it *wasn't* the only way.

"I could take her on the weekends," Lu-Lu was saying. Behind her, Philippe straightened, suddenly interested in what his future wife was saying.

"You'll what?" he said, his piercing blue eyes flashing. "Don't you think we'd better talk about this? Do I have to remind you she is HIV positive? I don't think you realize what you're getting into."

"I don't think *you* realize that she's family," Lu-Lu rejoined, accentuating each word. "Family," she repeated. "I'm not going to desert her."

Philippe's face darkened. "And what about us? I thought we were going to be family." They glared at each other, fighting a silent battle with their eyes. The rest of us looked away, waiting for what might come next.

"Maybe it's time to choose," Philippe said through gritted teeth. "Do you want me or them?" He flipped his thumb at us, his voice nearly a sneer. "It's time to make a choice," he said, shaking his finger at her. "I won't come in second to anyone."

Indignant words came boiling to the surface, but I bit them back; this was Lu-Lu's battle, one she had to wage alone. Those of us who loved her could only watch, lest our action drive her away from us forever. I saw the same emotions on Louise's face and in the way my husband's jaw tightened angrily. I put a restraining hand on his arm.

"It's not a question of coming in second," Lu-Lu said. Her voice pleaded for understanding. "My family needs me."

Philippe's face seemed to be carved from stone. "I'm leaving," he said flatly. "Are you coming?"

Lu-Lu's pleading turned to anger. "No. My brother's wife, my sister, is dying, and I need to stay here."

"Forget it, then," Philippe growled. "Forget it all." He turned and stomped to the elevator, reminding me of one of the twins in a tantrum. I bit my lip to stop an unbidden smile. Philippe entered the elevator and stared at us defiantly as the door clanged shut.

Lu-Lu's emotions transformed again, this time from anger to hurt, and she exploded. "My whole world is changing!" she wailed. "Why does everything bad have to happen at once?"

Louise hugged her daughter. "That's the way life is sometimes," she said soberly. But across her lips played the trace of a satisfied smile. I knew exactly how she felt; Lu-Lu may not understand it at the moment, but Philippe's leaving was the one good thing that had happened that night.

Lu-Lu took a shaky breath and stepped back from her mother. Jean-Marc's face caught her attention, and to my surprise she gave a short laugh. "You don't have to fight my battles, brother. I'm not five anymore."

Jean-Marc looked taken aback. Then he grinned somewhat self-consciously as he let his clenched fists relax. "He shouldn't talk to you like that," he said.

Lu-Lu's smile vanished, but she shook her head as if trying to clear Philippe's actions from it. "So about the baby," she said, turning to her mother. "Together we can do it—take care of her."

Jean-Marc glanced at me. "What do you think, Ari?" His tone told me he would accept any decision I made.

All eyes turned on me, waiting. Once again the world slowed and details stood out: the dark stain on the edge of the brown, low-cut carpet; the blinking lights above the elevator as it changed floors; the strained expression on Louise's face; the wrinkles on Simone's and the additional hair escaping from her bun; and above all, Jean-Marc's intense gaze. I shook my head slowly, wondering on some level why it suddenly felt so heavy.

"Jean-Marc and I will take care of her," I said. "I'm going to tell Paulette that we'll take both the girls as our own." There was a brief silence before the protests began.

"There ain't no need to be a martyr," Simone said.

"We want to help," Louise added. "We're her family, too."

"If I am going to be her mother," I said, "I need to be able to check on her at night, to make sure she's breathing and covered. I need to have time to grow to love her as my own." I paused, then added hurriedly. "And that doesn't mean I won't need your help; I will—probably more than I realize. But it will be as we"—I swallowed hard—"her parents, determine."

"We want to offer her a stable life," Jean-Marc added. "Just as any child has the right to live. That's all."

Louise and Simone were nodding. "Of course," Lu-Lu said. "Four homes could never be the same as one."

I was glad the whole thing was settled. Now I just needed to tell Paulette. I went to talk to the nurse at the desk opposite the door leading to the ICU. She called on the telephone. "Are you Ariana?" I nodded. "You can go back now. But just you. Don't forget to scrub."

I glanced over my shoulder and saw Jean-Marc watching me. "I love you," he mouthed. I smiled.

Only Pierre was with Paulette when I entered her room. "Where's Marie-Thérèse?" I asked.

"She went with Giselle," Pierre said. "It was getting a little too much for her in here. Giselle took her on a tour."

Paulette looked wretched and uncomfortable, but her eyes were shining. "They're bringing the baby," she said. "I'll get to hold her." Speaking brought a bout of coughing, and I cringed inwardly as Pierre tenderly wiped the blood from her mouth. She seemed so weak that I wondered how she would manage holding the baby at all. I opened my mouth to speak, but shut it again when the door opened and Dr. Orlan and a nurse entered with the baby.

"Here she is," the doctor said. He rolled the portable incubator close to the bed and opened it, lifting the infant out, once more wrapped in the pink blanket. She was awake and her bright eyes were open wide, taking in the new environment. Pierre propped Paulette up in bed, and Dr. Orlan laid the baby in the crook of her arm so that most of the tiny body was resting on the bed. It seemed odd to see her outside the ICU nursery, and I was glad the specialist was there in case something went wrong. The doctor and nurse withdrew and stood near the door, where they talked together in low voices.

"She's so beautiful," Paulette murmured, staring down at her daughter. "She looks a lot like you, don't you think, Pierre?" He nodded but said nothing. I noticed his gaze was fixed on Paulette, not the baby.

All of a sudden the baby started to cry—thin, wailing little sobs that bit into the heart. Paulette tried to rock her but didn't have the strength. In a minute, she lay back on the bed exhausted, rivulets of sweat on her forehead. She began to cry quietly. "I can't help her," she sobbed. I could only imagine how helpless she felt at being unable to comfort her child. "Help her, Pierre," she pleaded.

Pierre reached out for his daughter, moving his hands around awkwardly. After approaching the baby from several directions, he pulled his hands back in frustration. "I can't. She's so tiny, I'm afraid I'll hurt her. And I'm afraid I'll pull out her feeding tube. Or the wires."

Paulette's face turned to me. "Ariana?"

I gently picked up the baby, holding her against my body, careful not to pull on the wires. The crying stopped. I felt the bond between us, as I had the first time I held her. Now I understood what it meant.

"You never answered my question." Paulette's voice was strained. "I have to know."

"Of course I'll take care of them," I said. "As if they were my own."

Both Paulette and Pierre had relief on their faces. "They will be yours," Pierre said, "after I'm gone." His voice was devoid of feeling.

I gazed at the baby, aware of the powerful emotions of love and fear. She was so utterly precious, yet there was a certain danger in loving this infant. But I knew it didn't matter; she was already a part of me.

The doctor and nurse behind me moved restlessly, and I knew they would soon take the baby back to the nursery. I stepped closer to Pierre and placed the infant carefully in his arms. "Jean-Marc and I will fill in for you on earth," I said, "but never forget you will be her parents in the eternities." Pierre's eyes filled with gratitude.

"Thank you," Paulette whispered. "You can't know what this means to me."

"I think maybe I do—a little."

She smiled, and I could sense a peace about her. In her eyes I saw acceptance, and I knew that it stemmed from her great faith in her Savior. She coughed again, and this time the surge of blood fell to the blanket. Her body convulsed, and her eyes closed.

Pierre uttered a small cry before handing me the baby and turning to stroke his wife's face. "Paulette, are you okay?" There was no answer.

Dr. Orlan came to the bed, eyes scanning the monitor next to it. His face was grave. "Paulette?" he said. "Can you hear me?" Her eyes fluttered open briefly, unseeing, then closed. He punched the emergency button near the bed. In a few moments a second nurse came into the room. "You'd better call Medard," he said. She nodded and left. Dr. Orlan motioned to the baby. "We'd better get her back." The nurse took the baby from me and settled her in the incubator again. I felt a great loss without her. I couldn't help wondering, if I felt that way, how terrible Paulette must feel to be so far away from her baby.

As they took the infant away, Dr. Medard, Giselle, and another nurse crowded into the room, all wearing rubber gloves. They examined Paulette, calling out names and numbers I recognized only from TV shows.

I backed up near the door and out of their way. I was shaking and my cheeks were wet. Pierre's face was a mask of agony.

"She seems to be stable for now," Dr. Medard said at last, turning a kind face to Pierre. "But she's unconscious. It's only a matter of time." Pierre nodded numbly.

"There's nothing you can do here," the doctor continued. "Why don't you go home and get some sleep?"

Pierre shook his head. "I can't leave her alone. I promised." He sat down and grabbed Paulette's limp hand, ignoring the nurse who was changing the blood-stained blanket.

"It could be a while."

Pierre didn't appear to hear him. I walked to the bed and stared at Paulette. I expected to see suffering, but her face was calm. Suddenly I could see a glow around her, as if a door to a place filled with light was opening nearby. I glanced around but couldn't find the source. The others didn't seem to notice. Paulette breathed on, but the light disappeared.

I put a hand on Pierre's shoulder, squeezing it reassuringly. "Shall I stay?"

He shook his head. "I'd like to be alone."

"Then would you like me to take Marie-Thérèse home?" I asked. He nodded mutely. I squeezed his shoulder once more, then leaned over to kiss Paulette's white cheek, wishing I could hug her and tell her how much I loved her.

I left the room and walked dejectedly down the hall. I could see Paulette's laughing face in my mind, but the memories held no comfort. As I reached the door to the waiting room, Giselle caught up with me. Her brown face was wet with tears. "Ariana, it's going to be all right," she said. Her fingers on my arm compelled me to stop walking.

"Paulette's dying," I stated, facing her. "She may never wake up."

She nodded. "It was expected. The surprise is that she's holding on so long."

My teeth dug into the soft flesh of my lip. "I never told her goodbye." Could that voice be mine? It sounded like rocks grinding against each other.

"Yes, you did. You told her you would take care of her daughters, didn't you?" I nodded. Her eyes bore into mine. "Then don't you see? You did say goodbye. Until she knew they were safe, she couldn't let go."

I remembered then that when Paulette first discovered she had AIDS, she had asked me to help her. I had feared she meant helping her to die, and I hadn't thought I would be capable of such a thing. But in the end, it seemed I had—twice. By helping her understand and accept the AIDS two months ago, and by agreeing today to take her children, I *had* helped her to die.

"You have been a good friend to her," Giselle said.

"As she has always tried to be for me." I paused, then asked softly, "How much longer do you think Paulette will hang on?"

"I think Paulette is already gone," she said, "or nearly so. Once the light comes—"

"You saw the light?" I asked.

"It's not the first time. Are you surprised?"

"Yes."

"Why? Because I'm not baptized? I may not be a member yet, but I was living the gospel before I ever met Paulette, before Marguerite introduced me to those young missionaries."

I believed her. "Are you saying you are going to be baptized?" I asked.

Her smile was serene. "Yes. This Sunday. And I'll be forever grateful to Paulette. If she hadn't become sick, I might have never found the true Church. Her gift to me is most precious."

"I'd like to come," I said.

"I appreciate your support."

I took her hand. "Thank you, Giselle, for everything you've done for my friend."

"I need no thanks. She's my friend, too."

We smiled, and then I went through the double doors to the waiting room. Jean-Marc stood near the door with a sleeping Marie-Thérèse in his arms. His suit was wrinkled, but he didn't seem to mind. He and the others looked up anxiously as I entered. "Well?" Jean-Marc asked. "What's going on? Giselle came and gave me Marie-Thérèse and then disappeared. Did something happen?"

"Paulette has lost consciousness. It's just a matter of time now, the doctor says."

Simone gave a cry and buried her face in her hands. Louise and Lu-Lu tried to comfort her.

"She did get to see the baby," I said. "And I told her what she wanted to know."

Jean-Marc closed his eyes, holding tightly to the little girl in his arms. I saw in his face how he wished he could spare her the pain she would have to face, not once but three times, as those closest to her died from AIDS.

I set my jaw resolutely and wiped away my tears. I couldn't afford to be weak now. I had to take care of Paulette's daughter first. "Come, let's go home," I said. "She needs to be in bed."

"I'm stayin' here," Simone said. "I want to see my little girl again."

"We'll stay with you," Louise said. "I don't want to leave Pierre alone either."

"What about the drug clinic?" Jean-Marc asked Simone. "I thought you had to go back there."

Simone shrugged. "I don't care. It don't matter."

"I called and explained," Louise said. "As long as I am with her, it's okay. I'm sort of a companion, I guess. I'll take care of her. You two go on home."

We said goodbye and made our way to the car. As we left the hospital, I felt a ripping sensation in my breast, one that had nothing to do with

Paulette. We had left behind the little baby, alone in the hospital, with only the nurses to look after her. Although they were kind, their care could never match that of a mother's. What if she cried? What if she needed me? Now that I knew she was my responsibility, I felt her absence acutely.

I held my head in my hands and let the tears flood my body, purging it. Jean-Marc pulled over and we held each other until there were no tears left, then held my hand as he drove the rest of the way home. When we arrived, he carried Marie-Thérèse to our apartment. I carried Dolly, who had fallen out of the sleeping child's arms.

A short time later we laid Marie-Thérèse on our bed, removed her shoes, and tucked the covers up around her neck. Normally I insisted on the children wearing pajamas, but there were times when clothes were just as good, and this was one of those times. We slept that night with little Marie-Thérèse between us. During the late hours she awoke, crying for her mother. We soothed her the best we could, but only when Jean-Marc gave her Dolly did she finally return to sleep.

Early Thursday morning, Paulette died. Louise called us from the hospital to tell us she had passed, never again regaining consciousness. She sounded old and tired.

"Pierre doesn't look good," she said. "I'm afraid for him. He loved her so much."

"We'll help him," I said.

By the time Marie-Thérèse awoke, Pierre had arrived at our apartment. She was at the table eating, and wondering aloud when her cousins would be home.

Her eyes brightened when she saw her father. "Are we going to go see Mommy?"

Pierre shook his head. He took her in his arms and held her close. "Remember about the sickness Mommy had? Well, in the night Mommy couldn't hold on anymore, and she went to live with Jesus."

Marie-Thérèse cried with heart-wrenching sobs. Pierre cuddled her close for long minutes until they subsided. "Why don't we go somewhere together?" he said. "For a walk or something."

She nodded, her eyes red and swollen. "Can we take our baby?"

"She's too little to leave the hospital," Pierre said. "But soon."

"Can we go see her? She gets so lonely there."

"No, not now."

I imagined it was difficult for him to go to the hospital. When my baby died, the place had represented a nightmare.

"I can take you to see her later, if you want," I said.

Marie-Thérèse didn't look at me. "Okay," she mumbled. She laid her head against her father's chest.

They left, clinging to each other for support. "He's going to be all right," Jean-Marc said.

"I hope so," I said. But tendrils of worry crept up my spine. Pierre's face was unemotional, as if he had buried any residue of feelings so deep that no one could find them. Paulette had died, but I wondered if part of Pierre, the most vital part, hadn't gone with her. I prayed I was wrong; Marie-Thérèse and that helpless baby in the hospital needed him now.

CHAPTER EIGHTEEN

My mother brought our children home soon after Pierre and Marie-Thérèse left. Her eyes radiated sadness. "I'm so sorry about Paulette," she said. The children were dry-eyed, and more curious than sad.

"Do you think she's talking to Nette and Uncle Antoine?" Marc asked brightly.

"No doubt," Jean-Marc said.

"So where's Father?" I asked.

My mother shrugged. "He got up early and left. He didn't say where he was going. I assumed he was at work."

Jean-Marc shook his head. "I called to say I wasn't coming in, but he's not there. It surprises me. We have a big account to settle, and one of us should be there."

"Do you have to go?" I asked. So much for his promises of the day before.

But he smiled. "No. I told the secretary to cancel if your father didn't show up. I'm not leaving you today. We have to make arrangements for Paulette, and I don't think Pierre is the one to do it."

I hugged him. "Thanks for staying."

"He's my brother," he said. "And I meant what I said yesterday."

Jean-Marc was on the phone all morning, making arrangements for Paulette's funeral on Saturday. Mother stayed with us, and in the afternoon she watched the children while Jean-Marc and I went to the hospital to see the baby.

"Has my brother been here?" Jean-Marc asked the nurse as he cuddled the infant.

She shook her head. "We have everyone sign in when they come," she said. "He hasn't been here since Tuesday when he brought his wife in the wheelchair." She hesitated before continuing. "I'm really glad she has you two." She motioned to the baby. "She needs someone. I think she'll be ready to go home in a couple of weeks. She's nearly regained her birth weight, and she's having no trouble breathing. God must be looking out for this one."

I ran a hand over her so-soft little cheek. "I think you're right," I said. It was true she would develop AIDS, but her Father in Heaven had not abandoned her. I felt certain she had a mission to accomplish here on earth—an important one that only she could fulfill.

"Do you have a name yet for the baby?" the nurse asked. "We keep calling her Antoinette because of what her sister said."

"We'll talk to her father," Jean-Marc said. "I don't think they had decided yet about a name." I hadn't told him yet about Paulette wanting to call her Antoinette. There hadn't been time.

When we arrived home, the apartment was full of people. Marguerite and several of the other ladies in our ward were there with a huge dinner. Louise and Simone were also seated in the kitchen, looking somber. The twins stood near the counter, staring at a large cake, and André sat in my mother's lap chewing on a roll.

I hugged my old friend. "But how did you know, Marguerite?" Jean-Marc had called the bishop before we left for the hospital, but surely that hadn't been enough time for the women to put together such a feast. Besides the cake, I saw breads, pastries, cheeses, salads, and fruit on the table. On the stove were pans of soup, and through the window on the oven door I could see evidence of a main dish.

"Giselle called us this morning," Marguerite said. "But actually I started cooking last night after visiting the hospital. It makes me feel better to cook. We made two dinners, one for you and one for Pierre and Louise, but brought them both here when no one answered at Pierre's."

"Where is Pierre?" Jean-Marc asked quickly.

"Don't worry," Louise said. "He's here. He came back a little while ago. He said he couldn't bear to go home. Marie-Thérèse was asleep, and he looked tired so we made him lie down in your room. I peeked in a little while ago, and they were both sleeping."

Jean-Marc appeared relieved. He settled in the only remaining chair at the table, surveying the spread appreciatively. "This all looks good. I don't think we've eaten all day."

Marguerite put her hand on his shoulder. "That's to be expected." She glanced up at me. "We'll be bringing dinner for the next few nights. I'll call to make sure Pierre's still here."

I nodded, touched. When we needed them, the women of the Church were there. It helped to know someone was aware of our loss, and, recognizing our pain, were able to jump in and make sure that mundane things like food were taken care of. We hugged and thanked the women as they left.

"Where's Lu-Lu?" I asked.

Louise's expression darkened. "She went to talk to Philippe. I'd hoped she wouldn't, but I guess she loves him."

"Let's wait and see," I said.

"Can we eat now?" Josette whined. "I'm hungry for cake."

"Dinner first, my girl," Jean-Marc said.

My mother sighed. "I should go."

"No, stay. There's enough food, if that's what's worrying you," I said.

Her eyebrows drew together as she frowned. "No, it's your father. He's not home, and he still hasn't been in to work. I'm worried about him. I should go home in case he calls." There was fear in her voice.

"But he'll call here if you're not home," I said.

"Maybe he can't . . ."

Then I understood; it wasn't his call she feared, but the impersonal one, a strange voice like the one who had announced my brother's death that rainy morning so long ago.

"He was agitated after we left the hospital last night," she said. "I think what you said must have bothered him."

I felt my heart sink. All I needed now was to feel guilt for something I had said in my disturbed state. Still, there was one place he might go . . .

"I'm going to look for him," I said. "I think I might know where he is."

Jean-Marc pushed back his chair. "I'm going with you."

"I want to go," Josette wailed.

"Me too," Marc said. "You already went somewhere without us!"

I think what they were really saying was they needed us with them. Perhaps Paulette's death was real enough to them that they secretly worried about losing us, as well.

"You stay with them," I said to Jean-Marc, putting my hand on his shoulder to prevent him from rising. "They need one of us here, but I have to go find my father. Besides, Pierre may wake up and want to talk." He seemed about to protest, but little Josette climbed on his knee.

"Stay, Daddy."

He nodded. "I will." He reached out to clasp my hand. "But drive carefully." I felt the love in his eyes and bent to kiss his lips.

"I'll be back," I whispered as I drew away, feeling his hot breath mingling with mine. A thankful tenderness welled up inside me. How bittersweet it was to recognize the eternal nature of our relationship—bitter because of Paulette's death, but sweet because I could understand how it would continue forever, despite death's toll.

I drove straight to the cemetery and hurried up the cobblestone path. My father sat on the bench opposite Nette's tombstone. He stared into the air, seemingly alone and forlorn, his gray pin-striped suit wrinkled as if he had mistakenly put on a suit meant for the dry cleaner. He wore no tie, and the top buttons on his shirt were open, revealing the dark hairs on his chest. His dark hair and moustache were uncombed. While he didn't look like a vagrant, his appearance wasn't what I was used to from my meticulous father. My foot hit a loose stone and his head jerked up.

"Ari." His voice was low. He patted the bench, then turned to gaze again over the graveyard.

I settled beside him, and silence fell over us as it had so often over the years. The sun rested low in the sky and no longer sent its rays dancing through the leaves and over the tombstones. The late July air was warm and without the hint of a breeze.

"It's not Wednesday," I said after a time.

His laugh was short. "Or after lunch, either."

At his mention of food, my stomach growled loudly. "Was that my stomach or yours?" I asked.

"Haven't you eaten?"

I shook my head. "Have you?"

"I've been fasting."

"Paulette's dead."

His arm slid around me. "I know. I went to the hospital this morning, before coming here."

"Have you been here all day?"

He nodded. "Yes."

"Mother's been worried."

Remorse was etched on his face. "I've been so busy sorting things out, I didn't stop to think that she would worry."

"Well, she has been. She loves you."

His jaw clenched. "I know. I know. And only today did I discover how much."

I turned to stare at him. There was something different about my father, something I hadn't noticed before. "Why are you here?" I asked.

He gazed in the direction of my brother's grave. "I've been fasting—and talking to Antoine."

"Oh?" I hoped my father hadn't taken to seeing ghosts.

"What you said at the hospital touched me," he said. "When you stared at me with your righteous indignation, I realized you believed every word you were saying—that even in death Paulette was better off than me, and that I was standing in the way of us becoming an eternal family."

"I was upset," I said, rotating to face him. His arm dropped from my shoulder.

"But you believed what you were saying, and still do. Don't you?"

I thought about it, then slowly nodded, my eyes meeting his. "Yes, I do."

"I realized you meant it, and that decided me. I would fast and ask the Lord if what you said was true." He paused, his stare dropping to his hands, which were now twisting in his lap. "I know you've wanted me to do this for some time, but it seemed so ridiculous to fast about something I already knew was false." He chuckled and looked up. "Imagine my shock when I knelt down this morning in my office, before anyone had arrived, and discovered it was all true." His eyes gleamed with unshed tears.

Abruptly, I knew what was different about my father. He had felt the touch of the Savior's hand. He had a testimony! I smiled, feeling giddy. *My father knows the Church is true!*

"Oh, don't look so pleased," he said testily. "I feel absurd enough as it is. Imagine what I'm going to have to tell your mother. And to think she has put off her baptism because of me!" His head rocked back and forth in amazement. "I don't know if I would have done the same."

"It was you who asked her if she loved the Church more than you," I said dryly.

"That's my point," he said. "She picked me."

"The Church doesn't teach women to leave their husbands, no matter how stubborn they are. Maybe she had faith you'd come around."

"Well, I have. I only hope she'll forgive me."

"She will," I said confidently.

He smiled and stood, pulling me to my feet. "Then let's go get something to eat."

"The sisters in the ward brought dinner," I said. "There's plenty of food."

"Good. I'm starving."

He waited for me to touch Nette's stone in farewell, but paused and turned back to the bench when I began walking. I stopped short, watching him pick up a book which had been on the bench beside him, hidden from my view. The Book of Mormon.

He held it up. "Good reading, this. I'm about finished."

I smiled and leaned against him, breathing in the fragrant air. The evening was perfect. As night approached, the heat that always marked July dissipated, making the evening comfortably warm without being oppressive.

I smoothed the wrinkles in my father's coat. "This needs cleaning," I commented.

He stopped and put his hands on my shoulders. Once again I saw the sheen of tears in his eyes. He uttered a sound somewhere between a cry and a laugh. "Oh, Ari! My suit doesn't matter. It doesn't matter at all in the eternal scheme of things!" The laughter dissolved completely to tears, and for the first time in my life I saw my father convulsing with fervent sobs. "Today I learned Antoine is not gone forever, and that I will actually be able to hold your little Nette! Oh, Ari. It's all true!" He dropped his arms from my shoulders and closed his eyes before continuing in a whisper. "How grateful I am to God, and how unworthy I feel of his love! He never gave up on me, not even after all these years I've denied him. He loves me! He loves my family! I will never look at anything the same way again. Not ever." He opened his eyes and gazed into the western sky. The streaked mixture of oranges, reds, and yellows reflected off the few clouds until the heavens were lit more than they should have been—a bright, natural light, yet strangely poignant.

I reached out and touched his shoulder. I remembered so well my own conversion and how miraculous it had all been. Gratitude once again coursed through me. My father could now take his proper place at the head of our family. We could finally be sealed, and my mother . . . my thoughts stopped there. There wasn't room in my body for the emotions I felt.

"There's not room enough to hold all these feelings," my father said, as if reading my mind. His voice rushed on. "I want to shout, to stop strangers on the street, to sing at the top of my lungs. I want to do radical, outrageous, unheard of things to make people understand the love of God. I feel like Alma in the Book of Mormon, who wanted to shout it with a trumpet to reach the ends of the earth! I understand how he felt!" He whirled around with his hands in the air. Then he stopped, his happy smile subsiding. "It was all because of Paulette and her illness, and because of what you said. I went to tell her this morning, to have a nurse deliver the message if they wouldn't let me in, but she was already dead." He hugged me. "I'm so sorry. I know you loved her."

"Love her. I still love her."

"Of course. It's not the end, is it?" Joy covered the pain.

"Pierre's dying, too," I said. "Cancer. We've agreed to take the girls after . . ."

"We'll help you, Ari. I wasn't there for you when Antoine died, but I will be now."

"Jean-Marc won't be working so much," I said, resuming my steps on the path.

My father nodded. "He works too much, anyway."

"Not anymore. I don't care if it means less money."

"Once I would have been appalled, but you're right. Money means nothing. Absolutely nothing."

A faraway look shadowed his face. "Paulette," he said softly. "Can you picture her now, Ari? Wrapped in the arms of her Savior? I envy her that. Can you imagine the sheer bliss of that hug?"

I could, though perhaps faintly. When I had first learned that families could be eternally together, my jubilation had far exceeded anything I had ever felt.

We walked back to the parking lot in silence. My father turned to me before I opened the door of my car. "What is my new little grand-daughter's name?" he asked.

"I don't know yet." I still didn't want to name her Antoinette.

I drove through Paris, thinking about the baby. I wanted to stop at the hospital and be with her, but I knew my other children needed me as well. I prayed she would be watched over. I felt that she would; she had a special connection with heaven. Surely Paulette, now released from her frail, earthly body, was at her side, loving her and comforting her. The warmth of the Spirit flooded through me, testifying of the truthfulness of my thought. At that moment, I knew without a doubt that Paulette was happier than she had ever been on earth.

When my father and I arrived home, Pierre and Marie-Thérèse were sitting at the table with everyone else, finishing their meal. My father took my mother's hand and drew her close, kissing her tenderly.

"I'm sorry I worried you," he said. "But I have something important to tell you." My mother's face grew worried, but my father laughed joyfully. He knelt down on the hard, tiled floor and took her hands in his. "My dear, dear, Josephine. How much I love you! Thank you for not giving up on me!" The room had gone silent as we watched them, captivated by the strong love emanating from my father. Even the children were enthralled, and for once didn't interrupt.

"Will you do me the honor of being sealed to me for all eternity in the temple of the Lord?" he asked humbly. There was a stunned shock—everyone knew my father's views on how religion was simply a crutch for weak people.

My mother's eyes opened wide. "You mean—?"

He nodded. "Oh, yes. I do. It's true—all of it!"

Mother pulled him up and embraced him. This time her tears were from happiness.

"Why is Grandma crying?" asked Josette.

"Grandpa's getting baptized," I said, translating the adult conversation.

Cheers and clapping exploded into the room. Questions and comments shot out from all angles.

"It's about time."

"I can't believe it!"

"But he said he'd never be baptized!" little Marc said, not wanting to be outdone.

"Sometimes never is just around the corner," Jean-Marc said, fluffing our son's hair. "You just never know." Marc scampered out of the kitchen to look around the corner, and we all laughed.

My father gently wiped my mother's tears, then released her and walked over to Pierre. "I have your wife to thank for my conversion," he said. "It took this to make me find the answers. She was—is a wonderful person. I am sorry for her death, but glad that she is with the Savior." The laughter died, and once again the stark realization of Paulette's death hit us.

"Thank you," Pierre said. For a moment, peace seemed to light his face.

I grabbed a roll from the table and bit through the flaky crust to the soft inner white, but suddenly my appetite had left me.

"Can we go see the baby?" Marie-Thérèse asked. "I really want to see her."

Pierre was quiet. His expression was so agonized that I imagined we could actually hear his pain.

"I'll take you tomorrow," I said.

Her lips drew into a pout. "I don't want you," she said. "I want Daddy to go."

"Well, what ya goin' to name her?" Simone said, cutting into the silence left by Marie-Thérèse's remark. Her voice was rough with unspoken emotion.

"Did Paulette have a preference?" Louise asked.

"We didn't talk about it," Pierre said. "We didn't pick a name."

"Yes," Marie-Thérèse corrected. "Antoinette. Mommy wanted to name her after Josette's sister in heaven. She said she was really pretty."

"Are you sure?" Louise asked, glancing at me. I could feel my lips clamp tightly together, and I wondered if my expression showed my apprehension.

"Yes, it was Antoinette, wasn't it, Aunt Ariana?" Marie-Thérèse's eyes turned on me, challenging and angry. I couldn't understand her attitude toward me when we had always been such good friends, and this made me anxious to back her up, despite my reluctance to name the baby Antoinette.

"Paulette did mention it yesterday before she went into the ICU," I said. "Maybe we could name her Antoinette Pauline," I added, voicing a thought that had been in the back of my mind. "Then we could call her Pauline after her mother."

"It's perfect fer her," Simone said. "The name means 'small in stature but big in love.' That's why I named her Paulette in the first place. She was so tiny, but I felt so much love. It seemed to fit somehow."

We all waited for Pierre's response. "Fine," he said without feeling. "Whatever you think Paulette would like."

So Paulette's daughter became Antoinette Pauline Perrault instead of "the baby." Marie-Thérèse seemed content with the name, though she still kept her distance from me. I didn't know what to make of her new rejection, but I would give her all the time she needed.

It was Pierre who concerned us now.

CHAPTER NINETEEN

By Pierre's request there was a short viewing, attended only by members of the family and held Saturday morning just before the funeral. The funeral director opened the top part of the casket and left the room. I hadn't seen Paulette since I had told her I would take care of her babies. As then, she looked peaceful, though they had not gotten her makeup quite right. It didn't matter; she was no longer in the body.

For the first time, I saw Pierre cry. His body convulsed almost violently, and somehow I knew he stopped short of throwing himself over Paulette only because of Marie-Thérèse. Louise held him against her ample bosom until the wild shaking had relented. Then Pierre took Marie-Thérèse's hand and walked up to the casket. He kissed his wife's pale cheek, and silent tears splashed onto her face, smearing the makeup. Marie-Thérèse was crying, but she held out a trembling hand to touch her mother's red lips, then brought them to her heart.

"I love you, Mommy," she whispered. This time Paulette was unable to respond.

Pierre picked her up and stepped back into the semicircle we had made around the casket. Not a face was dry except for André, who didn't understand what was happening. *Or perhaps he understands better than any of us*, I thought.

"Shall we pray?" my father asked. It was strange to see him standing up as the patriarch of the joined families. Louise and Simone looked at him gratefully.

"May I offer it?" Jean-Marc said to his brother.

"Please." Pierre's voice was hardly more than a whisper. He clutched Marie-Thérèse as though he were drowning.

After the prayer, we each filed past the casket, bidding Paulette a private farewell. When all had said their goodbyes, Pierre tenderly covered Paulette's face with her temple veil and stepped back from the casket. The funeral director must have been watching from the door, because when we finished, he was quick to come in and close the lid. He reached under the curtain to unlock the brakes on the metal frame holding the casket, and rolled it into the main room where friends were gathering.

Marie-Thérèse was still crying. I longed to reach out for her, but when I tried, she shook my hand away. How was I to take care of her if she didn't let me? *I'll find a way*, I promised silently as they rolled Paulette from the room.

People gathered in the large room where the funeral would be held. Elisabeth and René, old friends of Paulette and the Perrault family, had come from Bordeaux with their two little boys. Monique, the nurse who had first introduced me to the gospel, also attended with her husband and three children. Many of the ward members were there as well, including the parents of the students in Paulette's former Primary class, the same ones who had shut her out from teaching. Their faces showed their regret, and this somehow comforted me. The mood was somber as people shared their memories of Paulette. Pierre took no part in the ceremony, but asked me to speak.

"Paulette has been my friend for many years," I began. "I know of no one who has so turned their life around, no one who is more pure. She gave up the time she had left on this earth to save her baby's life." My words stopped and sobs shook me. *My baby*, I thought. *She died early to save the baby she would give me to raise, as she hadn't been able to save Nette*. Pauline's sweet little face danced before my eyes, and the growing love I felt for her swelled even more in my heart because of Paulette's sacrifice. *What a precious gift!*

I don't know how long I stood there crying before Jean-Marc rose and gently led me from the pulpit. I clung to him. He settled me beside my parents, then took the stand himself.

"I know we all loved Paulette," he began. "But I can't help thinking that she might be a little upset at us today. We have remembered her, but not once mentioned the thing most dear to her heart besides her family. I feel I should do so now." He paused and stared out over the audience. An air of expectancy filled the room.

He continued, "If Paulette were here, I think she might say it like this: Once there was a child born who came to save the world, not in but from their sins. He loved us so much that he willingly gave up his life so that we can live again. So that Paulette can live again! Think of it! Think of families being forever. I know as surely as I'm standing here that Paulette is alive, that we will all see her again. I'm sure she would ask us to remember our Savior today, to lift up our hearts and sing with joy for His everlasting love!"

Of course! Jean-Marc was right. Paulette would have us remember the Savior. And who knew how many countless lives Jean-Marc's testimony would touch that day? Nonmember neighbors and friends in the room couldn't help but feel the Spirit bear strong witness of the truth. My husband had taken this somber occasion and turned it into a giant missionary discussion.

"Paulette has made her transition from mortal life to the eternities triumphantly," Jean-Marc declared. "Let us all redouble our efforts to obey the commandments and turn to our Savior." He concluded with his testimony. The mood in the room had changed from sadness to one of hope and love.

After the service, I gathered my children about me and headed for the car, steeling myself for the burial. At the cemetery, birds sang overhead, flying carelessly across the clear blue sky as the casket was lowered into the warm, protecting earth. This time I didn't feel the devastation I felt when Antoine and Nette died. I knew where Paulette was and that I would see her again. It made things much easier.

Nearby, I could see Louise holding Marie-Thérèse and whispering in her ear. I hoped she was telling her the things I would like to say, given the chance. My arms ached to hold her, to start fulfilling Paulette's last wish, but I would have to be patient.

The next day we attended church as a family, including both my parents. Only Pierre declined to attend. Marie-Thérèse took her cue from him, and reluctantly, we left them both home. Later we went to the baptisms.

We had settled in our seats in the chapel when Giselle and her grandfather entered. Giselle was beautiful and radiant, dressed in white, but it was Grandfather who held our attention. The white clothing across his barreled chest contrasted sharply with his ebony skin and yet matched the hair on his head. His countenance was regal, and a sense of unmistakable greatness hung about him. A row of dark faces, also dressed in white, trailed after him—his progeny. I found myself smiling.

Pierre should be here, Jean-Marc whispered, a grin covering his face. "He'd like this."

"But who's baptizing them?" I asked. Neither of the missionaries who had taught the discussions was dressed in white.

The mystery was solved when we went into the room with the font, and Grandfather took his place in the water to baptize Giselle.

"He was baptized earlier this week so that he could receive the Aaronic Priesthood," Marguerite explained from the seat behind us. "He said that to make sure none of his children doubted the truthfulness of the gospel, he would baptize them all himself!"

And so he did! His deep voice seemed never to tire as he said the words that would set his family on the path to salvation. After the baptisms, both Giselle and her grandfather came up to us.

"Congratulations," I said, hugging them.

"How are you doing?" Giselle asked.

"Pretty good, actually."

"Paulette told me to check up on you."

I felt a rush of emotion. It was as if Paulette were there in the room, telling me how much she loved me.

Grandfather bent down to talk to my children on their level. He and Giselle were the only members of their family to live within our ward boundaries, so the children knew him fairly well. He rose and addressed us. "Time with them now will save a hundred sleepless nights later."

"I'm beginning to understand that," Jean-Marc said.

"You know," Grandfather continued, "I have accomplished many things in my long life, but none equals the pleasure of having a righteous child."

"Well, I think you must be feeling pretty good then." Jean-Marc motioned to his descendants.

Grandfather's eyes twinkled, and a warm smile stretched his lips. "Yes," he said, nodding. "This is a pretty good day."

Pierre and Marie-Thérèse stayed with us while the workmen took down the wall in their kitchen that separated their apartment from Louise's. Louise hadn't wanted to move into our apartment because of its larger size, and she and Lu-Lu were staying with my parents until they found a smaller one. We put our apartment up for sale and began to pack. I was grateful for the activity, as it kept my mind from my troubles with Marie-Thérèse.

Lu-Lu had tried to make up with Philippe, but he refused to forgive her for her choice at the hospital. Unhappily, she called off the wedding and notified the guests.

"I'm so sorry," she said to me a week after Paulette's death. She had asked me to call the caterer and florist to cancel and get back what money I could.

"Why?" I asked. "It's not your fault."

"But it is. I shouldn't have upset him so. Then maybe he would still love me, and we would be getting married. Then you wouldn't have to call." Her voice sounded despondent.

"Don't be ridiculous!" I said. "Your only mistake was to become engaged to him in the first place."

"What!" Her eyes flashed angrily.

"At last, a spark of life," I said teasingly. "Don't you see how much pain you've been spared? The many times you would drag your kids to church alone because he refuses to go? You are so lucky."

"But I love him!" she cried.

"You can't go through life not being yourself around someone. With him you're afraid to speak your mind. You can't even be with us without endangering his self-confidence." I grabbed her hand. "Lu-Lu, that's not love. Believe me, I know. Please listen."

"I didn't know you didn't like Philippe. You never said anything before."

"Only because you wouldn't listen. But we've been praying so hard that what was best for you would happen."

She sniffed. "So have I."

"And our prayers have been answered," I said. She frowned abjectly. I shook my head. "Oh, Lu-Lu, there's so much more out there—so much that doesn't involve Philippe! Love will happen when you least expect it. Until then, look outside yourself and see who you can help. It will get your mind off Philippe."

"But it hurts!"

I hugged her. "I know. But it will go away, and you'll be able to look back on it with a different view. Just as someday we'll remember Paulette without the pain. You need to be happy within yourself," I added. "You can't rely on a man to make you happy, just on yourself and on the Lord. Only then can you be confident and whole enough to enter an eternal relationship. Until then, just take it one day at a time."

Her arms tightened around me. "Thanks, Ariana. It doesn't seem so now, but if you say so, I believe you."

"Good," I whispered. I only hoped Philippe wouldn't realize what he had lost before she was over him completely.

Pierre came into the kitchen for a drink of water. We said hello, but he appeared not to hear.

"Is he always like that?" Lu-Lu asked, coming out of her self-absorption.

I nodded. The whole time Pierre had stayed with us he had said little, walking around as if in a trance. We had given him André's room for privacy, moving the little boy's crib to ours. Now Pierre spent most of his time in the room, sleeping or simply staring at the teddy bear wallpaper. He didn't visit little Pauline in the hospital or leave the apartment at all, except for doctor's appointments and his radiation treatment. I didn't know what to do for him.

Daily, I visited Pauline, who was growing stronger and gaining weight steadily. She took more milk at each visit and used the feeding tube less. The doctor was sure she would be able to go home soon. Marie-Thérèse accompanied me on my increasingly longer visits, but only to see her sister. She refused to speak to me during our outings or at home, and even with her father she had become reserved and cautious. Only with Jean-Marc was she her old self. She talked incessantly to him and insisted on sitting next to him at the table. Josette began to feel displaced in her father's affection, and it showed in her treatment of her cousin.

"I want her to go home," she said on Monday during family night, almost two weeks after Paulette's death. She glared at Marie-Thérèse, who sat on Jean-Marc's lap, clutching Dolly in her arms. We were in the front room playing a board game—always a difficult challenge with the twins. As usual, Pierre had retired to his room early, claiming exhaustion.

"Josette!" I reproved her sharply. My daughter had made no attempt to lower her voice, and Marie-Thérèse glared at her.

"But she gets all the attention. She still has a dad, but she only wants mine."

Marie-Thérèse was crying now, and Jean-Marc comforted her. He looked sternly at Josette. "That's enough. You and I will discuss this later."

Josette's tears began at her father's tone, and in frustration I started to cry—but in loud, fake sobs. The girls looked up immediately to see if my tears were real. Grinning, little Marc did his best pretend wailing, then Jean-Marc joined us. Soon only André was quiet, staring at us curiously. Despite herself Josette laughed, accompanied by Marie-Thérèse, though she resisted looking at me.

When all the tears were giggles, Jean-Marc fixed his eyes on the children, moving slowly from face to face. "We're a family now," he said. "We're all staying together. We'll be moving next week to Marie-Thérèse's house, only it's bigger now because they've finished taking out the wall to Grandma Louise's old apartment. You four children will live like brothers and sisters. That's the way it is."

"And my baby?" Marie-Thérèse asked.

"She'll be coming, too," I said.

Marie-Thérèse, staring at her hands, appeared relieved. "Good. I really want her."

What she wanted was to not lose any more loved ones from her life. My feelings echoed hers.

"But before we get the baby, we'll need a bigger car." Marc's tone was matter-of-fact. "We don't have enough seat belts."

Jean-Marc smiled. "How about us men going to look for one tomorrow?" he said.

"Yeah!"

"I want to go!" Josette said.

"Me too!" Marie-Thérèse added.

Jean-Marc looked at me, but I shook my head. "You got yourself into it, and now you're stuck. I've done it before with all of them." I smiled and added helpfully, "I'll keep André."

He grimaced, but I could tell he was enjoying the idea. "Okay, I'll take you all." The children cheered.

"I get the front!" Marc shouted.

"No, you had it last time!"

"It's my turn!"

My husband's eyes met mine and we both sighed. But inside I felt happy.

Moving day, the Tuesday three weeks after baby Pauline's birth, came sooner than expected. Pierre had returned to work the day before, but Jean-Marc and my father took the day off to supervise the movers. Louise, Simone, and Marguerite were in our new apartment, cleaning and putting things away as they arrived. Josette and Marie-Thérèse squealed excitedly at having their own room away from the boys, and Marc stoically accepted sharing with little André. Both rooms were in the part of the apartment that had been Louise's.

I went into the nursery Paulette had so painstakingly arranged for her darling baby. We had taken Marie-Thérèse's old room next to where the baby would sleep. On the other side of the nursery was Pierre's room—the same one he had shared with Paulette. I had removed all of her things, either giving them away or keeping them for the girls when they were older. Pierre hadn't wanted to return to the room, but I insisted he be where he could hear his baby cry and go to her, should she need him.

When I had made the suggestion, he stared at me, looking strange without the thick head of hair he had sported before starting the chemotherapy. "She won't need me," he said. "She'll have you and Jean-Marc."

I wondered if perhaps we had been wrong in stepping in to help Pierre so much, in spite of Paulette's wish. But then I thought of Pauline's precious little face, and I knew I had to do it for her. I couldn't let her feel abandoned. Still, I hadn't expected that Pierre would try to completely abdicate his responsibilities.

At one o'clock, Jean-Marc, Simone, and I took the children to the hospital in our new van, leaving my father and Louise to finish things at the house. Pierre was notably absent, as he had insisted he couldn't take any more days off work.

In the nursery, I dressed Pauline in a warm but frilly outfit Marie-Thérèse and I had bought the day before. She was still tiny, just under two-and-a-half kilograms, and the clothes were big. We laughed as I wrapped her in the baby quilt Paulette had made from material left over from the new curtains. I fingered the pattern, remembering how many times I had seen the material in Paulette's loving hands as she worked on it.

I carried Pauline to the van, wrapped snugly in her mother's love. It felt wonderful, and not just a little strange, to be holding my new baby without all the wires and the feeding tube. I buckled her into the new car seat next to André's, then sat on her other side to make sure she wouldn't cry. The children bounced on their seats with excitement, and I felt like joining them.

"Now remember what we've taught you," Jean-Marc said as he started the engine. "What do you do if the baby spits up?"

"Tell Mom or you so you can watch while we put gloves on and clean it with a cloth," Marc said.

"Then we put it in the special basket," Josette added. "And throw the gloves away."

"Or if it's a lot, we let you clean it," Marie-Thérèse said.

"Then what do you do?"

"Wash our hands with soap," said the chorus.

"And what if you see blood? Do you touch it? Or try to clean it up?"

"No!" all three children said emphatically.

"What about dirty or wet diapers?"

"Only with gloves," they said.

Jean-Marc continued to drill them on everything that might happen with the baby. They knew all the answers; it seemed we had them prepared well. We had tried not to instill fear, but caution. We wanted them to love Pauline, and to be prepared to help her for however long she would be with us, and not to turn away from her because of the infection.

Despite all my worrying about the virus passing to the healthy children, the doctor had been much more worried about our caring for the baby. "Since her immune system is damaged, keeping her free from sickness will be your chief concern," he said. "You need to watch for signs such as cough, diarrhea, or any odd behavior that might signal an infection. Anything at all needs to be reported immediately."

We had been told to keep Pauline inside and away from people outside the family until she was stronger, at about six or seven months, and then she could go out only if it was good weather. It wasn't only because of her HIV; most premature babies were too fragile to fight off even the normal germs coming from outsiders. As with any premature baby, anyone who did stay with Pauline was required to take a CPR class; all the adults in our family took it, including Pierre. I was hopeful we would never have to use it.

As we gathered for dinner, Pierre came home from work. He glanced around at the changes in the apartment, and I thought his face showed relief; I had altered things enough so the memories of Paulette wouldn't assault him at every turn. Then his eyes rested on the baby in her carrier sitting on the large kitchen table. He studied her, and for a moment I thought he might go to her, but he didn't. He slumped to a chair and stared at his food listlessly.

"Daddy," Marie-Thérèse said, "I missed you." She climbed onto his lap. As usual, she carried Dolly in her arms.

Pierre managed a smile. "Missed me? But I was only gone to work."

"Do you have to go again?"

"Yes, tomorrow."

"We brought Pauline home. Isn't she beautiful? I've never seen a baby so beautiful."

Pierre grunted. Marie-Thérèse tried to turn in his lap. Clutching the doll made her clumsy, and she knocked Pierre's fork to the floor.

"Marie-Thérèse!" he said sharply.

Her face fell. "But I love you, Daddy," she wailed.

"Pick up the fork," he said. She slid off his lap and retrieved the fork, her face puckered in a fearsome scowl. Pierre took it but made no move to comfort her. I longed to go to her, but I knew she wouldn't accept me. I met Jean-Marc's eyes over the table, begging him to do something. He shook his head at me.

"I love you, Daddy," Marie-Thérèse said again.

"I love you, too," Pierre said.

"I want to hug you." Marie-Thérèse held out her arms. Pierre sighed wearily but did as she requested. Then he pushed his chair back from the table and lurched to his feet.

"I'm not hungry," he said. "I'm really tired." He left the kitchen, and I stood staring after his ever-thinning frame. The doctor had warned us he would change as the effects of the cancer progressed, not only in body but in spirit, but surely not this soon. And why his utter rejection of Pauline?

"I just love him," Marie-Thérèse said softly. It was a phrase that had become common on her lips since her mother's death. If her father showed even the slightest irritation, she would say the words over and over, whining, until he gazed directly in her eyes and responded with his own feelings of love. It was irritating at best and grated on us all, even though I knew it was only because she was not getting what she desperately needed. But Paulette wasn't coming back, and Marie-Thérèse wouldn't let me fill her place. There was only Pierre, who seemed too wrapped up in his own private misery to notice his daughter's cry for help.

Jean-Marc picked up Marie-Thérèse and danced her around the kitchen. "I bet I can eat dinner faster than you," he taunted, coaxing a reluctant smile. The tension dissolved and we passed the rest of the evening in peace. At bedtime we gathered the children around us, as we had begun doing since Paulette's death, and read the scriptures. We sat on the floor in the girls' room and Jean-Marc read aloud, acting out some of the parts to keep the children's attention. This was how I had always imagined life with my family. Jean-Marc had so far kept his promise to me and tried to place us first, though some nights he still had to work late.

Pauline wriggled faintly in my arms. She opened her eyes and stared at me with eyes seeming far too wise for someone only three weeks old. She was still so tiny, yet I sensed a strong spirit there. Pauline—little, but big in love. The name fit her well.

I cuddled her close, loving her. I felt a soft touch on my shoulder and looked up to see André watching me. He reached out and stroked the baby with surprisingly gentle fingers, his face bursting into a grin. "Baby," he said. I helped him sit in my lap and placed the baby on top of his short legs. His smile grew wider. "Baby," he said again.

That night, we put Pauline in her crib and turned on the small machine we had purchased to monitor her breathing. Because of her size and the HIV infection, we had felt it best to keep it on her, just in case. We bought another device that allowed us to hear any sound in the room. It comforted me to know that though she was so far away from me, I could hear even her tiniest cry at night. My other children had always been in the same room with us for at least the first few months, but with Pauline we had to consider Pierre. "He has to have a chance to know her," Jean-Marc said when I had reconsidered putting her in the room alone. "And he won't if we keep her in our room." Reluctantly, I agreed.

The days went by quickly with my new responsibilities, and sometimes I wondered if I would make it through. I had forgotten what work a new baby was, and how much time was necessary for her care. Though she had completely captured my heart, Pauline quickly turned into a demanding, fussy baby, with a surprisingly loud voice for one so small. The burden grew heavier as Pierre became more sickly and could only work part-time. He spent more time in bed than out of it, staring at the wall and only grunting in response to my questions. He never thanked me for the care I gave him, and each day he withdrew more from Marie-Thérèse.

Louise and my mother came over often to help, as did Simone on her days off. Still, it was all I could do sometimes to keep my sanity. Even with the relatives helping, Pauline's care fell mostly to me and Jean-Marc. When he walked in the door at night, I usually plopped the baby in his arms, crying or not.

"And to think I once complained because you wouldn't let me take care of the children when they cried," he said one day when Pauline was six and a half weeks old. The baby was crying, and nothing I did would stop her.

I glared at him. "I've had it! Do you know what your sweet little children did today? They colored all over the kitchen walls with crayons while I was rocking Pauline!" The baby had stopped crying as I said the last words, and my voice seemed conspicuous in the abrupt silence.

Jean-Marc's eyebrows drew together, and he made a sympathetic noise.

"And we've no food," I added. "We're eating leftovers again."

He shifted Pauline to one arm and put the other around me. For once, the baby didn't cry. "I love you," he said. "And we'll get by somehow."

"This too shall pass, eh?" I quoted.

He smiled. "Something like that. Why don't I watch the children while you go out for a while?"

"I could go to the grocery store."

A key turned in the lock and Pierre entered. He had only gone into work shortly after lunch, but already appeared exhausted. "What's wrong?" he said, immediately noticing my flushed face. I saw him glance at the baby and away again quickly.

"The children wrote on the walls in the kitchen," Jean-Marc said.

Pierre's mouth twisted in his gaunt face, and he stomped down the hall, making more noise than I had believed possible for a man who had grown so thin. I followed him, with Jean-Marc close behind.

Marie-Thérèse looked up from the wall she was cleaning with a rag. She saw her father's grim face and dropped the wet cloth onto the white linoleum floor. "But I love you, Daddy," she said before he could speak.

"You know better than this," he said. "After you clean up, you'll go to your room."

She began to cry. "I don't love you, Daddy. Never, never!" Tears streamed down her cheeks as she faced him defiantly. "And I don't like you, either!"

Pierre gave a strangled gasp, then whirled and made his way down the hall. Marie-Thérèse stared forlornly after him.

I ran after Pierre. I reached his room before he had completely shut the door and elbowed my way in. "She didn't mean it, Pierre!" I said. "She just needs you. You haven't been here for her, and she's afraid of losing you like she did Paulette."

"She *is* going to lose me," Pierre grated sarcastically. His face seemed heavily marked by the black of despair. "I'm dying. I can barely work anymore. The doctor says I probably have only a few months left. Before long, I won't be able to get out of bed!"

"You're not so sick that you can't love your daughter," I retorted.

"She won't let me do it; you're the only one."

He pulled up the leg of his trousers. Covering his calf were strange growths, standing out dark and ugly against his thin, white leg. I gasped and recoiled.

He laughed mirthlessly. "Another opportunistic cancer," he rasped. "It's eating away at the outside, while the other cancer eats at the inside."

"How long have you had it?"

He shrugged. "A month now."

"Does it hurt?"

His smile was bitter. "Oh, yes." His eyes narrowed as he added, glancing toward a large picture of Paulette and Marie-Thérèse hanging on the wall above his dresser, "But it is nothing compared to the feeling in my heart."

I felt his hopelessness, but I was also fighting for my best friend's child, my child. "And you're a grown man," I said acidly. "How do you think Marie-Thérèse feels? She's hurting just as badly as you are, maybe worse, because she feels she's lost you as well." He glared at me but I wasn't through. "And Pauline needs you, too. Don't for a minute think that she's too young to feel your rejection. You and Paulette wanted a baby, and it was Paulette who made the decision to save her life when no one else wanted to." I shook my finger at him. "You have to come to grips with that. *Your* wife chose to give *your* baby a chance at life. It's not Pauline's fault. Stop blaming her for her mother's death."

"She's going to die." Pierre's face was stricken.

"We're all going to die someday. Our job is to survive until then and try to be happy." I purposely made my voice hard. "And don't tell me you're enduring to the end. Enduring isn't standing idly by and letting life sweep you away. It's making the best of what you've been given. If you ever want to see Paulette again, maybe you should think of that. Eternal families take work." I turned from him and strode from the room, feeling the muscles tensing in my body.

Outside in the hall, Jean-Marc waited with the baby. "Did you hear what I said?" I asked.

"He had to be told," Jean-Marc said. "It should have been me."

"No, you love him too much," I said. "He's your brother. But I love the girls more than I love him."

"Where are you going?" he asked as I passed him.

"To see Marie-Thérèse. We've something to settle between us."

He nodded, and I felt perhaps he stopped himself from saying it was long past due. I felt a stab of guilt; he was right. She was just a child, and whatever it was that stopped her from letting me love her, it couldn't continue—especially if Pierre wouldn't come to his senses.

I found Marie-Thérèse alone in her room. The door was slightly ajar, and I pushed it open far enough to squeeze in. She sat on the floor, facing the window, holding her doll to her chest and rocking it as she sang. Her voice was thin and high and shook with feeling.

"Heavenly Father, are you really there? And do you hear and answer every child's prayer?" I realized the song they had learned at church was actually Marie-Thérèse's prayer.

"Please, send my mommy back," she whispered when she couldn't remember any more words to the song.

I must have moved, because she turned. Her lips drew together as she saw who I was, and she turned back to face the window.

"We need to talk," I said, sitting on the floor beside her. She said nothing, so I plunged ahead. "I know I can never take the place of your mommy, but we've always been such good friends. Can't you tell me what's wrong? Why are you angry with me?"

Marie-Thérèse's face darkened, and she clamped her lips together tightly.

"I love you," I said.

"No you don't."

"Yes, I do. And before your mom died, I promised her I would take care of you. That's why we all live together now. I'll always love you, no matter what."

Her face turned in my direction, eyes challenging. "You said my mommy wasn't going to die, but she did."

Of course! I had told her that, and I had believed at the time she wouldn't die—at least not right then. How was I to know Paulette would die so abruptly? But at least I now understood the problem. In Marie-Thérèse's eyes, I had lied. How could she believe me when I said I would always love her?

I sensed a waiting about the child, as if she wanted to give me a chance. "I thought I was telling you the truth," I said. There was passion and conviction in my voice, but I wondered if she would understand it. "I didn't think she would die, not for a long time. I just kept telling myself she wouldn't. I guess I thought if I said it enough, it wouldn't happen."

Marie-Thérèse watched me for a moment before saying softly, "She could come back. Heavenly Father could make her come. He can do anything. Can't He?" The last two words were spoken tremulously, as if she was afraid this too was a lie.

"He can, but He won't," I said. "There are certain laws He also lives by. Because your Mommy got AIDS, she had to die, no matter how much we hurt, or how much Heavenly Father hurts with us. Now we have to show how we can grow strong and learn how to get along without her. And you needn't worry about your mommy. She's with Jesus now, with no more pain or hospital beds, and she's looking down on all of us, waiting for us to be together again."

Her eyes dropped, and I thought I had lost. "Oh, please, Marie-Thérèse! Please, let me love you. I miss your mommy so much. Can't we help each other? I don't know if I can do this without you!"

I saw the tears on her lashes and reached out to draw her close. To my extreme relief, she didn't pull away. "I love you so much," I said, just to make sure she understood. "And I'll always love you. Always."

She still didn't meet my gaze, but now she clung to me, letting her rag doll slip to the floor. As at Giselle's baptism, I felt Paulette's presence warming me, and I knew she was with us.

"We're fine," I told her. "Just fine."

CHAPTER TWENTY

Sunday, several days after my confrontation with Pierre, dawned bright and tense. He hadn't emerged from his room all the day before, though I thought I had heard someone in the kitchen during the night. An air of expectancy had seemed to settle over the house. The children were abnormally quiet—except Pauline, who cried a great deal, as usual, squeezing her tiny fists together and howling with all her might until I gave her whatever she desired. Lately, she wanted only to be held in the rocking chair in her room, and to be rocked back and forth. The automatic swing we bought wouldn't do; she wanted human contact. She demanded almost constant attention, as if she had too much energy for her little body. Tomorrow she would be seven weeks old, though she was still smaller than most newborns.

I hummed to myself that morning as I rocked Pauline in her room. André sat on the floor in front of me, dressed in his Sunday clothes and playing with some toys. Jean-Marc was in the bedroom dressing the children. As usual, Josette was whining because her tights weren't quite right, and Jean-Marc sounded exasperated. I knew he was tired from lack of sleep—we had both paced the floor with Pauline last night—yet I stilled the urge to rush to Josette and take over. My husband had been right about me never letting him solve the problems with the children, and I had been practicing sitting back and watching. It seemed to be working. More and more often the children turned to him when he was home, leaving me more time for the household—or, more accurately, for Pauline.

I stared at her face. She wasn't sleeping, just watching me. I knew if I stopped rocking she would cry. She favored Pierre instead of Paulette, with abundant dark hair and intense brown eyes. There was no hint of illness yet about her, only the urgency to experience life.

André lurched to his feet and held onto my knee, swaying as I rocked. A grin nearly split his face. "Such a big boy," I cooed. As usual when looking at him, I marveled at how good he was. Then it hit me; my Father had known all along I would be raising Pauline, and so had given me the steady and serene André because he had known I would be overwhelmed. I reached out and patted his tousled brown locks. "I love you, André," I said. He giggled and reached out for my hand. In my arms, Pauline gave a small cry, as if suspecting my attention had shifted.

"Well, we're ready," Jean-Marc said, coming into the baby's room. It was his turn to go to church with the children. Since the baby could not leave the house except for doctor's visits, we took turns staying at home with her. Pierre was usually in the house too, as he hadn't returned to church since Paulette's death, but we were afraid to leave her with him since he had never looked twice at her in the same day.

"Remember to come home right after, just in case Simone is late," I said. "She's working and was worried about getting here on time. I may not have time to get there on the metro." Today at the baptisms after church, my parents would become members. Since the day of Paulette's death, my father had been taking the missionary discussions and searching out every minute aspect of the Church, as was his thorough nature. Finally, he and my mother were being baptized. Simone had agreed to watch Pauline while Jean-Marc and I attended together. I felt comfortable leaving the baby with Simone as I had never imagined I might. The subtle changes that had begun in her since entering the clinic had continued, though she still refused to accept the missionaries.

"I'll be here," Jean-Marc assured me. "And if Simone's not here, you'll go on ahead and I'll meet you at the church."

"And probably miss the baptisms," I said.

He kissed me. "Don't worry about it. Since I'm baptizing them, they won't start without me."

"Don't be too sure," I said lightly. "My father's pretty determined now that he's learned everything he can. If Simone is late, maybe I should stay." I grimaced even as I said the words.

"It'll work out," Jean-Marc said confidently. His grin was infectious. "Now kiss Mom, kids, and let's be on our way." The twins came exuberantly, Marie-Thérèse shyly, and André sedate as usual. I felt especially grateful for Marie-Thérèse's acceptance of me. Her little face seemed less tragic now. If only Pierre could be there for her.

Pauline had fallen asleep, but I didn't move from the rocker. I was content to hold her and enjoy these moments of peace. Later, I warmed a bottle. As I fed her, I held her close and studied the tiny, perfect features so superbly masking the time-bomb ticking away inside her.

The minutes turned into hours, and when my family arrived home from church, I jerked awake in the chair. My body felt stiff and sore, and I tried to stretch my back. Pauline awoke with the movement and smiled as she always did after a good sleep. I grinned back, helplessly drawn to her charm.

The phone rang and I stumbled to my feet to answer it, but Pierre had come out of his room and beat me to the kitchen. "Okay, I'll tell her," he said into the phone.

"What?" I asked.

He didn't meet my gaze, and I sensed an embarrassment about him. "Simone can't come. She says she has to stay at work."

I groaned. Jean-Marc came into the kitchen with André in his arms and the others scattering around his feet like little yellow chicks. Except for Marie-Thérèse's slightly lighter hair on a head poking an inch above the others, the three could pass as triplets. "Then Pierre will have to watch his daughter," Jean-Marc said firmly.

Pierre's eyes widened and he shook his head, backing away. "I can't."

"Yes, you can." Jean-Marc let André slide to the floor and took Pauline from my arms. "You know how to rock her and feed her. If you don't remember from when Marie-Thérèse was little, you have seen us doing it enough." He tried to give the baby to his brother, but Pierre retreated down the hall. He went into his room and slammed the door. I heard the lock click firmly into place.

"She's your daughter," my husband yelled through the door, "and it's about time you took your responsibility. You've had time to adjust. Now stop feeling sorry for yourself and do something with the time you have left. Is this how you want your daughters to remember you—a man whose spirit has been broken by trial? What kind of example is that?"

There was no answer. "Well, we're leaving," Jean-Marc said through the door. "Ari's parents need our support today, and we haven't left this apartment together since we brought your baby home. *Your* baby, Pierre! We're going to leave her in her crib, and you're taking care of her!" He stomped away from the door and into Pauline's room. Gently, he laid the baby in her crib, stroking her cheek for a moment so the sudden change wouldn't make her cry.

"No!" I whispered. "What if he doesn't take care of her?"

"Ari, I know what I'm doing," he said. "Please take the children and wait in the hall." I wanted to rebel, but his eyes pleaded.

"Come on, children." I ushered them out, stopping only to collect my purse on the small table beneath the mirror in the entryway.

As I opened the door, Jean-Marc ducked into our room for an instant, then out again. He glanced over his shoulder. "We're leaving, Pierre," he declared loudly.

I heard Pauline start wailing in her room, realizing she was alone. My heart constricted, and I tried to go back into the apartment.

"No," Jean-Marc said, stopping me. The children watched us with anxious faces.

"I'm her mother," I said. "I won't leave her without knowing."

Jean-Marc shut the door and put his arm around me. "Of course we won't leave her," he said. Out of his pocket he drew the baby monitor and held it out to me.

I grabbed it and switched it on quickly. Now we could hear Pauline's shrill cry even more loudly. Marie-Thérèse's eyes held tears; I too wanted to cry. We huddled together in the hall around the monitor in Jean-Marc's hand.

"Let's go get her," little Marc said, voicing my feelings.

"Wait a minute more," Jean-Marc said. His tearful gaze met mine. "It's the only way, Ari. They need each other, and this is the only way I know. It's like me with our children. I need to be with them and take care of them, even when they are being difficult—no, *especially* when they are being difficult."

The resentment building in my heart dissolved. Leaving Pauline alone, so little and helpless, was hard for him as well, but we had to balance her needs now against a possible relationship with her father for however long they had left.

The crying went on and on, seemingly forever, though it could only have been a few minutes. Then a new sound: stiff steps, a low mumbling. "They left," came Pierre's puzzled voice. "They really left!" Pauline screamed even louder.

"Shhh, baby," he said. "Be quiet. Just be quiet." His voice was rough, and I wondered if he might hurt her.

Jean-Marc saw my thought. "It's Pierre," he reminded me. "He loves her. He's her father, whether he likes it or not."

"Pauline!" Pierre's voice came through the monitor, sounding frustrated. "Please stop crying!" Then, "Okay, come here." The cries changed slightly, but didn't stop. "There, there," Pierre mumbled.

"I've got you. Don't cry." The cries lessened to a whimper, then ceased completely.

"See? It's okay. I've got you. You're not alone." Pierre's voice sounded odd now. "Don't worry, I'm not going to leave you alone." Again we heard crying, soft sobs, but they came from Pierre and not Pauline. "Hi, little one," he murmured. "I guess it's time we meet. I'm your daddy. Yes, I am." He paused before adding hoarsely, "And I love you. I'm so sorry, Pauline. I love you so much!"

I looked up to see Jean-Marc watching me. His hand was gentle as he touched my cheek, wiping a stray tear. "It's going to be all right, Ari," he said. "He just needs time alone with her."

I nodded. "You're right."

"So are we going?" Marc asked. Now that Pauline was no longer crying, his child's brain had moved on. "I don't want to miss Grandpa getting baptized."

"Me either," Josette said.

Jean-Marc glanced at me questioningly, and I gave a sharp nod. "Okay," he said. "Go push the button on the elevator."

"It's my turn!"

"No, mine!"

I left Jean-Marc to sort it out and focused on Marie-Thérèse. She still stared at the white monitor in my hands. Pierre was singing a song, so softly I couldn't make out, the words or recognize the tune.

"He's singing 'Tell Me Why," Marie-Thérèse said, a smile playing on her lips. As she said it, I recognized a few lines from the song I had known as a child:

Tell me why life is so beautiful.

Tell me why life is so happy.

Tell me why, dear Mademoiselle.

Is it because you love me?

"He used to sing that to me before Mom—" She broke off and transferred her gaze to me. "Is he back?" she asked. Her expression was hopeful, but tinged with caution. "Do you think he'll love me now?

I hugged her. "He always loved you," I said. "He just misses your mom, and he's a little scared like you are. But I think he's back. I think everything's going to be okay now."

She seemed relieved. "I'm glad. I missed him."

"Me too," I said. "Me too."

The elevator chimed and I picked her up and carried her inside, where the others waited. There would be time later for her to be with Pierre. Right now, he and Pauline needed to get to know each other without interruptions.

I didn't know if I was right about leaving Pauline with Pierre; it didn't matter. I was only doing the best I knew how; it was all any of us could do.

At the church, my father was pacing in the hall, already dressed in white. "Oh, you're here," he said. Jean-Marc went to change while my father led us to where my mother was seated. Louise and Lu-Lu were with her.

"They look so happy," Lu-Lu whispered to me.

I smiled. My parents were holding hands, and occasionally their eyes met and held as if exchanging deepest thoughts. "They know they'll be together forever," I said.

"Do you really believe that?" Lu-Lu asked.

The question startled me. "Don't you?"

"I—I guess so. I just didn't realize how important it was. When Philippe and I were getting married, I just thought about now, and about how much I loved him. But take your parents. They've been together so long, and yet they nearly broke up because of their different beliefs. I wonder if that's what would have happened to Philippe and me."

"You never know. But it seems likely, given his attitude toward the Church."

"I could never imagine choosing the Church over a man I loved," Lu-Lu said. "But maybe I was wrong. I mean, like with Paulette and Pierre, their love will go on forever. Had Philippe and I been in their position, our love would have been over, with no hope."

"Do you have a testimony of the Church?" I asked.

Lu-Lu paused in thought. "I don't think I did, or I would never have settled for marriage outside the temple," she said. "But I believe now."

"That's a beginning," I said. "Now what are you going to do about it?"

"What do you mean?"

I laughed. "Don't look so startled. All I mean is that a secure knowledge of the gospel always leads people to want to help others. Do you remember when my father decided to be baptized? Well, when I found him in the cemetery that day, I thought I might have to stop him from jumping up on a park bench somewhere and proclaiming the gospel with one of those loudspeakers."

"Really?" Lu-Lu giggled at the idea.

I nodded. "It wasn't a bit like him. Do you know he passed out a Book of Mormon to everyone at the bank?"

"He didn't!"

"He did. The board members weren't too happy when they heard."

Her eyes grew wide. "What did he do?"

"He gave them each a long overdue raise—and a Book of Mormon!" The idea of him doing so made us both laugh.

"Shhh, you two," my father whispered. "It's beginning."

I turned to say just one more thing. "Family is one of the most important things we preach in the gospel," I said. "I never realized how important family was until I went on a mission. It was then I knew that the best work I could ever do was at home, with those I love. Don't settle for what won't make you happy in the long run. It's not worth it!"

She nodded. "I think I've been luckier than I deserve," she said. "My family has always been strong. I wonder if I . . . " Her voice drained away. "Thanks, Ari. I've got some thinking to do." She turned to listen to the speaker.

A short time later, when my father emerged from the water, I knew I had never been happier in my entire life. *We did it, Antoine*, I said silently. *Our family is whole!*

Jean-Marc met my gaze from where he stood in the font, waiting for my mother. *I love you*, he mouthed.

Life was sometimes hard, but so worth it.

When we arrived home, Pierre met us at the door with tiny Pauline asleep in his arms. His face was worried.

"What's wrong?" I asked anxiously, checking Pauline for any visual signs of sickness.

"It's Simone," Pierre said.

"What?"

"The clinic called. She's supposed to be here or at work, but when they were doing random checking, they found out she's not at either place."

I frowned. "Oh, no! For over two months she's been without drugs.

Two months! What if . . ." My voice trailed off.

"I don't believe it," Jean-Marc said. "She was doing so well."

"Was she?" I asked. She had been upset at Paulette's death, but less than I expected. Perhaps stark realization had finally struck. "I have to find her," I said.

Jean-Marc nodded. "Pierre and I will stay with the children."

"No, I want to go with Ariana," Pierre said.

"Are you sure you're up to it?" I didn't try to keep the surprise from my voice.

He nodded once, decisively. "Yes. She's Paulette's mother. It's time I took responsibility for my family and their happiness." He handed Pauline to Jean-Marc and knelt near Marie-Thérèse. "I'm going to find Grandma Simone, and when I come back, you and I are going to have a talk."

Marie-Thérèse beamed. "What if I'm asleep?" she asked, her smile fading.

Pierre kissed her nose. "Then I'll wake you right up."

"Thank you, Daddy. And I love you." Her arms went up around his neck.

I bid farewell to the twins, and Jean-Marc blew me a kiss. I grabbed it in mid-air and slapped it on my cheek. Pierre pulled on a cap over his bald head and opened the door.

We started by searching the bars and cafés near Simone's house, then near ours and the clinic. We found nothing. It was embarrassing entering the places reeking of alcohol and smoke, but we plunged doggedly on. We began checking the small stores lining the streets, though many were closed for the Sabbath. The afternoon sun began to fade.

"Where could she be?" Pierre said.

I shook my head. In his eyes I saw the same guilt I was feeling. If only we had been more supportive, if only we had paid her more heed. "It's not our fault," I said. "It's her choice to change or not."

"Like it was mine to reject my daughter."

I said nothing, just watched him.

"You were right all along," he continued. "You and Paulette. That baby is a gift from God."

"Shall we pray?" I asked.

He grinned, and I could see the old Pierre shining through. "May I offer it?" We stood together and prayed in a little alleyway off the main street. Afterwards we walked on.

"Now, where might she go?" I mumbled. I couldn't help feeling that the answer was within my grasp.

"She wouldn't try to hurt herself, would she?" Pierre asked. "Like throw herself in the Seine or anything."

I grabbed his arms. "The Seine, yes!"

Without explaining, I propelled him back to the car. I drove straight to the Quai de Montebello and the booksellers' stalls. We left the car and hurried to the stone wall overlooking the Seine, eyes searching through the thin crowd of tourists.

"There!" Pierre pointed, and I saw her, looking out over the water.

"Simone!" I cried. She turned her head and watched our approach.

"Where have you been?" Pierre said. "We've been searching every-where."

She turned her gaze back to the gentle waves below. "I've been watchin' the water," she said. "And wonderin' how God made it."

"What?" Pierre said, but I smiled.

Simone focused on Pierre. "Ya thought I went to a bar, didn't ya? Or back to drugs?" Pierre nodded, shamefaced. There was no trace of substance abuse in Simone's manner. She laughed. "Don't feel bad. I almost did." There were tears in her voice. "I was missin' Paulette and thinkin' about yer little baby. I got depressed and planned to go to a bar and order a vodka and a couple joints to begin with, but then I stopped here first. A man came up to me, and we got to talkin' about how water is made—you know, them molecules and stuff. He told me how the world always has the same amount of water in it, and how it recycles. It evapo-rates, goes up and comes back as rain, or people use it. It was so fascinatin', such a perfect system. I knew God made it." She glanced my way briefly. "So I prayed." She stopped.

"And?" Pierre asked anxiously.

"He answered, of course," Simone said. "I guess I'll be seein' them missionaries of yers after all. And don't be shocked, but I ain't too sure if I won't go back to school, study science or somethin'."

Pierre hugged her. "Paulette would be proud."

"Proud?" Simone asked doubtfully. She thumbed heavenward. "More than likely, she's up there askin' what the h—, uh, beans took me so long."

We took Simone back to the clinic. She had to undergo a drug test, but given the circumstances of her daughter's recent death, the personnel were understanding—especially when the tests came out negative. Pierre and I went home, exhausted but happy.

"We have been blessed," Pierre said to me. "Don't let me ever forget it."

CHAPTER TWENTY-ONE

After his baptism that Sunday, my father threw himself into church work like a man starved for any touch of the Spirit. Through his efforts, the genealogical line I had been sporadically working on doubled in size the first week. My mother blossomed with her newfound happiness. "I'll never ask for another thing," she vowed. "The Lord has been so very good to me."

My parents were the only ones newly baptized, but they were not the only ones who began a new life. That day it seemed we all started anew—learning from the past, throwing out everything that held us back, and holding on to only that which made us strong and sealed us as survivors.

Pierre's budding relationship with Pauline healed something inside him, something none of us could reach. It made him stronger physically, as though the love inside helped fight the cancers that ate at his body. Even with his growing strength, he didn't return to work full-time. He wanted to spend whatever moments he had left with his little girls, building memories to last them the rest of their lives. He unearthed the videotape recorder Paulette had made him buy, and we spent outrageous sums on videotape in order to record every moment we wanted to hold dear.

In November, when Marie-Thérèse turned five, we celebrated at the house. At nearly four months, Pauline was still too small to go out in the cold weather, so we contented ourselves in having a family party with more presents than any little girl had a right to. Josette couldn't hide her envy, but Marie-Thérèse was more than willing to share her bounty.

One of Simone's presents turned out to be the best. She had carefully wrapped a certificate the bishop had filled out for her baptism that coming Sunday. She had originally planned to wait until her drug program was complete, but she decided that having the Holy Ghost with her would make the last six weeks in the clinic easier to bear. She had been clean for four and a half months.

Marie-Thérèse handed Simone a money bank I had given her. "Then you'll need this," she said. "To save money for a trip to the temple."

Simone hugged it to her body. "Oh, thank you!"

"Well, that's all the presents," I said, stooping down to gather wrapping paper from the floor in the sitting room.

"I have an announcement," Lu-Lu said suddenly. She had been bursting with a secret since she arrived, and I felt dread at hearing it, fearing that Philippe had come to his senses and wanted to marry her after all.

"I'm going on a mission," she said brightly. "I'm tired of waiting for something good to happen. I'm going to be like Ari, and go out and try to make a difference." She turned to Jean-Marc. "And who knows? Maybe I'll meet my future spouse on my mission, like you did." We hugged her, offering congratulations. I saw sharp relief on Louise's face. She, too, had been worried by the impending announcement.

My father stared at Lu-Lu enviously. "I wish I could go," he said. Abruptly his eyes glazed over and he seemed to be far away. "Why, I *can* go! Not yet, perhaps, but retirement is not too far away." He faced my mother. "What do you think?"

She laughed. "You? Retire? I'll believe it when I see it."

"You've got another ten years before you can even think about retiring," Jean-Marc said.

My father's eyes glistened with a fervor which before I had only seen him demonstrate toward his work. "It's not too soon to begin planning," he said. We laughed. To think that less than four months ago, my father had never even read the Book of Mormon! A miracle had happened before our eyes.

"Enough of this," I said. "Who wants cake?" A chorus of voices shouting "I do!" followed me into the kitchen.

Lu-Lu helped me serve. "So what made you decide to go on a mission?" I asked.

"I want to help people understand how much God loves them," she replied. "It's just like you said. Once I began to understand how important and true the gospel is, I wanted to share it."

"Kind of like a virus, ain't it?" Simone said inelegantly. "Ya know, catchin'." I wasn't sure I liked the analogy, but she had a point.

The phone rang. "It's for you, Lu-Lu," Jean-Marc said.

"I'll get it in the sitting room," she said. "There's too much noise here."

When she had left, Jean-Marc came up to me. "It's Philippe," he said quietly. "On the telephone."

I groaned and closed my eyes. "Not now." I went into the large entryway where I could see Lu-Lu talking in the sitting room. When she put the phone in its cradle, she was crying.

"Are you all right?" I asked.

"He wanted me back," she said. "And I wanted to say yes. I still love him. But I know the Church is true. If he wants me, he'll have to come on my terms. I'm not trading eternity for what I can see right now. Like you tried to tell me when your parents were baptized, it's not worth settling. There's too much at stake."

"I'm proud of you," I said.

She came to me and buried her face in my shoulder. "I'm all right. I really am. It just hurts because I know that Philippe won't be changing any time soon."

"I guess it's good you're going on a mission then, isn't it?"

She smiled. "Yeah, I guess so."

A feeling of love pervaded the room, drying Lu-Lu's tears. I knew there would be hard times yet ahead of her, but more than half the battle was already won. We joined the others for a beautiful evening of family togetherness. Love and laughter filled the apartment as never before.

"Happy?" Jean-Marc asked, pulling me close in a tight embrace.

"Oh, yes," I said. I knew that our happiness was ever so much more precious because it hadn't come easily.

The evening had gone well, but later, long after the children were in bed, I started from a sudden sleep, my heart pounding frantically. I hurried out of bed and into Pauline's room. Had she become sick? She had seemed so well earlier. *Not my baby!* I cried silently. *Not yet, it's too soon!*

Jean-Marc was already in the room, staring down at a sleeping Pauline. "She's all right," he whispered. "The crying isn't coming from here."

Now that I knew Pauline was safe, I smiled in wonder that Jean-Marc, who had once slept so soundly, had awakened before me. Pauline certainly had us all trained. "Let's check the others," I said.

We met Pierre coming from the girls' room. "It's Marie-Thérèse," he said, wringing his hands. "She's crying. I can't get her to stop." He looked up at the ceiling, blinking rapidly, and in the dim light I could see the tears. "She's calling for her mommy."

I pushed past him and into the room. Marie-Thérèse was sitting up in bed, clutching her rag doll and rocking back and forth, whimpering.

"Mommy! Oh, Mommy, where are you?"

I sat on the bed and drew her unresisting body onto my lap. "I'm here, Marie-Thérèse. I'm here for you. It's going to be all right." She clung to me and the whimpering stopped, but her little chest still shook with silent sobs. I held her, not knowing what to do. I had thought she had accepted her mother's death, but it seemed that acceptance was not a complete healing.

After a long time the shaking subsided, and Marie-Thérèse spoke. "I can't see her anymore."

"What do you mean?"

"In my mind, when I close my eyes. She's not there. Her face isn't there. I don't remember what she looks like."

I had experienced the same thing myself. At times I could see Paulette so clearly, but at others I could only remember the way she had made me feel.

"Are you afraid you're going to forget her?" I asked. Marie-Thérèse gave a large sniff and nodded. I hugged her. "You know, sometimes when we're not with a person, we can't remember too well what they look like. But that doesn't stop us from loving them. Not ever. We can hold them in our hearts, even if we can't hold them in our minds. Our hearts will never forget."

Then I had an idea. I picked Marie-Thérèse up and carried her into the hall. "We need a picture of Paulette," I said to the brothers who hovered anxiously near the door. "And a flashlight."

"I'll get the flashlight," Jean-Marc said.

I glanced at Pierre. "I want a good picture," I said. "A large one we can hang near Marie-Thérèse's bed."

He disappeared, and I carried the little girl back to her bed. Soon the others were back. We hung the picture and gave Marie-Thérèse the flashlight. She turned it on, shining it onto her mother's face. It was the large picture from Pierre's own room, taken at the time of Marie-Thérèse's birth. Paulette was staring down at the new baby with love etched unmistakably on her face.

Marie-Thérèse nodded, her expression solemn. "Now I won't forget."

I pointed to her chest. "Remember what I said. You won't ever forget her in your heart, even if you can't remember her face."

She nodded, then reached out a finger and touched my lips, closing her hand tightly and bringing it to her heart. "Thank you."

Her special link with her mother, and she had used it with me! For a moment I could only stare, marveling at the miracle. Then I brought my own finger to her lips and held it to my heart. "I love you, Marie-Thérèse," I whispered.

She smiled, and for a moment I saw Paulette in her face. "I know," she said simply.

I kissed her and stood up to leave. Jean-Marc did the same, but Pierre settled on the floor beside the bed. "I'll stay here for a while, until she falls asleep."

The rest of the night passed quickly, with only Pauline's feedings to break it up. When it was my time for one of the three nightly feedings, I checked in on Marie-Thérèse, but she slept soundly. Pierre was asleep on her floor, and I covered him with an extra quilt.

Early in the morning, I heard someone enter Pauline's room. I listened to the monitor, but heard nothing more, so I arose and went in. Marie-Thérèse stood on the bathroom stool near the crib. The bright morning light streaming in through the windows made an aura of light around her body, bringing out the highlights in her hair like a halo. In her hands, she held the cloth doll Paulette had made.

She glanced up as I entered. "She's awake," she said.

"Did you sleep okay?" I asked.

She nodded. "Do you know why I'm here?"

"You wanted to say good morning to Pauline?"

The little head shook. "No, I came to give her a present."

"What is it?" I asked, wondering which of her new birthday gifts would go to the baby.

"You'll see." Marie-Thérèse stared at her sister. "I have something for you," she said softly. She lifted the rag doll over the side of the crib and settled it next to the baby. "Mommy made it. She would have made one for you, too, but since she can't, I want you to have this one."

Her face was somber, and I wondered why she would give away something that meant so much to her. She felt my gaze and looked up at me.

"Pauline won't remember Mommy at all," she explained. "She won't even remember when she sees a picture. I want her to have a part of Mommy."

I put my arm around her. "You're a wonderful sister," I said. "And I'm sure if you ever want to borrow Dolly for a while, Pauline won't mind."

The baby had discovered the doll, and her tiny hands reached out for it clumsily, pulling it closer. Since she was born prematurely, her development was behind that of a normal baby her age, so the motion was unexpected. Marie-Thérèse gave a cry of delight. "See? She likes it! She's trying to get it! She never did that! Do you think she knows Mommy made it?"

"Who knows?" I said. The diffused light in the room seemed to grow stronger, though I knew it was only my imagination. This, I decided, was a little piece of heaven on earth. This quiet moment alone with my new daughters.

February came with its endless wetness and melancholy grays. The twins turned five, and Lu-Lu left on a mission to the south of France. Pierre's condition had worsened, yet he clung to life, despite the pain, if only for his daughters. By May he was completely bedridden, and Louise moved into our house to help me care for him. "There's no sense in getting a nurse," she said as she settled her belongings into Pauline's room. "I'm his mother, and I want to do it."

Jean-Marc moved Pauline's crib into our room, and the baby monitor became Louise's way of knowing if Pierre needed her. I worried that despair would fall over our household, and some days it did, but it never stayed for long.

"It seems as though I can see right through him to heaven," Jean-Marc said to me one day. The children were in bed, and we sat cuddled together on the sofa. I could feel his breath on my neck.

"I know what you mean," I said. "It's as if heaven is closer than we ordinarily know. It's a comfort, and yet—"

"He doesn't even look like himself."

I knew what he meant. Pierre was so thin now that he seemed hardly bigger than a child under the blanket. His gaunt face resembled a skeleton more than a living human, with dry skin stretched taut over his face.

A sob shook Jean-Marc. "I don't want to let him go."

"I know." There was nothing I could do but hold him.

"Have I kept my promise to you?" he asked abruptly. "To be the husband you wanted?"

I faced him. "You're not perfect," I said. "But neither am I. And you have come home on time at least half the time." I kissed his lips. "I am happy, if that's what you're asking."

"It is. I want you and the children to be happy for as long as we have left."

"We have eternity," I said.

"I know," he agreed. "But sometimes it's hard to remember."

"We have to remember," I said. "We *have* to."

The children enjoyed having Pierre at home all the time. He often read them stories of Jesus, filling our house with enough hope to get us through the hard days.

"It's all in the attitude," he said to me at the end of June. The children were sitting around him on the double bed he used, holding handfuls of books for Pierre to read. "We can choose to be happy in any circumstance. We can choose to have faith. It's our choice! I feel so grateful to the Lord for everything."

He appeared tired, so I motioned the children off the bed. "Let's go make Pierre some lunch," I said. The twins and André jumped off the bed and raced each other from the room. I picked up Pauline, who was nearly eleven months old.

"Can I carry the food, Mom—I mean, Ariana?" Consternation filled Marie-Thérèse's face at the slip. Pierre and I glanced at each other with concern. Though I had longed for this day, I feared anything I might say would make the situation worse.

"Come here." Pierre motioned to his daughter. She climbed onto the bed next to him, her face downcast. "Are you worried because you called Ariana Mom?" he asked. She nodded. "I know what you mean. It's hard not to call her that when she does all the stuff mothers do."

Her light-brown eyes lifted to meet his. "Do you think Mommy would be mad?"

He shook his head. "No. It's kind of like how you call Simone, Louise, and Josephine Grandma. They don't mind that you call the others that, too; it doesn't take away from them."

"But they *are* all my grandmas, except Grandma Josephine. She's not my real grandma, she's Josette's and Marc's."

Pierre's eyebrows drew together slightly. "Well, I've got a better example then. You know how Heavenly Father and Heavenly Mother are your parents in heaven?"

She nodded. "Yeah."

"You see, they lent you to your mom and me to raise here on earth. Do you think they mind if you call me Father or Daddy? Of course they don't. And with Mommy, it's just like that. She's lending you to Aunt Ariana to raise. I'm sure she wouldn't mind if you called her Mom." Marie-Thérèse didn't seem convinced, and Pierre continued quickly, "If you're still worried, maybe you could always refer to your mommy as Mommy, and you could always call Ariana just plain Mom. That way they would each have their own special name, like your grandmas. Does that sound good?"

A slow smile spread over her face. She slid off the bed, glancing up at me shyly, waiting.

"I would love that," I said. She ducked her head and ran out of the room, giggling self-consciously.

"Thank you, Pierre," I said. I wondered if he realized what he had imparted to both his daughter and to me. By giving Marie-Thérèse permission to call me Mom, he had paved the way for many future transitions.

"Paulette knew this day would come," he said softly. "And she was right; a child needs a mother."

Pierre died two weeks later, passing away in his sleep, his pain at last ended and the torment on his face forever stilled. After a brief time of grieving, the children rebounded, but Jean-Marc seemed to go into a depression. Once again he began to spend long hours at work. I knew he was only trying to forget his loss, but after waiting three weeks for him to return to normal, I called him on his cellular phone.

"It's time to come home," I said. "You're taking a vacation."

"I am?"

"Yes. I've cleared it with the boss."

His chuckle was low. "I'm doing it again, aren't I?"

"Yes."

"Why didn't you tell me?"

"I *am* telling you. Now come home."

His step was a little lighter as we carried our suitcases to the van and set off for a long-overdue vacation, just us and our five children.

We made the long drive to Deauville, on the western coast of France—a crowded, internationally famous seaside resort where the children could play in the ocean. There was also horse racing and boat sailing to keep people occupied, but my interest was simply to spend time with my family; it didn't matter what we chose to do.

"Hmm," Jean-Marc said when we arrived in Deauville the next morning. "Isn't that the place with the balcony?"

"The very one," I said with a smile. I had in fact reserved the same suite we had stayed in the night the twins were conceived.

We settled in the rooms and headed for the beach.

"Thank you," Jean-Marc said. "This is exactly what I needed."

"It's what we all needed," I said.

"I love you so much, Ari." His voice was gruff. He reached out and cradled my face with one hand, his thumb moving under my eye and wiping off the sand clinging to my cheek.

A loud crying spoiled the moment, and I jerked away to focus on Pauline, who was trying to spit out a mouthful of sand.

"I told her not to eat it," said Josette.

André grabbed a cloth from the picnic basket and with clumsy fingers tried to sweep the sand out of the one-year-old's mouth. I noticed he was careful not to get the saliva on him, though such an amount would never pass the HIV virus; we had taught him well. At his ministrations, Pauline cried harder.

"She needs a drink," little Marc said helpfully.

I sighed and pulled Pauline onto my lap. "Spit it out," I said.

"Hold it there! What a great picture!" Jean-Marc pulled out both the camera and the videotape recorder.

"Me too! Get me too!" chorused the other children.

"Can I be by you, Mom?" Marie-Thérèse asked.

"Sure," I said.

I posed for the camera, for some reason remembering the day I had filmed Paulette making the baby curtains. As always, I felt a stab of heartache when I remembered my friend. It wasn't the aching grief I had felt when she died, but more the longing for what could have been, for what would be one day. Until then, I would do my best to satisfy the role that had been thrust upon me.

"Smile!" Jean-Marc said, poking the camera in my face.

Upon us, I amended silently. Paulette had given us a gift most precious: this little toddler in my arms. I lowered my face to her soft halo of brown hair and breathed deeply the baby scent of her. She was so precious to me. In dying, Paulette had given me more than what had been taken away—just as the eternal gift of her testimony had forever changed the lives of so many others who had been important to her.

Jean-Marc put down the camera and came to my side. We held hands as we watched our children playing in the sand, dancing barely out of the waves' reach, as if taunting the ocean. Their cherished faces crinkled in wide smiles, and laughter sounded over the crowded beach.

I felt alive as I never had before; every moment seemed priceless. How incredibly beautiful the world was! How unique! I would live each moment to its fullest.

Pauline's tears had ended, along with her patience, and she wriggled, trying to leave my lap and crawl to the gritty sand. For a moment I resisted, thinking of the future. As yet she had shown no signs of the illnesses that marked AIDS, and though it might seem like holding water in my cupped hands, I would try to hold on to her forever. Hold on to her as I hadn't been able to do with my beloved little Nette. At least until the time came to say goodbye.

In the meantime, the future always held chance of a cure. I never let go of the hope—or the faith that the Lord knew what he was doing, what He was building in us. And who knew but that the time would shortly come when the Savior himself would put His hands on her head and make her whole?

I let Pauline go, and she giggled softly as she reached the end of the towel. Promptly, she picked up a handful of sand and tried to bring it to her mouth. "Oh, no you don't," Jean-Marc chided, reaching for her.

I laughed softly and gazed out over the ocean. The waves lapped lazily onto the shore in steady repetition, reminding me of the gentle waves in the River Seine. I watched, recalling vividly what Simone had said the first day we had met at the stone wall above the riverbank near the booksellers' stalls.

"The water is us," she had said. "We're helpless against the trials that come. We can't push them away; we can only go where we're pushed. What good is life when we can't control anythin'?"

I smiled at the memory, understanding much more than I had that day. We *were* like the river water as she had suggested, being tossed to and fro by the wind and wakes of the boats. But when the boats were gone and the wind ceased, the water remained in its place. Like the water, we too remained when the problems and trials were over, falling back into our lives as before until the next waves came to test our endurance. And always, we were cradled in the banks of our Father's firm hands.

"Do you think it might rain tonight?" Jean-Marc asked, scanning the sky hopefully. "I thought we might sleep out on the balcony," he added, his voice teasing.

"You want to get wet?" I asked, jumping to my feet. Laughing, I pulled him to the frothy waves. In his arms, Pauline giggled.

Yes, water was mighty and resilient, like we were. We, the children of God!

ABOUT THE AUTHOR

Rachel Ann Nunes (pronounced *noon-esh*) learned to read when she was four and by age twelve knew she was going to be a writer. Now as a stay-at-home mother of five, it isn't easy to find time to write, but she will trade washing dishes or weeding the garden for an hour at the computer any day! Her only rule about writing is to never eat chocolate at the computer. "Since I love chocolate and writing," she jokes, "my family might never see me again."

Rachel enjoys camping, spending time with her family, reading, and visiting far off places. She stayed in France for six months when her father was teaching French at BYU, and later served an LDS mission to Portugal.

Rachel has fifteen published novels and one picture book entitled *Daughter of a King*. All of her books have been best-sellers in the LDS market.

Rachel lives with her husband, TJ, and their children in Pleasant Grove, Utah. She enjoys hearing from her readers.

You can write to her at P.O. Box 353, American Fork, UT 84003-0353 or rachel@rachelannnunes.com. Also, feel free to visit her website at www.rachelannnunes.com.

9 26575 76461 4